ELEMENTARY

BLOOD AND INK

ALSO AVAILABLE FROM TITAN BOOKS

Elementary: The Ghost Line

ELEMENTARY™

BLOOD AND INK

ADAM CHRISTOPHER

BASED ON THE CBS TELEVISION SERIES
CREATED BY ROBERT DOHERTY

TITAN BOOKS

ELEMENTARY: BLOOD AND INK
Print edition ISBN: 9781785650277
E-book edition ISBN: 9781785650284

Published by Titan Books
A division of Titan Publishing Group Ltd
144 Southwark St, London SE1 0UP

First edition: April 2016
10 9 8 7 6 5 4 3 2 1

TITANBOOKS.COM

For Sandra, always.

"How often have I said to you that when you have eliminated the impossible, whatever remains, however improbable, must be the truth?"

I

THE ADVENTURE OF THE POISONED
PRESERVE POT

"Of course," said the great detective, "it was the emeritus professor's tiepin that was the final clue, the last piece of the puzzle that had, thus far, proved to be so very elusive."

Sherlock Holmes leaned back in his leather chair, practically vanishing between the high wingbacks of the seat, his elbows locking as his hands pulled tight on the uppermost knee of his crossed legs. With a slight smile, he glanced to his left. There, standing next to him, Joan Watson lifted her hand and opened it, before walking forward to show the rest of the assembled group. Lying across her palm was a silver tiepin set with a brilliant purple gem.

"Amethyst," said Watson. She raised an eyebrow and cocked her head at the old man with mutton-chop sideburns who stood, slack-jawed, against the mantelpiece on the opposite side of the room. "Your birthstone, isn't that right, Professor?"

The gasp that followed did a complete orbit of the room, passing from one person to the next as the revelation sank in. Watson half-turned to glance at Holmes, still ensconced in the ridiculous chair, and she saw his eyes move with the sound, traveling around the group they had assembled in the luxurious expanse of the penthouse suite of the Starling Hotel—the lounge of which, Watson thought, was actually far larger than most of the apartments in the buildings that surrounded the exclusive and discreet hotel on Manhattan's Upper East Side.

As Watson watched her colleague survey the group, she knew that behind those eyes and the cool, unflustered expression, the synapses of his remarkable brain were firing, one final round of observation to confirm what he already knew to be correct.

Because they had solved the case. They had found the killer and they had discovered how she had done it. Already Watson knew this was a case Holmes would keep in the forefront of his mind for years to come, a case to be savored and recalled when the moment struck. Complex, twisted, intriguing; a case that highlighted the lengths a person would go to, the depths of evil into which they would plunge, if they had reason to.

Watson turned back to the emeritus professor, a wiry man in his mid-seventies with an expansive bald head and face framed by those wild sideburns. For a moment the professor stared at her palm, open-mouthed, before reaching a tentative hand forward. He snatched the tiepin and examined it, holding his hand away from him, as if the tiepin were electric. Then, with a sheepish look to the woman standing next to him—Mrs. Eleanor Pyr, a twenty-something socialite dressed like a 1940s Hollywood star, complete with nearly intact fox draped around her shoulders—the professor slipped the pin back onto his tie, which he then straightened. He cleared his throat and stood with his hands neatly clasped, as if nothing had happened at all.

Watson, the professor, and Mrs. Pyr were the only three people standing. Holmes sat in the wingback chair; across from him, separated by a marble-topped coffee table about as big as a king-sized bed—on which was set a classic afternoon tea, complete with delicate bone china cups and teetering cake stand, upon which a selection of patisseries and dainty English scones were so delicately balanced—sat Hal Clarke, a retired something-something from the US Air Force who was as old as the professor, if not older, but who looked to Watson to be twenty—no, *thirty*—years his junior.

Next to Hal was Bradley Grant, a young man with a thick neck, square shoulders, and a haircut to match, a man who didn't say much but who had been of invaluable help during the case. He sat with his legs spread wide, the heel of one boot tapping to a rhythm only he could hear.

At the end of the table, separate from the rest, was Olivia Peel. She was young—maybe Watson's age, maybe a little younger, but dressed in the simple, elegant black-and-white uniform of hotel management, her makeup and hair immaculate, she looked a lot older. Like Holmes she had her legs crossed but unlike Holmes, she was leaning forward, balanced on the very edge of her chair, her entire posture uncomfortable, tense.

Which is entirely understandable, thought Watson. Because she knew what was coming, she knew what Watson and Holmes had uncovered, what they had observed, what they had *deduced*.

It was to Olivia that Holmes slowly turned, sliding his whole body into a new angle on the leather seat so he could see the hotel manager past the chair's wing.

Nobody else moved. Half the people in the room had their eyes fixed on Holmes; the others all stared at Olivia.

Then the emeritus professor cleared his throat, and the spell was suddenly broken. Mrs. Pyr sighed and adjusted the fur around her neck. She looked at Holmes, then at Watson, then sighed a second time. Now everyone was looking at her.

"Well?" she asked. "Can't we just get on with it? All this melodrama just makes me hungry."

She ducked forward and picked up a small cake plate from the table. Then, lifting the silver tongs from the base of the cake stand, she went for one of the English scones that sat in a proud pyramid on the very top tier, before laying her plate on the table with a heavy clatter. She reached for the open jar of strawberry preserve from a nearby tray, a silver spoon deeply embedded in the bright, sticky jam.

"I would suggest a honey cake instead, if I were you, Mrs. Pyr."

Eleanor Pyr froze. Holmes hadn't moved, his eyes still locked on the hotel manager's. But the tone of his voice left no doubt as to his warning. Mrs. Pyr dropped the preserve jar back onto the tray with a shriek and retreated quickly to the mantelpiece, flexing her fingers as though the cold preserve pot had somehow burned her. Beside her, the professor began puffing his cheeks like a steam engine, his eyes wide in horror. Seated on the other side of the table, Hal Clarke exchanged an uncomfortable look with Bradley Grant.

There was a single knock from the double doors of the penthouse lounge. Watson turned as the doors opened, and two men entered. They were each the size of football linebackers and were squeezed into identical tan suits. The one in front caught Watson's eye; she gave him a slight nod, which he returned. Behind them, in the penthouse entrance hall, Watson could see two uniformed police officers.

Watson walked over to Olivia and looked down on the hotel manager—the *fake* hotel manager, in the stolen uniform, with the stolen passkey, the stolen money and a grudge she had kept for more than a decade.

Olivia Peel, the murderer.

Justice was served.

"Once we had discovered the professor's gambling debts,"

Watson said, "it was simple to trace your own involvement back to the Bratislava crime syndicate."

"But even they might be surprised to find out who you are *really* working for," said Holmes. "Lacing the strawberry preserve with strychnine was an effective, if old-fashioned, method of eliminating your CIA handler, Dormer."

The group gave a second collective gasp.

"It must have been a shock when you found Dormer undercover as a hotel porter," said Watson. "Especially after you found him and the professor arguing in the elevator that night."

Olivia Peel said nothing. She just looked up at Watson with cold, narrow eyes. Watson returned the look, then nodded toward the door. "I think your house detectives would like a word with you."

Holmes nodded sharply. "And after that, the good detectives of the New York Police Department, as well. Oh, and if you are very, very unlucky, the enforcers of the Bratislava syndicate, should you be unfortunate enough to escape the protective custody of the NYPD."

As Olivia was escorted out by the two house detectives, the others all watched in stunned silence as Holmes untangled his legs and slid forward in his seat, reaching for the teapot. He poured himself a cup of steaming tea, and then, balancing his teacup and saucer on one knee, the tip of his tongue poking out of the corner of his mouth, carefully chose one of the fruit tarts from the bottom tier of the cake stand.

"Help yourself, everyone," he said. "I think we have all earned this." He leaned back, and then he quickly jerked forward again. "But, ah… avoid the scones and jam," he said, almost as an afterthought.

Then he turned on a broad smile.

"Chin-chin!" he said, sipping his tea.

2

DEATH'S FINE HAND

"Nice of them to give us a souvenir," said Watson, as she and Holmes exited the elevator and headed out across the acre of dark oak paneling that formed the Starling Hotel's impressive—and, in Watson's mind, *oppressive*—lobby.

Next to her, Holmes smiled and lifted the silver preserve spoon in his hand. It was elegant, and quite possibly a genuine antique, given the particular echelon of society the hotel catered for, although Watson hadn't had much of a chance to take a look. What she did know was that the fine metalwork of the spoon was curled and fluted, the flat head set with a disc of striated blue-green stone—perhaps agate—and that there was a hallmark on the underside.

Holmes stopped and lifted the spoon between finger and thumb, finding the perfect balance point.

"A fine specimen of kitchen cutlery, *yes*, although the plastic variety from corner bodegas fulfills much the same function."

Watson sighed. Okay, so now Holmes was in one of *those* moods. "Would it hurt so much to, I don't know, just sometimes be *appreciative*? It's not often that you actually get to keep the murder weapon from a case."

Holmes pursed his lips and nodded, and then he glanced at his companion, a furtive smile floating around the corners of his lips. "Quite true, Watson, quite true." He tilted his head as he turned back to the spoon, lifting it high in the air. "But what is this, really? A spoon. An implement. True enough, it was used to dispense the poisoned strawberry preserve, but *after* the crime is committed, what is it? Is this truly the means by which a vicious, evil act was committed, or is it just an innocent bystander, one merely caught in the machine of evil, unaware of the new use to which it has been put?"

Watson blinked a couple of times and watched Holmes as he looked at the spoon with what was quite possibly reverence.

"I think you've had too much sugar today," she said, finally. "How many of those preserve pots did you have to taste test to prove your theory?"

Holmes's eyes narrowed and he jutted his chin out in what Watson knew was annoyance. "It was not a *theory*, Watson, it was a *hypothesis*. You of all people should know the difference between the two."

"Okay, fine—"

"And it was twenty-six. At first I found it oddly moreish, but I admit that even I have a limit to my sweet tooth. But, as I believe you are aware, I am the foremost expert on all types of poison, and not only that, I have over the course of many years of careful and controlled dosing developed a tolerance to many toxic agents, several of which can only be detected by *taste*, by which point it is far too late for the intended recipient. I had to taste every preserve jar coming out of the kitchen— there was simply no other way to conduct the screening."

There was an insect-like buzzing from Holmes's pocket. He pushed the spoon unceremoniously on Watson while reaching with his other hand into his jacket to extract his phone. He cast a cursory glance at the screen, then nodded to himself, before thumbing the answer button.

"Captain Gregson."

As Watson waited, she slipped the silver preserve spoon into her shoulder bag. Looking back at Holmes, she saw him frown, then glance sideways at her. He looked around the hotel lobby, phone still pressed to his ear, then he gestured with a nod toward an alcove near to where they were standing, occupied only by an ornate antique table topped with an extravagant arrangement of fresh-cut flowers. Together they moved into the small space for a little more privacy. Holmes lowered the phone and hit the speaker function.

"Watson is listening, Captain."

"Hey," said Watson. "What's going on?"

"Oh, just the usual," said Gregson, his voice small and thin as it came from the phone's speaker. "I need you both up here ASAP. We have an active crime scene, and I think you'll want to take a look."

Holmes bristled, bouncing a little on his heels as he held the phone in one hand, his eyes scanning the lobby.

"And where is *here*, Captain? *Please* try to be a little more precise."

There was a pause. Watson shook her head.

"Ignore him, he's had a lot of sugar today," she said. "I'm assuming you're talking about a homicide?"

"There's been a murder, yes. We're in room 262 of the Athena Hotel in Washington Heights. And it's a real nice place, rooms by the hour and everything. I'll text you the address."

"Does this really require our assistance, Captain?" asked Holmes. "Crime is unfortunately not unusual in hotels that rent rooms by the hour, no matter what mythical Greek goddess they're named after."

"Oh, I think you will want to see this. The hotel may be a dive, but the victim has been identified as one Gregory Smythe, the Chief Financial Officer of a hedge fund firm called Mantis Capital Investment."

Watson frowned and looked at Holmes. "A hedge fund? What was he doing at a place like the Athena?"

Holmes snorted. "Money can buy you a lot of things, Watson. Sometimes such proclivities are only available in certain kinds of establishment and require a certain level of discretion."

"Yeah, well, if that's the case then these 'proclivities' have got our Mr. Smythe killed," said Gregson.

"As I said, Captain," said Holmes, "this is a big city. Crimes happen, whether it be homicide in Washington Heights or financial corruption in the boardroom of a hedge fund management firm."

"Look, Holmes, I know you don't like big business—"

"Captain Gregson, we will make a detective of you yet."

"But listen, this is not just another murder. Whatever reason Smythe was up here, he was stabbed to death."

Holmes's jaw opened a little, then closed. Watson raised an eyebrow. Whatever her partner's views of hedge funds— and merchant bankers, investment lawyers... in fact, anyone involved in the financial industry—he couldn't resist a mystery. And when Captain Gregson said the victim was *stabbed* to death...

"I'm assuming the murder weapon was not a knife," said Holmes, his voice suddenly quieter as he voiced the very thought Watson had.

"No," said Gregson. "It was a fountain pen. The victim was stabbed through the eye, and the weapon is still here." There was a pause. "Like I said, I think you will want to see this."

Holmes nodded. "Captain Gregson, we shall be there presently."

Holmes ended the call without a goodbye, then hefted the phone in his hand a couple of times before returning it to his inside pocket. Then he turned to Watson. And...

There.

She could see it. The light in his eyes, the way he was holding his mouth, the set of his jaw, the tendons on the side of his neck now just a little more defined.

Sugar overload or not, Holmes was on the case.

His phone buzzed again. He pulled it out, then tilted the screen so Watson could see. Gregson had texted the address of the Athena Hotel, Washington Heights.

"Come on," said Holmes. "We can take the A train most of the way, then we are on foot. The walk will do us good."

Holmes patted his stomach, then strode out of the alcove and across the lobby of the Starling.

Watson adjusted her bag on her shoulder and followed.

3

THE MEN IN BLACK

The evening was drawing in by the time Watson and Holmes reached the Athena Hotel. Holmes had been right, his encyclopedic knowledge of New York City leading them on the A-train subway all the way to 168th and Broadway. From there, it had just been a short walk to the hotel.

Gregson had been right too. The place was… well, it was a dive. In her time with Holmes, Watson had seen her fair share of the seedy side of Manhattan, but the streets here were a real mess, a mix of industrial, low-rent office space, and apartment buildings that were practically tenement blocks. The entire island was being gentrified, but that insidious process had yet to reach this particular part of the city.

The building they were heading toward was the same as all the ones around it—pale brick blackened by decades of grime and pollution, the structure only five floors in height but narrow, making it look taller—and gloomier—than it really was. The sign over the entryway—which said THE ATHENA and HOURLY RATES AVAILABLE at an angle that didn't seem quite right—was only half-lit, the remaining neon letters faint and flickering. There was a drugstore next door and that at least was brightly lit, but Watson wasn't really sure that was much comfort.

The detectives stopped on the corner across from the Athena. Holmes frowned, his nose crinkling as he looked around them. Watson knew exactly what it was he was concerned about.

The street was narrow and there were only a few cars parked—some of which looked like they hadn't been moved in quite a while. Right outside the Athena were two police cruisers and another unmarked car that Watson knew would have brought the captain and Detective Bell to the scene.

But farther along, parked nose-to-tail with not an inch between them, were two very large, very black SUVs, the windows of which were just as dark as their bodywork. To Watson they looked like the kind of vehicle the government used for shady federal agencies—something, unfortunately, she had had firsthand experience with.

The doorway of the Athena was recessed into the building and had a dark-green awning stretched over it. The awning had a tear down the middle and ATHENA HOTEL stenciled in dirty white block letters.

Standing underneath that awning was a young, tall man with blonde hair, wearing a black trench coat that hung open, under which was a black suit with a crisp white shirt. Completing the ensemble was a tie, which was also black, as were the sunglasses wrapped around his eyes—an entirely unnecessary accessory given the darkening evening.

Watson also spotted something else, something patently obvious from the way he stood, hands clasped over his belt buckle, shaded gaze remaining resolutely forward.

Whoever he was, whatever agency he represented, he was *armed*. That in itself was not necessarily a problem, but as Watson peered at the man, seeing the curled wire of an earpiece snaking down the back of his neck and disappearing under his collar, she wondered what the hell was going on.

Because one thing was for sure—he wasn't the police.

Holmes turned to look at Watson, his expression set, his mouth a firm, straight line. Watson inclined her head, indicating she had no doubt been thinking exactly what he had been.

They headed across the road, Watson wondering what they were about to walk into.

There were two men in black suits and glasses, earpieces in place, stationed in the hallway just outside of the hotel-room door, with a third out by the elevator. They didn't move an inch when Watson and Holmes emerged into the hallway. Holmes remained silent, but Watson could sense him bristling at the presence of the mysterious agents. The very fact that they were ignoring her and Holmes suggested to Watson that they weren't, in fact, part of any official group—federal agents were usually very quick to make their authority known, asking for identification while wheeling you out of their way. These men, whoever they were, looked more like Secret Service than FBI for a start, and the glasses and earpieces were certainly an overblown cliché.

Watson thought back to what Gregson had said about the victim, and who he worked for. Were the men in black actually security agents from Mantis Capital Investment?

Room 262 of the Athena was much as Watson had expected it to be: a small, narrow space with a bed that barely qualified as a double, the carpet hard underfoot, the walls mostly thin blue-painted fiberboard panels over cinder block, which was exposed around the room's single window. The view outside was hardly that, the blank gray wall opposite—perhaps part of the same building, perhaps not—almost within touching distance.

There was a chair and a table that would have counted as retro chic if Watson wasn't so certain they'd been in the room since they were new in the mid-1960s. The TV was big but old and it sat on a sideboard of the same vintage as the other furniture. There was a cupboard with no doors next to the bed on the opposite side of the tiny room. Inside the cupboard was a grimy plastic tray. What the cupboard once held—a tea kettle perhaps—Watson couldn't tell.

But the details of the room and its meager contents were very much secondary; it was the victim that drew her full attention.

Gregory Smythe, former CFO of Mantis, lay face-up, stretched horizontally on the floor at the foot of the bed. His mouth was open, his face seemingly frozen in an expression that looked more like one of surprise than pain. His left eye was open and staring at the ceiling.

His right eye—in fact, most of the right side of his face— was a bloody mess. The eye itself was gone, and protruding from the ruined socket was exactly what Captain Gregson had described—the fat black shaft of a fountain pen.

The small room was amply filled by a uniformed officer, Gregson, and Detective Bell, conferring as they stood in the doorway to the tiny bathroom. The uniformed officer was excused, Gregson and Bell giving their consultants a nod of greeting. Holmes virtually ignored the two policemen, instead moving swiftly around to the other side of the body, where he dropped into a crouch, arms awkwardly folded as he peered closely at the victim's face, his own creased in concentration as he examined the man's injuries with grim fascination.

"Thanks for coming up," said Gregson. He glanced over his shoulder toward the door, where the two mystery men in black were stationed, then turned back, giving a slight shake of the head. "We've got a real handful here."

Watson leaned in to the captain and lowered her voice. "What's going on here? Who are those guys?"

Detective Bell blew out his cheeks and, sticking his elbows out, adjusted his belt. "Just a little jurisdiction friction."

Watson frowned, her mind racing with a dozen different options. Maybe her initial assessment had been incorrect. "Are those guys FBI? They're parked outside and there are more down in the lobby—they didn't stop us coming up, but they never said anything to us either."

"Oh, don't worry, they're under strict instructions now," said Gregson.

"Yeah," Bell added, "after we threatened them with obstruction."

"Mantis Capital Investment."

The three of them turned to Holmes, who was still crouched by the body. The consultant bounced a little on his haunches, then looked up. "Private security from the victim's firm, I assume." He gestured to the body. "This man was a valued, high-profile employee, after all. I imagine they are here to ensure that news of this crime does not yet become public knowledge."

"Actually," said Bell, tapping his notebook on the knuckles of one hand, "they were here before us."

Watson frowned. "But how did they find out their CFO had been murdered? Surely the police didn't contact them?"

"No, we most certainly did not," said Gregson. "In fact, it was a Mantis agent who discovered the body in the first place."

"Only they weren't the ones who called it in," said Bell. "It was a member of the hotel staff."

Watson shook her head in confusion. "What?"

Gregson turned and nodded toward the security guarding the doorway. "According to the hotel staff they just arrived without warning. A few headed up here while the rest took up positions in the lobby. It wasn't until thirty minutes later that the police were called. Nobody even knew there was a body up here until we arrived and secured the scene."

"Wow, that's pretty strange," said Watson. She folded her arms and looked back toward the doorway. The two security agents didn't appear to have moved a single muscle since she and Holmes had arrived, and if they were listening in to the conversation, they certainly weren't giving any indication. Watson turned back to Gregson. "Strange, if not *criminal*. If they knowingly failed to report a crime—"

"Oh, don't look so shocked, Watson," said Holmes. He stood and joined the others. "The hubris of the financial industry knows no bounds. If a firm like Mantis Capital believes it can operate above and beyond the law when it comes to their day-to-day business practices, then it would be of no surprise to discover that they would decide not to report the death of one of their own if they could help it. Nothing more destabilizing to their investments than *murder*."

Gregson folded his arms tightly and turned a raised eyebrow in Holmes's direction.

"Have you heard of this Mantis Capital? Something you're not telling us?"

Holmes pursed his lips but didn't answer. Instead, Watson shook her head and waved her hand in her partner's direction. "Don't listen to him. He's eaten his body weight in sugar today. He doesn't know anything about Mantis." Then she frowned and looked at Holmes. "Uh... do you?"

"No, I do not." He rolled his hands expressively. "I was merely voicing an opinion about such institutions. I do believe the laws of this country allow me to do so."

Beside Gregson, Bell shook his head, licked his lips, and buried his nose in his notebook. Holmes meanwhile turned back to look down at the body.

"As a point of fact, I haven't heard of *Mantis Capital*

Investment at all," he said, pronouncing the name with exaggerated clarity, as if the words were in an unfamiliar foreign language. "And this is despite my thorough survey of hedge funds and other investment companies throughout the borough of Manhattan. Indeed, the first I had heard of the firm was when you called me, Captain."

Just then, a man and a woman in NYPD windcheaters, each carrying a large box-like case, entered the room, skirting past the security agents. Bell closed his notebook and moved over to the two forensic technicians, one of whom placed their case on the bed and clicked the catch open.

Watson moved around the already crowded space to give the techs more room. "Okay, so nobody working at the hotel knew there had been a murder in one of their rooms, but the men from Mantis did, and they weren't planning on calling the police anyway."

"Which begs the question," said Holmes, "of how Mantis knew that their CFO had met his untimely end, and where."

Gregson lifted his own notebook and checked the most recent page. "Now that we do know. When we arrived, the head of Mantis security, one David Gallop, was here. Bell and I asked him a few questions about their operation."

Bell nodded and moved back to join them, leaving the techs to their work. "Seems they tracked the victim's cellphone. Mantis are super tight on security and secrecy, to the point where they routinely monitor the GPS location of their employees by their phones."

"When Smythe didn't show up for an important meeting at the office this morning, and didn't answer either his cell or the phone at his residence, Mantis security tracked him here," said Gregson.

"Presumably the address was something of a surprise," said Holmes, casting a look around the dingy hotel room.

"On that point, Mr. Gallop was less forthcoming," said

Gregson, with a small sigh. "But at least they did a good job of securing the crime scene. They knew not to disturb it."

"As far as we know at present," said Holmes. "I would like to speak to this Mr. Gallop."

"He left," said Bell. "But don't worry, we'll be talking to everyone here and at the company."

Holmes nodded, then turned back to the body. Watson moved to his side and watched for a moment while one of the forensic techs began taking close-up photos of the wound, and of the weapon still lodged in it.

Holmes bent at the waist, ducking left and right, crinkling his nose as he watched the CSUs at work. Pulling his phone out, he reached into another pocket and slipped out the magnifying attachment for the phone's camera. Fitting it, he sidestepped over the body, directly in the way of the CSU's camera. Holmes held both hands up in what to Watson looked like some kind of apology; the tech looked at Gregson, clearly confused and not a little annoyed. The captain nodded, but waved him aside anyway. The tech stepped back with a frown.

Holmes dropped to his knees on the hard carpet as he leaned over the body, bringing his nose within an inch of the fountain pen embedded in the victim's eye. Then he shifted position, and rested his cheek on the victim's chest, apparently to get a clear, perpendicular view of the pen's barrel. Watson and Gregson both shuffled on their feet as they watched, Bell returning his attention to his notebook as the CSU tech with the camera muttered something to his colleague, who stood back, watching with folded arms and a raised eyebrow.

Careful to keep his head still, Holmes brought his phone up and, magnifying lens practically touching the pen, he snapped a series of photographs.

Then, in a single fluid movement, he pulled himself to his feet and he took a step back, his heels touching, legs together.

He gestured with an expansive wave to the corpse.

"You may continue," he said to the body. Behind him, the CSU techs looked at each other, then stepped forward to continue their interrupted work.

Bell peered over Holmes's shoulder as the consultant began swiping through the photographs he had just taken.

"Anything?" asked Bell.

Holmes snorted a laugh, then, pausing on one photograph, he turned his phone around and pinch-zoomed in on the picture.

"Quite the murder weapon," he said.

"Not every day someone is killed with a fountain pen, sure," said Bell.

Holmes nodded and turned the phone around to the others. Watson looked closely at the image, a close-up of the pen's fat barrel. The etched make and model of the pen was clearly visible.

"Not every day someone is killed with a fountain pen worth as much as a mid-sized family car, no."

With that Holmes tilted the phone again and tapped the screen, zooming still further. Watson squinted, trying to read the writing without her glasses.

"Jacques... LeFevre?"

Holmes nodded. "Swiss manufacturers of some of the finest writing instruments in the world. The typical retail price of a LeFevre is somewhere north of $20,000, but, based on the shape of the barrel, the patina of the surface, I suspect this one is a vintage model and may be worth considerably more than that. But it requires further examination to place it precisely."

"Could it be Smythe's own pen?" asked Watson.

Bell sniffed. "People really spend that much money on a *pen*?"

Watson nodded. "Pens like this are more common than

you'd think. Back when I was a resident I worked with several consultants who prided themselves on their pen collections."

"And as CFO of a place like Mantis," said Gregson, "the victim's salary would probably have easily financed a pen like that."

"Nothing like an investment piece you can put to practical use," said Holmes. He thumbed through a few more photographs, then pocketed the phone, lens *in situ*. "Has the body been searched yet?"

Gregson nodded. "Pockets, yes. The room too. We have his wallet, driver's license, the usual."

"No cap?"

"Cap?"

"Yes, *cap*," said Holmes. "The fountain pen will have a cap. LeFevre introduced serial numbers to their writing instruments in 1986, engraving them on the cap's clip. I can't be sure what precise vintage this pen is without further examination, but if it was made any time after the mid-eighties, the serial number will help in identifying the instrument and its rightful owner. The purchase of a high-value item such as this pen should be relatively easy to trace."

"Nobody has found the cap yet," said Bell, extracting his phone from his jacket. "But we have a team at Smythe's apartment." He nodded at Gregson. "I'll give them a call, see if there are any more pens there like this one."

"Excellent, Detective," said Holmes. "There are other ways to identify fountain pens—the wear on the nib, for example, can be as unique as a fingerprint. If we can match the angle of wear on the murder weapon with a pen from Smythe's apartment then we will know if the pen was his or not."

Gregson raised an eyebrow. "Okay, we can take a look back at the morgue with the medical examiner."

At this comment, Watson saw one of the Mantis security agents at the door, still facing away from them, touch his earpiece and incline his head. Were they listening in? They had to be. Watson wondered who they were reporting back to. It made her distinctly uncomfortable—this was a crime scene, one the NYPD were controlling. Any interference would complicate things, potentially jeopardizing the investigation.

Holmes must have noticed the security agent too, as he glanced toward the door and licked his bottom lip, before turning back to the captain.

"I think we can find out much quicker than that," said Holmes, his voice low. He moved to the bed and pulled a pair of blue latex gloves from the open CSU case, then moved back to the body, muttering a brief "excuse me" before reaching down for the fountain pen.

The tech protested, but it was too late. Holmes tugged once, then twice, then the pen slid free. Watson winced, knowing the slick sucking noise she heard was entirely in her imagination.

Holmes returned to the others, blood-covered pen held as delicately between forefinger and thumb as the silver preserve spoon had been earlier that afternoon. Gregson nodded at the weapon, his nose crinkled in disgust.

"Couldn't that have waited until we got the body back to the morgue?"

"A delay that would have been quite unnecessary," said Holmes. He held the pen up to his eye, examining the end that had been embedded in the victim. Watson could see the gold nib of the pen was fairly clean. The point looked decidedly sharp.

An ideal weapon.

Still holding the pen level, Holmes scrabbled in his jacket with his other hand and extracted his phone again, magnifying lens still in place. Flicking the phone's bright

LED light on, he moved his eye close to the screen as he rotated the pen under the lens.

"What are you looking for now?" asked Bell.

"Fingerprints," said Holmes. "There were none on the pen's barrel. It's possible there were some farther down the shaft, but unfortunately the various humors of Mr. Smythe's right eyeball have done a fairly good job of cleaning the evidence. Here. Swipe through the filters, you'll see."

With that he handed the phone to Watson. Bell and Gregson leaned in as she scanned through the photos Holmes had taken. In the bottom toolbar of the picture app was a series of edit functions. Selecting the filter option, Watson cycled through a number of different automated enhancements. In each case, the color of the pen's barrel and nib changed slightly, but Holmes was right. The telltale swirls, whorls and loops of a fingerprint were distinct by their absence.

"The killer was wearing gloves perhaps," said Watson, handing the phone back to Holmes. Then she looked around the hotel room. "They cleaned up after themselves too. If there was some kind of struggle, I can't see it."

Bell nodded. "Either there was a struggle and the killer cleaned the scene when he was done—"

"Or," said Holmes, interrupting, "there was no struggle because the victim knew the killer. It's possible Mr. Smythe was taken by surprise. Who booked the room?"

"We've got people checking the records downstairs. They can fill us in when we join them," said Gregson. "But what we do know is that the room hasn't been slept in. We've been over it top to bottom and there's nothing in here. Whoever had the room never stayed in it."

"Of course," said Holmes. "This was merely a rendezvous. And what better place to pick, an unsavory hotel in an unsavory neighborhood where people have a tendency to turn a blind eye. And the very last place anyone would suspect the CFO of a major financial investment firm, not to mention a highly secretive one, to be visiting." He looked down at the body, then gestured to Watson. "Time of death?"

Watson took a pair of gloves from the CSU case and pulled them on before kneeling down by the body. She gingerly felt the limbs, flexing the arms until she met resistance, then she pulled one of the deceased's sleeves up and examined the skin on the underside of the forearm.

"Well," she said, lowering the arm and then standing, "sometime last night, at a very rough guess. Certainly he's been dead for less than twenty-four hours, based on lividity and rigor mortis. We'll know more when we get him back to the morgue."

"That would tally with the GPS data Mantis have from his phone," said Bell. "According to their security chief, the victim got here sometime late last night."

"Curious that the killer didn't take Smythe's phone," said Watson, "which suggests he or she didn't know about how Mantis tracks their employees."

Holmes nodded. "I think we should go down and talk to the hotel staff, including the person who called the police. It's possible that even a rundown establishment such as this has at least *some* video surveillance. If we are very lucky we might even be able to get a look at the killer."

Holmes strode from the room, Gregson and Bell at his heels. Watson followed, but paused just inside the room. Out in the hall, her friends were almost at the elevator, where one of the Mantis security agents stood, impassive, silent, unmoving. Watson stepped through the doorway and glanced back at the two agents similarly positioned outside the hotel room where Gregory Smythe had met his death. Both of the agents were young men, haircuts razor-short, eyes completely hidden behind their opaque glasses.

Mantis Capital Investments. Watson turned the name over in her mind.

Whoever they were, she didn't like their methods one little bit.

4

THE SUSPECTS

"What was that you were saying about getting lucky?"

Holmes glanced sideways at Watson, one arm wrapped around his chest, the other hand stroking his chin, before returning his attention to the very small and very cheap LCD monitor on the desk in front of them. The back office behind the front desk of the Athena Hotel was small and, occupied by Holmes and Watson, Gregson and Bell, and Cynthia the receptionist, a young woman barely out of her teens with teased black hair who was apparently in sole charge of the building, rather cramped.

The image on the screen was green-tinted monochrome and washed out almost to the point where half of the picture was nothing but a bright glow. The angle of the video feed was also less than ideal, showing a three-quarters view of the lobby that didn't include the street entrance or the elevator on the opposite side. Of course, Watson knew at once why the camera was positioned as it was, focused mostly on one half of the front desk—the half where the cashbox was kept. The security camera was less for the safety of hotel guests and more to keep a watchful eye on untrustworthy staff.

Holmes reached forward and held down the right arrow key on the dirty keyboard in front of the monitor, and the replay of surveillance footage sped up. After a few moments of nothing, there was a blurred movement. Holmes released the key, wound back a few seconds, then stood back and studied the footage.

A man appeared from the bottom left of the screen—street side—dressed in a dark suit, the front of which flapped open as he marched with some speed and purpose across the lobby. There was a receptionist on duty—not Cynthia, Watson noted—who glanced up as the man passed, and then leaned out across the desk as the strange visitor collided with a young couple making their way from the elevator side of the lobby. The visitor, in some hurry, apparently ignored the pair, even though the collision had spun the woman around and the man had turned, arms outstretched, mouth working in silence as he berated the visitor. While it was a shame there was no sound on the footage, Watson wasn't sure they would have learned anything more from it if it had.

But the video surveillance did have a timestamp, and although only his back was visible to the camera, there was no mistaking the identity of the visitor in the smart suit.

That man was Gregory Smythe, and when he entered the building it was eleven minutes past eleven the previous night.

"He sure was in a hurry," said Watson.

Holmes nodded. "Have you spoken to the couple he nearly knocked over, Captain?" he asked, not taking his eyes from the screen. The video surveillance now showed an empty lobby, Smythe out of view by the elevators and the receptionist having disappeared into the very back office they were all now standing in.

"Still looking for them. They're a couple of backpackers from Germany who checked out this morning. We think they're on the road somewhere, a little hard to contact."

"What about the guy on reception?" asked Watson. She turned around to face Cynthia. Standing between the two policemen, the morning receptionist crinkled her nose and glanced nervously at Captain Gregson, who smiled and gave her a friendly, encouraging nod.

"Ah, that was Gerry," she said. "He told me about the dead guy when I came in this morning. Gerry has the night shifts this week, I'm on days." She shrugged. "Sorry, I don't know any more than that. He just said the guy was in a hurry. The others arrived—they came in and just stood there for ages and ignored him, he said. More of them went up in the elevator and didn't come back down. Eventually he went up and had a look himself. That's when he saw there was a body in 262 and called the police." Cynthia shuddered.

While she spoke, Holmes had rewound the footage to the point where Smythe would have entered the building, but rather than stopping there, he kept going back. As Watson watched the timestamp spin into the past, a number of ghostly, blurry shadows flitted across the screen as people came and went through the hotel lobby.

"I expect you see a fair few businessmen in expensive suits," said Holmes. "Hotels that offer rooms by the hour often do."

Watson frowned. "You think he was here meeting a *prostitute*?"

Holmes sniffed. "Or to get his fix. Maybe this was a drug deal gone wrong, his supplier stabbing him in the eye, perhaps not necessarily to kill." Holmes mimed a stabbing motion with one arm while he stroked his chin with the other hand, his eyes getting that faraway look that Watson knew all too well. "The video surveillance shows any number of possible candidates entering and exiting the building during the day."

"If the victim had any drugs in his system then it'll show up in the tox report," said Bell. "But he wasn't carrying anything. That also doesn't explain how the room was cleaned up. If it was a fight and he died accidentally, the killer would more likely just have panicked and fled the scene."

"And there's also the fact that the murder weapon is a twenty-thousand-dollar fountain pen," said Watson.

"Which we have yet to discount as the victim's own," said Holmes. He waggled a finger at the computer monitor and craned his neck around to look at Cynthia. "This is the only surveillance footage available, yes?"

Cynthia nodded, her fingers curled together tightly in front of her as she spoke. "Uh, yeah. There are no other cameras in the whole building, I think." She crinkled her nose again. "Sorry."

Holmes spun on his heel to face the young woman. Cynthia took a half-step back and looked at Watson for support, clearly unnerved by Holmes's twitchy behavior.

Watson didn't blame her *at all*.

"I understand you were on duty when the people who booked room 262 checked in," Holmes said. It wasn't a question, it was a statement.

Cynthia nodded. "Yeah. That was me."

"Well then," said Holmes, suddenly turning on a dazzling smile. "I suggest we take a look at the hotel's ledger."

Watson flicked through the last couple of pages of the Athena Hotel's check-in ledger, which seemed to be about the same vintage as everything else in the building. The book was long and rectangular, the cover greasy to the touch, the yellowed pages within divided into the usual fields for guests to sign in—name, address, phone number, even a column for email address (*not so ancient then*, thought Watson). The book was half-filled, and on the left-hand center page, where the binding showed at the spine, was the entry for the last people to check into room 262.

"Josephine and Harold Banks," she read. "The address is a little hard to read—looks like—" she peered closer at the spidery scrawl, knowing full well that the handwriting was deliberately rough to obscure the details "—North Carolina? There's a cell number but no email."

"All fake, of course," said Holmes. "Names, address, contact details." He slid the book out from in front of Watson and spun it around on the front desk. Behind it, Cynthia had resumed her usual position as receptionist on duty, while Gregson and Bell were standing together on the lobby side. Watson, realizing she was on the far left of the counter, turned and looked up into the corner of the lobby where the wall met the ceiling. There was a smoke detector there—a fake, inside of which was the low-quality security camera the hotel owners used to monitor their front desk staff.

Holmes tapped the entry in the ledger then looked up at Cynthia. "The couple. Can you describe them for us?"

Cynthia shrugged. "Well, I guess. They were, uh, old. I mean—" she looked around the group assembled in front of her "—well, not as old as all of you, but she was in her thirties and he was in his fifties maybe."

Watson raised an eyebrow and glanced at Detective Bell, who was having trouble hiding a smirk.

"Uh, she had dark hair, kinda long," Cynthia continued. "He was kinda big. Blonde hair, he had a goatee I think." She waved a hand around her own chin as she remembered his features.

"Big as in *fat*?" asked Holmes.

"Oh, no, like, he was *big*," said Cynthia. "Y'know. Big. Strong. Like a football player maybe."

"According to the ledger they checked in the day *before* yesterday, around four in the afternoon," said Watson.

"Which leaves about thirty-one hours before the victim arrived," said Gregson.

"And whoever Jo and Harry are," said Bell, "they never actually stayed in the room."

Holmes looked over the ledger again, lips pursed as he ran his fingers down the entries. Then he pulled his phone from his pocket yet again and took a couple of snaps of the check-in of interest before pocketing the phone and looking back up at Cynthia. "I'd like a copy of the video surveillance footage please."

Cynthia frowned. "I thought we just checked it?"

"Some, yes, not all," said Holmes. "And I want *all* of it."

Cynthia glanced at Watson again. "I… I'm not sure how to do that. I mean, don't you need some kind of warrant or something? I've seen this kind of thing on TV."

"Well, you're not on TV now," said Gregson. He leaned over the front desk, resting both arms on the counter top. He cocked his head. "We can get a warrant if you like, but how about you just help us out. You called *us*, remember?"

"Um, sure, okay," said Cynthia. She glanced over her shoulder. "Oh, um… it's just… I'm not sure I know how to…"

Watson smiled. "It's okay, we can do it."

Watson lifted the hinged section at the end of the counter and swung the bottom section open, then, stepping through, gestured for Cynthia to lead them all into the back office. Once there, Holmes seated himself at the computer desk and took a small black object—a USB stick—from his pocket before sliding off the seat and disappearing under the desk to connect it to the computer itself.

As Watson waited, she heard the elevator ding out in the lobby. There was a rattle, like something heavy on wheels was being pushed over a bump, and then she heard Bell's raised voice.

Holmes banged his head on the underside of the desk as he extracted himself from underneath it, and emerged, rubbing his crown.

"What's going on?" he asked, looking up at Watson.

"I'm not sure," said Watson. "I'll go check."

Bell stood with his hands on his hips, blocking the main doors of the hotel, his jacket pulled back to show the NYPD badge on his belt. In front of him was a procession of black-suited security agents in sunglasses from Mantis Capital, and behind them came a wheeled stretcher with a body bag—containing Gregory Smythe—pushed by two New York Fire Department paramedics. Through the main doors, beyond Detective Bell, Watson could see the red bulk of a fire department ambulance parked at the curb and Captain Gregson, now talking to another officer just outside the hotel. As Watson watched, the captain glanced back into the lobby, then broke off his conversation and walked briskly back inside. He took one look at the scene and, stuffing both hands into the pockets of his coat, tilted his head at his colleague.

"There a problem here, Detective?"

"The problem here, Captain," said Bell, "is deciding whether I charge these guys with obstruction of justice or tampering with a crime scene. I gotta admit, it's a tough one. Maybe I'll just go for broke and charge them with both."

Watson looked between the police detectives and the Mantis security agents. Behind them, the two paramedics with the stretcher looked decidedly unimpressed.

Surely Mantis weren't trying to take the *body* away?

Watson turned back to Bell. "What's going on? This is a police investigation, isn't it?"

"Oh, don't worry about that," said Bell. "That much they've acknowledged, and the body is going to the morgue. But our friends in the sharp suits here are refusing to hand over the victim's cellphone."

Holmes nodded, then turned to the lead Mantis agent. He stepped close, until he was practically touching the agent's nose with his own. The agent didn't move. It didn't even seem like he was *breathing*. Watson moved around until she could see Holmes and the rest of the group reflected in the agent's black glasses.

"You do realize you are interfering with a *murder* investigation, don't you?" Holmes asked, his voice barely a whisper, his back ramrod straight and his hands curled into tight fists by his side. He narrowed his eyes and moved his head around, almost like he was trying to see beyond the opaque sunglasses, before straightening up. "Your lack of cooperation certainly suggests a certain involvement in your CFO's death, at the very least. If I was of a conspiratorial mindset, I would even suggest some kind of corporate cover-up. Wouldn't be the first, won't be the last."

"I can assure you there is no cover-up, sir."

Holmes, Watson, and the two police detectives turned to face the new voice, one that belonged to a man with red hair and a red beard who had just entered the hotel from the street. He was dressed in a black suit similar to the Mantis agents, but Watson could see the cut was different, the fabric finer. As the man reached out to offer Holmes his hand, a cufflink with a jewel the size of a pea glittered at his wrist. "David Gallop, Mantis Capital. And you are…?"

Holmes looked down at Gallop's hand, but then rather pointedly clasped his own hands behind his back. "Annoyed and in need of a cup of tea."

Gallop gave an odd sort of half-laugh and looked at the others, turning his hand instead toward Gregson. The captain raised an eyebrow at Holmes before shaking the other man's hand.

"Good to see you again, Captain." Watson remembered that Gallop had been at the Athena when the police arrived.

"Mr. Gallop. I have to tell you, your staff are on the verge of causing an obstruction."

Gallop clicked his heels and dropped his chin onto his chest. "Captain Gregson, I must apologize on behalf of our company. My staff can be somewhat... enthusiastic, shall we say, about the tasks to which they are assigned."

"Tasks including covering up a *murder*?" asked Holmes, his eyes wide, a smile playing over his lips like he'd just asked the other man if he'd had a nice weekend.

Gallop laughed nervously again, then glanced at Gregson, his own eyebrows raised.

"This is Sherlock Holmes and Joan Watson," said the captain. "They are consultants to the NYPD."

"Fascinating," said Gallop. He glanced at Holmes, then turned his attention to Watson, sensing perhaps she was the more reasonable person to talk to.

"Consultants, eh? Well, I can assure you that my staff will be cooperating fully with your investigation."

He snapped his fingers and held out a hand to the lead security agent, who immediately handed his boss the victim's cellphone, which he had been holding behind his back, still sealed in its police evidence bag. Gallop took the object and, smiling at Watson, immediately offered it to Holmes.

Watson couldn't resist a small smile herself. It was a classic move, she thought, seeking to regain Holmes's trust.

But she wasn't smiling at that. She was smiling because she knew exactly the kind of reaction this would get from her partner.

Holmes looked down at the bag, the smile still on his face, but he didn't touch it. Then he looked back up at the other man, the smile suddenly evaporating.

"We will need to talk to you and your 'staff', Mr. Gallop."

"By all means. It is vital we get to the bottom of this, and as I say, you have our full cooperation." He turned to Gregson. "I can arrange passes for everyone to come to our office tomorrow morning. You will be free to interview anybody and everybody in the building."

He then offered the bag-wrapped phone to Gregson, who took it with a muttered thanks. Gallop gave a small bow, then he snapped his fingers again. The black-suited agents began filing out of the lobby. Once the agents had exited, Gallop spun on his heel and turned a smile on for everyone, then followed his men out.

"Well," said Watson, "that was... weird."

Bell clicked his tongue. "You're telling me," he said, with a shake of the head. Then he turned to the paramedics waiting by the stretcher. "You're good to go."

As the stretcher was rolled out, Holmes snatched the phone from Gregson's hand.

"Hey!"

Holmes ignored him, instead grabbing the side of the stretcher, bringing it to a halt.

"One moment," he said. Then he opened the bag and took the phone out. Waking the device from sleep, he then unzipped the body bag all the way to the victim's waist, reached inside, and pulled the right arm out. Pulling the stiff thumb as straight as possible, he held the pad against the home button—which doubled as a fingerprint reader—on the phone, which, a second later, beeped. Holmes then dropped the arm, waving at the paramedics as he began fiddling with the phone. The paramedics stood still for a moment, no doubt wondering what the hell was going on, before swinging Gregory Smythe's lifeless arm back into the bag and zipping it up.

"I wonder if Mr. Gallop would have been so agreeable to let us keep the phone if he thought I would be able to unlock it?"

"Well, it's not like he had a choice," said Gregson. "Our techs would have unlocked it eventually."

Holmes peered at the screen, moving his thumb around as he navigated the contents. Watson went up on her toes to get a closer look.

"You really think they are trying to hide something?" she asked.

"Mantis Capital Investments appear to work in their own little world, so the answer to that question is undoubtedly yes," said Holmes. "The corollary of that question is whether what they are trying to hide has any bearing whatsoever on the death of their CFO." He paused. "Aha."

Bell flipped his notebook open, pen poised. "Found something?"

Holmes tapped the screen and tilted it so the others could get a look. Watson saw a long list of calls made and received.

"Gregory Smythe," said Holmes, "received a very long call from a number that is *not* in his contacts. Nearly forty minutes, in point of fact. Look at the rest—every other call he received was from people already listed in his phone—people he knew. Co-workers from the Mantis office, the others presumably clients."

Holmes tapped through the list, each number coming up with a contact card, nearly all of which, Watson saw, had the full details of the person entered, including a photograph.

"Is that the only mystery call?" she asked.

Holmes pursed his lips and scrolled back through the call list. "Apparently so." Then he exited the call log, and opened the message app. There were only a handful of messages listed. But the latest one caught Watson's attention.

"There," she said, pointing to the screen. "That's the same number."

Holmes opened the message:

PLAN CHANGED. 2HRS. B THERE.

"That message was sent at 8.29 P.M. yesterday," said Holmes, "a full four hours after he received the call from the same number."

"And the footage from the security camera shows him coming here just after eleven," said Watson. "No wonder he was in a hurry. He was late."

Holmes *hrmmed*, then he thumbed the call button and held the phone to his ear. Gregson frowned.

"What are you doing?"

"Eliminating the obvious," said Holmes, pulling the phone from his ear then pulling his own from his pocket. With the two side by side, he manually entered the number from Smythe's phone and hit the call button then the speaker button. The number didn't even ring, going instead straight to an automated voice.

"The number you have dialed is no longer in service. The number you have dialed is—"

Holmes killed the call. Moving to the reception desk, he pulled the ledger around, traced the number left by the non-existent Josephine and Harold Banks, then entered it into his phone.

"The number you have dialed is unavailable. Please try again. The num—"

"The number they checked in is fake," said Watson.

Holmes nodded. "While the one they called Smythe from likely came from a burner phone, one most probably now sitting at the bottom of the Hudson River."

"Well," said Bell, "we'll still run a trace on both, just to be sure." He pointed with his pen to the hotel ledger. "I'm assuming that the address is a fake too."

"Easy enough to check," said Gregson. He took one last look around the hotel lobby. "I think we're done here. Let's leave CSU to get on with their job. I'll text with a time for our visit to Mantis. Ah, may I?" He held out his hand. Holmes handed over Smythe's phone, his lips pursed and eyes narrow.

Watson wished the two detectives a goodnight, and watched as they headed out. Holmes stood by the front desk, his head tilted to one side as he watched Gregson and Bell disappear through the hotel doors.

"Do you really think Mantis will be cooperative when we go see them?" she asked.

"That is what we shall find out, Watson," said Holmes. "I'll certainly be fascinated to find out more about this autonomous nation-state they call a company."

The pair left, Watson thinking over what Holmes had said many times on their journey back to the brownstone. Were Mantis hiding something? Did that have anything to do with the murder of their CFO, Gregory Smythe? She could understand the importance of controlling the situation—if Mantis was a hedge fund management firm, then the news that one of their senior executives had been murdered was sure to send ripples throughout the financial industry. Add to that the circumstances of Smythe's death, the time and location, then a scandal would be sure to brew. Perhaps she didn't blame their head of security, Gallop, and his miniature army of black-suited agents. They were remarkably zealous... but then perhaps that was also understandable. They were unlikely to have encountered a situation like this one before.

In any event, tomorrow was going to be an interesting day.

5

THE LION'S DEN

The offices of Mantis Capital Investment were pretty much exactly as Watson had expected. Secluded in a tall glass and steel skyscraper in midtown Manhattan, just one of many such anonymous structures that formed the skyline of the city, to say the company just occupied the top floor of the building was doing them something of an injustice. With high ceilings and an external wall that was entirely composed of apparently seamless plate glass, offering incredible views of the city, the Mantis office was as impressive in design as it clearly was in cost. The entire design aesthetic was one of European minimalism, with everything from the sofas in reception to the coffee pots and matching cups delivered on trays to the boardroom in which Watson and Holmes currently sat; clearly very, very expensive. What wall space there was that wasn't plate glass was covered with modern art, which, if not instantly recognizable, was at least obviously original.

What Watson *hadn't* expected was the half-hour procedure they had been put through just to get into the building. Common to many inner-city office blocks, access just to the building's expansive lobby required the doorman on duty behind the desk to check who was requesting entry before manually operating the door's remote lock. As Holmes and Watson, together with Captain Gregson, made their way across the lobby, the space cavernous and gray, every surface dark polished concrete, the ceiling slanted in interesting architectural angles, the doorman murmured into a phone pressed tightly to the side of his head, observing the approach of the visitors. Once at the desk, the group was asked to present their official IDs and sign in, and were then shown through a turnstile entry barrier to a hall of elevators nearly as big as the lobby again. The doorman pressed the elevator button, and when the car arrived, the door opened to reveal one of Mantis's black-suited security agents—possibly one from the Athena Hotel the day before, although Watson found it hard to be sure with their identical haircuts and dark glasses—who exited and then gestured for the group to enter. At the thirtieth floor, the elevator stopped and the group exited… and Watson's shoulders dropped as she saw there was yet another security desk and turnstile to pass through.

This desk was different to the one downstairs. Mounted on an adjustable arm was a camera, and below that, a wide, angled pad. Watson recognized the set-up immediately; it was nearly identical to immigration counters found in every major airport, ready to take photos and fingerprints from weary travelers just off their plane.

Signing in just to enter the main office took another full fifteen minutes. One by one, the visitors were photographed, fingerprinted, their IDs scanned and then studied with apparently great interest by the man behind the desk while a small printer spat out a passport-sized photograph of each of them. This picture was mounted in a clear plastic sleeve, along with a small printed card, which each person was required to sign before the guard stamped it. The plastic sleeve was about the size of a playing card and had a clip at the top, and printed as a transparent overlay was a giant red letter V—for visitor, Watson assumed. She and Holmes went through first, and waited for Captain Gregson in a plush area beyond the security barrier that was filled with sofas the size of large family cars and a tripod coffee table that would not have looked out of place aboard the USS *Enterprise*.

"Mantis sure are serious about security," said Watson as she sank into the sofa.

Next to her, Holmes remained standing, motionless, his hands deep in the pockets of his steel-gray jacket, his own ID badge clipped to the breast pocket, as he watched the security guard adjust the camera on the desk to get the best mug shot of Gregson.

"I would go a step further and suggest that Mantis Capital have ventured beyond seriousness and are now well into the realms of paranoia."

"You can't blame them," said Watson, gesturing at the set-up. "A lot of companies are starting to invest in this level of security. And look at this place. Mantis must have a healthy client list to pay for all of this."

"Smoke and mirrors, Watson," said Holmes, rocking on his heels. He glanced around. "The glowing light of the anglerfish, waiting for a meal. The baited hook, the beauty of the angler's fly—"

Watson sighed. "Okay, I get the picture, thanks."

Security cleared, Gregson joined the pair, the captain adjusting his company-issued ID that sat next to the NYPD badge clipped to his lapel. Watson extracted herself from the sofa, and the three of them stood for a few seconds in the waiting room before an internal door opened and a familiar man joined them.

"Gentlemen, *lady*."

David Gallop walked into the waiting room, his hand already outstretched to welcome the visitors. Holmes stepped forward and grasped it, pumping the security chief's hand firmly—much, as Watson could see, to the obvious surprise of Gallop, no matter how much the security chief tried to hide it behind a smile.

"Mr. Gallop, it is a pleasure," said Holmes. "I must congratulate you upon your remarkable security screening."

"Ah well," said Gallop. He glanced at Watson, one eyebrow heading upwards. Watson gave him a tight smile, noting, as he clearly did too, Holmes's apparent decision to now be polite to the man. Gallop then looked back at Holmes.

"Better safe than sorry," he said. "We manage the portfolios of a number of rather important clients for whom discretion is key."

"Indeed," said Holmes. "Discreet to the point of obfuscation."

Oh, thought Watson*, there it was. Of course Holmes wasn't being polite. He was being sarcastic.*

More fool me.

"Your company website is a *single* page with a *single* paragraph of text and a *single* contact email address," Holmes continued. "After a further six solid hours of online research, the only information about Mantis Capital Investment I was able to ascertain was the address of this building. A remarkable feat in this digital age."

Gallop frowned. "Obfuscation?"

Holmes smiled. "Don't take that the wrong way, I meant it as a compliment. Keeping an entire company and its staff *offline* must be quite the undertaking, and as I said, you are to be congratulated. Shall we?"

Holmes gestured with an open hand to the doorway through which Gallop had come. The security chief was confused for a moment, then he smiled, adjusted his tie, and mirrored Holmes's gesture.

"Oh, please," he said, "after *you*."

Holmes might have been right about how the public areas of Mantis Capital Investment were the alluring bait for potential clients, but if Watson was honest, she couldn't see much difference once Gallop had led them beyond the internal door. The main working office space followed the typical layout, one Watson had seen time and time again in the big city companies she and Holmes visited often in the course of their work: a large, open-plan array of desks, some separated from the others by low cubicle walls, others entirely free-standing, orbited by a series of offices and meeting rooms, some with glass partitions, some entirely hidden behind more walls on which more of the Mantis collection of modern art was proudly displayed.

The office was busy, too. Life—*work*—must go on, thought Watson, particularly in a place such as this, in a company not only dealing with unimaginable sums of money but trying very, very hard not to let their clients and investors know, for as long as possible, that something was very much awry. But still, as Watson followed the others, security chief Gallop in the lead, she sensed a nervous tension in the air. Those workers not on phones or glued to computer displays watched the group as they made their way across the floor. Watson could see the body language, sense the mood. People were shaken, nervous, afraid, upset, angry. Their company had been *invaded*; something had happened that was out of their control, and with terrible consequences. And sooner or later, that news would have to go public, and they would have to deal with whatever fallout came their way.

Gallop led the trio into a large meeting room, this one with a glass partition wall fitted with louver blinds for privacy. Once inside, Watson paused and, despite the familiarity with her home city, had to take a moment as she crossed the threshold to admire the view. Outside, seen through floor-to-ceiling plate glass, midtown Manhattan stretched out in a nearly one-hundred-and-eighty-degree vista.

Gallop stopped at the head of the table and rested his hands on the chair in front of him. He gave the room a look over, sucking his cheeks in as he did so, like he was checking that everything was as it should be.

"You can use this as your operations room," he said. "You need anything, just ask. You have carte blanche. I'm free to assist with the interviews."

Or free to listen in on them, thought Watson.

"Thank you very much, Mr. Gallop," said Holmes, nodding as he looked around the expansive meeting room. "This will do very nicely indeed." Then he turned to face the security chief, the grin on his face suddenly freezing in place. "I think we can start with you, if you don't mind."

Despite the bizarre secrecy, the over-the-top security screenings, and the swarm of make-believe G-Men who had gathered at the Athena Hotel—security agents just like the one that had met them at the elevator—Watson had to admit that Mantis Capital were being cooperative. *Very* cooperative. She, Holmes and Gregson had been talking to Gallop for nearly forty minutes, and if anything, the security chief was positively enthusiastic as he and Holmes went over the firm's simple but effective cellphone tracking system.

Holmes nodded in his chair, the movement traveling down his entire body, as he peered at the laptop Gallop had placed in front of him. Seated next to him, the security chief pointed to the screen, which showed a map of the entire tri-state conurbation. Scattered across the map were a couple of dozen tiny red icons, the largest cluster of which were in midtown— the Mantis office building.

"So as you can see," said Gallop, "we can identify and track any employee using the GPS in their company-issued cellphone, and our own custom human resources app."

"And presumably," said Holmes, his own finger tapping his bottom lip, "your system provides both real-time location data and historical tracking records?"

Gallop nodded. "Oh yes. Absolutely." With a finger and thumb, he executed a shortcut on the keyboard; as he repeatedly tapped, the red icons all disappeared, replaced instead by a single, larger icon that appeared and disappeared across the Manhattan and Brooklyn areas of the map as he cycled through the movements of an individual Mantis staff member—which, according to the data tab at the top of the map, was Gallop himself— over the past week. Then the security chief reached into his jacket pocket to pull out his phone. Holding it up, he tapped the laptop keyboard again with his other hand. A single large red icon showed over the location of the Mantis building; another tap, and his phone dinged an alert. "Real-time tracking, and we can ping phones—useful if you've lost it down the back of the sofa."

At this, Holmes burst into laughter along with Gallop. Watson frowned and glanced across the table at Gregson, who merely raised an eyebrow.

"How far back does the historical tracking data go?" asked Holmes.

Gallop laid his phone down and pulled the laptop a little toward himself. "We hold a complete record." His fingers flew over the keyboard, and then he pushed the laptop back toward Holmes and executed the earlier shortcut. His own red indicator began jumping around the screen again, moving too quickly to be seen clearly, and then the entire map zoomed out to show the United States as a whole, with the red icon appearing over Los Angeles.

"As you can see, this time last year I was in Burbank, California, for a meeting."

"Very thorough," said Holmes.

Captain Gregson tapped his pen against the table. "Sounds like a pretty big invasion of privacy to me."

Gallop shrugged. "If your phone has a GPS chip, it can be tracked whether you agree to it or not. Likewise your car, your computer, your tablet. Location tracking is part of the employee contract here. Everyone signs up to it. And besides, you're a member of the NYPD. Your current location is known by... how many people back at your precinct?"

Gregson tilted his head, acknowledging the point.

"But what do you need this level of security for?" asked Watson. "I mean, I get it, you're a hedge fund management firm. But there must be dozens of financial institutions like yours within just a couple of blocks of this building. I don't imagine many of them have their own private version of the secret service."

Gallop sat back in his chair and steepled his fingers under his chin. "This was all actually Gregory's idea."

Holmes sat back in his own chair, deliberately mirroring Gallop's posture, fingers in an equally thoughtful pose.

Gaining his confidence, thought Watson, *without Gallop even knowing it*.

"Tell us about Mr. Smythe," said Holmes. "How long had he been the Chief Financial Officer?"

"Ever since Mantis Capital was founded," said Gallop. "We're a relatively new company, only started six years ago. Our CEO will be able to give you the full history when you interview her."

"Oh, don't worry," said Gregson, "she's next on the list."

"Forgive me," said Holmes, "but high-level security doesn't seem to be within the purview of a CFO."

Gallop nodded. "You're right. Before Gregory joined Mantis he was a security analyst. He worked for a federal agency initially but then moved into the private sector."

"And then," said Holmes, "he had a late change of career, switching to the financial industry?"

Gallop gave a frown, but he nodded, indicating that that was just how it was. "Some people have an aptitude for many different types of work. He was smart, I'll say that much for him."

"And he brought his past experience in security with him," said Watson.

"Not just experience, Watson," said Holmes. "An entire *mindset*. He wanted his new venture to be the most secure and secretive in the hedge fund universe. What better way to entice the most lucrative of clients? Demonstrate that their personal data and portfolios are held by the most secure, the most secret institution, and the richest investors will flock from all over the world."

"So we have the victim himself to thank for the discovery of his own body," said Gregson. "Smythe doesn't show for a meeting, doesn't answer his phone, so you track it and discover he's been murdered before the hotel staff even know anything's happened."

"Exactly right," said Gallop. Watson watched as the security chief worked on the laptop, selecting Smythe's profile in the GPS tracker then cycling through the records.

"On the day that poor Gregory was killed, he was in lower Manhattan, then midtown, back to downtown, then up to Washington Heights."

"Where he remained," said Holmes quietly. He pointed at the screen. "Can you go back further? The last two weeks."

"Sure," said Gallop. Watson watched as he cycled through the longer time period, Smythe's red icon leaping around all over the map.

"Manhattan, Brooklyn," said Gregson, leaning in to get a better look at Smythe's journeys. "Jersey City, back to Manhattan. Okay. Can you give us a readout of each of the locations he was traced to?"

"To the exact address," said Gallop.

"In your initial review of your CFO's movements, is there anything that strikes you as out of the ordinary, Mr. Gallop?" Holmes asked.

Gallop sat back again and pursed his lips, shaking his head. "I don't think so. Gregory normally travels quite a lot, but there was nothing in the calendar that I can recall in the last few weeks. These locations on the tracker correspond to the office here, his apartment in Central Park West. His trip to Brooklyn could be anything, maybe a restaurant, visiting friends, shopping. Same with New Jersey. Honestly, there's nothing that jumps out at me."

"Thank you, Mr. Gallop," said Holmes. "You have been most enlightening." He looked at Gregson. "Captain, perhaps you can enlist some of your fellow officers to start talking to the staff out on the floor while myself and Ms. Watson have a chat with the CEO."

Gregson nodded. "I'll get started," he said, standing from the table and adjusting the buttons on his jacket, his cellphone already in one hand.

Gallop stood and moved to the door, swiping his security card in the reader to allow it to open.

"Wow," said Watson. "You even need a security card to get *out* of a room?"

Gallop smiled. "You can never be too secure."

"And if there's a fire?"

Gallop indicated the red button below the card reader.

"Emergency door release," he said. "But it's linked directly to the fire alarm. Now, if you would like to follow me, please."

6

NO LOVE LOST

I f the Mantis Capital security chief, David Gallop, had been the definition of helpful, the company's CEO was anything but. Early fifties, with long gray hair falling in two elegant, symmetrical waves onto the shoulders of a pin-sharp blue suit, Darcy Kellogg sat behind a desk half as big as the table in the meeting room Watson and the others had just spent the last hour in. Behind the desk, the CEO's office came to a point, the building's corner a right angle of plate glass offering the best view available—in this instance, looking directly down a corridor of tall buildings toward Downtown Manhattan. In the middle distance, centrally framed between the skyscrapers, the Empire State Building shone in the morning sun.

"So you have absolutely no idea *whatsoever* why your Chief Financial Officer, arguably *the* most important member of staff of your company, with an annual remuneration package that I can only imagine would make the average man—or woman—on the street weep in despair at the injustice and inequality of the world, was in a roach-infested dive hotel in the very seediest quadrant of this island?"

Kellogg blinked at Holmes's question, but didn't answer

it. Instead she looked at Watson. Watson remained impassive. If Holmes had a point, he would get to it soon enough. Out of the corner of her eye, she saw her colleague's mouth twitch at the corner.

Oh yes, he had a point all right. And, if she was honest, she didn't blame Holmes for his change in temperament. The CEO's demeanor was more than just calm business efficiency. It seemed like she was barely controlling her annoyance that her routine was being interrupted by something as inconvenient as the murder of her right-hand man. Being forced to talk to the two NYPD consultants was merely the icing on the cake.

"Or," Holmes said, tilting his head to look at the company CEO with narrow eyes, like she was a shimmering mirage on a distant horizon, "perhaps you are of the opinion that he was nothing more than a jumped-up accountant, and whatever trouble he had landed himself in uptown in Washington Heights, it was his own fault?"

Kellogg laughed and gave a slight shake of the head, as if she couldn't believe she had to entertain what she clearly thought was a ridiculous question. "I know what he was doing in Washington Heights," she said. Her eyes darted between Holmes and Watson, before settling back on Holmes.

There was a hardness there, a defiance. While Watson didn't much like the CEO, she could only imagine the business battles Kellogg had had to wage. The woman clearly had decades of experience, and while Holmes may have been used to discombobulating witnesses and suspects alike with a mix of genius insight and unsettling directness, Watson could tell that in Darcy Kellogg he had perhaps met his match.

Holmes lifted his chin, his eyes wide, clearly indicating that Kellogg needed to elaborate. The CEO snorted a laugh. "What else do you do in a hotel where you rent a room by the *hour*, Mr. Holmes? Our dear old Gregory was probably meeting a woman of, how shall I put it, *negotiable* affection."

Watson frowned. Wow, the CEO *really* didn't like her CFO. "You think he was seeing a *prostitute*?"

Kellogg shrugged, looking a little less like she could give a damn by the minute.

"An astute theory," said Holmes, "and it is possible that your CFO had a taste for a little bit of rough, shall we say. But a man of his position, money meaning nothing in the slightest, would have any number of high-class prostitution options available in lower and midtown Manhattan. Professionals of the highest caliber, offering the utmost discretion and secrecy as a matter of course—*precisely* the kind of arrangement a former security analyst in a prestigious position would no doubt prefer."

Holmes turned in his chair to Watson, and crossed one leg over the other as he leaned toward his colleague. "I speak from experience, of course—never trust a source that is not the primary one. I have in fact conducted a personal and, I can assure you, quite thorough survey of such services offered in this very area."

Watson frowned. "Of course you have."

Holmes nodded briskly. "Strictly for research purposes, you understand."

"Right."

Holmes beamed and turned back to Kellogg. "And personal relief, of course."

Kellogg's expression slipped, just a fraction. She glanced at Watson, her eyes a little wider than they had been. Holmes merely sat there, radiant smile still in place.

Watson closed her eyes, took a breath, then slid forward in her seat. It was time to steer the interview back to the subject at hand.

"Ms. Kellogg, we'll need to see your personnel files. We'll need to canvass everyone in your company, see if anyone had anything against Mr. Smythe, or any possible motivation for wanting him out of the way."

Kellogg shifted in her chair, her back straightening just a fraction. "I'm afraid that's out of the question."

Holmes jerked a thumb over his shoulder. "It's too late for that, Ms. Kellogg. New York's finest are already conducting interviews. Another couple of hours and they should have met with everybody."

"No," said the CEO, "I meant the personnel files. We take privacy very seriously here—"

"As we have gathered."

"And I can't possibly let you have access to that data."

"You seem to forget we are investigating a *murder*, Ms. Kellogg. A crime you and your company seem not particularly concerned about."

"I didn't kill Gregory, if that's what you're suggesting."

"I'm not suggesting anything of the sort," said Holmes. "What I *am* suggesting is that I call Captain Gregson of Special Crimes in here and suggest that *he* calls a judge and we get a subpoena to take a very great deal more than just your personnel files."

Kellogg's mouth was a tight line. She and Holmes shared a very long look, neither of them blinking. Then she reached for the phone on her desk.

"Yes," she said into the mouthpiece. "Get Gallop in here."

A moment later came a soft knock at the door and David Gallop leaned in.

"Ms. Kellogg?"

Kellogg stood from the desk and walked toward him. "Give them everything they want," she said.

And then she left her own office.

7

DEAD ENDS

While Gallop prepared the company files they had requested, Holmes and Watson took a look around Gregory Smythe's office. At half the size of his CEO's, it was still an impressive workspace, complete with yet another designer coffee table and two big easy chairs facing the plate glass windows overlooking the city, while the wall behind the mammoth desk was lined with bookcases in dark wood. Watson moved behind the desk and walked along the rows, reading the spines. Most of the volumes on display covered the minutiae of the financial and accounting industries, along with a few business management tomes that looked even drier. Light reading, they were *not*.

The books on the shelves were immaculate, first divided into subject category, then arranged alphabetical by author. Neatness was evident in the whole room—the desk had an all-in-one personal computer in brushed aluminum, a leather-bound notebook, and absolutely nothing else on it.

As Holmes wandered off to the coffee table area on the other side of the room, Watson turned back to the desk and began a survey of the drawers. There was paperwork—most of it neatly filed in folders that appeared to be color-coded, and some bits and pieces of office stationery: more notepads; colored cubes of sticky notes still in their cellophane wrappers; a box of paperclips; a staple remover; and a solar-powered calculator that had seen better days.

The second drawer contained more of the same, although most of the stationery consisted of packets of envelopes in three different sizes.

The third drawer Watson tried revealed something far more interesting.

"Hey, look at this..."

The office was empty.

"Sherlock?"

Holmes's head appeared from around the bottom of one of the easy chairs. He pulled himself to his feet and walked over to the desk.

"Amazing what people will drop under a sofa," he said.

"Did you find something?"

"Ah, alas not," said Holmes. "I was speaking purely theoretically. Our victim was fastidious in his neatness, it seems."

"Tell me about it. I've never seen a desk so tidy. But it seems our victim *didn't* use fountain pens."

Watson held up her discovery—a small oblong box of white card. There was an open flap at one end, with a scuff and tear indicating where a piece of tape had once sealed the opening. Watson shook the box, and it rattled. Then she peeled back the flap and turned the opening toward Holmes so he could see.

Holmes pursed his lips. "Pen refill cartridges."

"*Ballpoint* pen refills," said Watson, extracting a thin gold cylinder between a finger and thumb. "And the box has been opened. This looks like it's come from the office stationery cupboard—no marking or label, so probably from a bulk supply."

Holmes glanced at the desk. "But no sign of any pens, ballpoint or otherwise."

Watson reached for the leather-bound notebook and flipped it open. The page she landed on was filled with notes, even little drawings which, at first glance, looked like some kind of outline for a slide presentation.

Leaning down to get a better look, Watson lifted the edge of the book and tilted the page away from herself. Peering along the edge, with her other hand she ran a finger across the writing.

"Ballpoint," she said. Standing straight once more, she quickly flipped through the rest of the notebook. "The whole thing is in ballpoint."

Holmes nodded. "Indeed. But no cheap, disposable biro to be tossed away when it runs out—look at the stroke, this is a quality writing piece. Which is why he chooses to refill it from that pack you found." He placed a finger on one page, stopping Watson from flipping to the next. He slid his finger to a point about two-thirds of the way down. "Here. You can see where it ran out," he said, and he was right. The writing at the end of the line was faint, but the impression on the page was deeper, like Smythe was pushing down hard. On the next line, the blue ink was deep, nearly black. He'd changed the cartridge in his pen.

Watson frowned. "But like you said, there are no pens in this office. I guess he had a favorite he carried around with him."

"And yet," said Holmes, "the only pen found at the crime scene was embedded four inches into the man's cranium."

"A pen that apparently wasn't his."

Holmes cocked his head at Watson. "Apparently so, although hardly a concrete deduction."

With this, he strode to the office door and stepped through, quickly. Watson followed, but by the time she reached the doorway Holmes was far ahead, striding out across the open-plan area of the main office.

Watson stopped in the doorway to watch. As Holmes came to each desk in the main office, he paused, casting an eye over it with a look of grim determination, before moving to the next. If there was a person at the desk, he ignored them—and their protests—even when his search involved wheeling a chair—with the worker still on it—out of the way to pull open a drawer. After a few moments of this everyone in the office was watching him along with Watson.

As Holmes completed a circuit of the office, Watson headed around the other side to head him off.

"What are you looking for?" she asked.

Holmes stopped, his arms ramrod straight by his side. "The murderer," he said, before ducking to Watson's left to continue his bizarre mission down the center aisle of desks. At the first he stopped a little longer to examine the contents of two drawers before moving to the next.

Then Watson realized what he was doing. Gregson, meanwhile, appeared from a nearby meeting room, attracted by the commotion; through the open door, Watson could see another Mantis staff member seated for an interview in front of Detective Bell, who had arrived on the scene to lend a hand.

"I know I'm going to regret asking this," said Gregson, as he made his way to Watson's side, "but what's he doing now?"

"He's looking for pens," said Watson. "We think Smythe used refillable ballpoint pens exclusively, but at an office like this, there should be at least a few people who have fountain pens, even if they're just used as desk dressing."

Standing in the meeting-room doorway, Bell poked his tongue into his cheek. "Call me crazy, but spending twenty grand on a pen just for it to be some kind of office status symbol seems a little much."

By this time, Holmes had returned to the group, leaving

a trail of bewildered employees murmuring to each other in his wake. His eyes flicked between Watson, Gregson, and Bell, but Holmes didn't speak. It seemed like he was holding his breath.

Watson knew what that meant: frustration.

"No pens then?" she asked.

"On the contrary," said Holmes. "Pens aplenty. Ballpoints that come in five-dollar packs of ten. Ballpoints that cost the same as a small yacht you park outside your beach house in Montauk."

Bell raised an eyebrow. "And fountains?"

Holmes gave the detective a curt nod. "Two Mont Noir, three Boatman. Price range in the low hundreds to one number used by a gentleman—who is having an affair with a sommelier from Finland that he thinks his wife doesn't know about, but she does and is preparing divorce papers as we speak—that cost the same as a rather nice but not ostentatious small family home in the Midwest."

Watson sighed. "But no LeFevre pens."

"Indeed not. Nothing even in the same *league* as a LeFevre."

"You really think someone here killed their CFO?" asked Gregson. "We've spoken to most of the staff here, and so far, no red flags."

Holmes shrugged. "Yes. No. Maybe. We are hampered by a lack of evidence. There are no suspiciously timed absences in the office today. There is no indication that anyone here has lost a pen or is hiding their collection of valuable writing instruments. Everyone apparently liked the victim, and more than a few have been traumatized by his untimely death. In fact, I would recommend the company brings in a counselor to help those most in need."

At that moment, Detective Bell's phone buzzed. He excused himself as he stepped away from the group to take the call.

"I know one person who isn't too cut up about it," said Gregson, glancing over his shoulder toward the biggest office over in the corner of the building. "The CEO."

"The CEO, yes," said Holmes. "But in general it takes a little more motivation than a casual dislike to knock off a valuable colleague in such a violent manner."

"Well, I got more news," said Bell, returning to the group, cellphone in his hand.

"By your tone I am not anticipating a surprise resolution to the case," said Holmes.

"Uh, no," said Bell. "That was the CSU techs. As we thought, the phone that called Smythe then texted him with the change of time and place was a burner and is untraceable, and the number that was entered at the Athena Hotel register was a fake. We've also started a canvass of stores that stock LeFevre pens—plenty of sales but so far nothing that matches the model of the murder weapon, although it would be easier if we had the cap and serial number."

"I guess we expected that too," said Watson. "A pen like a LeFevre might be a practical writing instrument, but it's also an investment piece. It could have been bought a decade ago, anywhere in the world."

"Indeed," said Holmes, "and it seems unlikely that the murderer would have bought it especially for the task."

Bell sighed. "Hey, just covering the bases here. You want us to stop checking stores?"

"Not at all, Detective," said Holmes. "Just because an event is *improbable*, it does not mean it is *impossible*." Then he lifted his chin, and turned on a smile as he saw something over Watson's shoulder. She turned just as the Mantis security chief joined them.

"Here you are," said Gallop, holding out a slim black USB stick. "Complete personnel files, going back the full six years, as requested. These contain background checks and security records as well as employment history for everyone who has ever worked here."

Gregson took the stick. "Very thorough, thanks. I'll get the team to start running through the files, see if anything pops." He looked at Holmes. "I'll get you a copy if you want to take a look yourself."

"Actually," said Holmes, turning his smile onto Gallop again. "I would like a copy, but on paper, if you please?"

Gallop blinked, and glanced at Watson and then back at Holmes. The chuckle that came next was somewhat hesitant.

"Um… paper?"

Holmes nodded. "Paper. As convenient as our modern world is, paper still usurps digital for the collation and retention of data. I find the tactile nature of a manual review helps stimulate and focus the mind." He lifted both hands and circled his index fingers around his temples as he spoke.

Watson wondered if he realized just what that gesture was normally shorthand for.

Gallop stared at Holmes for a moment, then cleared his throat. "Well, okay, I'll see what I can do. It might take a while to get everything collated though."

"Excellent, Mr. Gallop, your company has been most helpful. There is no need for us to loiter. You may deliver the documentation directly."

Holmes's hand shot out, his calling card already held between his fingers. Gallop took it, glanced at Watson and Bell, then nodded and walked away.

Holmes watched him go, then turned and headed in the opposite direction.

"Hey," Watson called out. "Now where are you going?"

Holmes turned on his heel. "*We* are going to the victim's apartment. This office is bereft of information. I hope his residence proves to be a more rewarding destination."

8

THE SECRET IN THE DIARY

Gregory Smythe's apartment was a penthouse in a fashionable building on Central Park West, and, much like his office, it met Watson's every expectation.

The doorman and lobby staff of Smythe's building were being assisted by more of the black-suited Mantis security agents, and as at the Athena Hotel, there were two more agents guarding the approach to the apartment itself up on the top floor, steadfastly ignoring the steady stream of NYPD officers and forensic technicians that came and went, the entire penthouse being meticulously examined, the contents fully catalogued in case there was anything within of relevance to the case.

The apartment itself was huge, with a total square footage that easily eclipsed that of the Brooklyn brownstone Watson and Holmes shared, roof garden included. The penthouse was split-level, with a veranda that encircled the entire floor, accessible from several points around its circumference, including Smythe's home office, which commanded yet another truly spectacular view of Central Park and the city beyond from behind a mammoth desk. The walls of the office were polished concrete, the bookshelves that lined three of the four walls black wood, the floor boarded with wood in a contrasting lighter shade. The rest of the apartment, as much as they had yet seen, was done in the same style. Watson, taking in the scene from the office doorway, wondered if Smythe himself had been responsible for the decor back at Mantis Capital too.

Holmes, hands deep in the pockets of his jacket, mouth set in a firm pout, did a brisk circuit of the room before moving to the desk, where a number of items already bagged by the police forensic team lay in neat order. Meanwhile Watson moved to the huge folding doors—currently closed—which led out to the veranda, as she went over what they had discovered so far from the short time they had looked around the victim's residence.

"So Gregory Smythe was fifty-seven years old, and a lifelong bachelor," she said, "with a taste for modern art, modern decor, and, going by the collection in his cellar, wine."

She turned and folded her arms as she looked around the office. It was all so elegant and modern—except for the desk. It was *elegant*, yes, but far from modern. Sitting as it was near to the center of the room, it was an incongruity, solid oak and massive, more like the kind of furniture you would expect the President of the United States to sit behind as he steered the country toward a bright and hopeful future.

Watson had to admit that it was a beautiful piece, and one that clearly had some considerable age to it. It was just so out of place, and when she voiced this opinion aloud it elicited a laugh from Holmes.

"It seems Mr. Smythe was a traditionalist when it came to certain things," he said. "A rich man with a taste for modern interior design and art, and yet he allowed himself the odd indulgence now and again." He gestured at the desk with the wave of a hand. "French, eighteenth century. Restored in the early 1950s by one of two fly-by-night antique dealers based in Queens. Whether Mr. Smythe knew that or not when he bought it is perhaps academic now."

Watson knew better than to ask how Holmes knew not only about the restoration of the desk, but the likely craftsmen responsible. Having worked with Holmes for so long, she simply took his observation, deduction, induction, whatever it was, on face value.

"Okay," she said, "so he liked working at a big old-fashioned desk."

"That's not all," said Holmes. He waved a hand in the air. "There is no computer here, and no sign there ever was. No cables, no chargers, USB sticks, nothing. *And*—" he took his phone from his pocket and held it high in the air, his nose crinkling as he peered at the screen "—not even a home Wi-Fi network, or at least not one that belonged to Smythe himself, unless he is a member of the Central Park West brony brigade." He lowered his phone, and then gestured to the desk again. "But we do have these."

Watson stepped around the huge piece of furniture to join Holmes behind it, and cast her eye over the bagged contents on display.

There were pens. Lots of pens—Watson counted sixteen—each in an individual evidence bag, each, at first glance, appearing to be unique. Nine of them were gold, six were silver, their barrels narrow and fluted, while the final pen had a fatter barrel fashioned out of a dark wood with a deep grain.

Watson nodded as she ran her fingertips over the bagged display.

"Refillable ballpoint pens," she said. "A nice collection, too."

Holmes pointed to them again with an open palm. "CSU were kind enough to gather them for us from all over the penthouse. According to them, there is not a single fountain pen anywhere to be found."

Watson shrugged. "That as good as confirms it then. Smythe liked expensive ballpoints."

"And he liked *paper*," said Holmes, picking up the only other item on the desk—a leather-bound diary. Holmes tugged a pair of latex gloves from his pocket and put them on before slipping the diary from its bag. Holding it with the spine flat against one palm, Holmes opened the book at a random page. "With his expertise and experience as a security analyst, it seems Mr. Smythe had an aversion to technology, at least in his private life, and instead liked to do things the old-fashioned way." Holmes smiled. "As I said back at the Mantis office, paper is a superior and far more secure form of data storage. It appears their CFO agreed with me."

"It looks like he kept a pretty full schedule, too," said Watson, looking around Holmes's shoulder as he leafed slowly through the pages, all of them packed with appointments, notes, dates, times, phone numbers, and dinner engagements in tight, tidy handwriting.

"The life of a CFO is a busy one." Holmes flipped to the back of the book, where the pages were blank, and started working backwards until he hit the newest entries. Watson watched as the pages—each representing a single day—flipped back in time. Each page was more or less the same. Eventually Holmes reached the beginning.

Watson shook her head. "So he was good at record keeping. What were the last entries he made?"

Holmes skipped back to the most recently used page, and the two of them stood in silence for a few moments as they read. More appointments, more notes. Nothing that seemed particularly interesting for, according to the date at the top of the page, the last day of Gregory Smythe's life.

Holmes frowned, and began flipping back through the pages again. Going back three days, something caught Watson's eye, and she reached out to stop Holmes's hand.

Then Holmes clearly saw it too, his fingers sliding to the bottom of the page, where they stopped, and tapped at the paper.

Three lines of text, at the very bottom of the page, squeezed into a blank space on an already full page.

The second and third entries were a mystery:

KRONOS PLAZA. 9th 8PM
KRONOS 10th 8PM

But it was the first that made Watson's blood run cold:

ATHENA H, WASHINGTON HEIGHTS, 9th <u>1AM</u>

Watson and Holmes looked at each other. Neither of them spoke. Then Watson turned back to the diary and read the entries again, as though she expected them to be different a second time.

"The Athena Hotel," Watson whispered.

"Indeed," said Holmes. "The date and location of his own murder, with the original time of the appointment, before it was brought forward by two hours by the mystery text message."

Watson frowned, her head spinning at the revelation. Gregory Smythe had gone to the Athena Hotel to his death—to a pre-arranged meeting.

"Kronos Plaza," she read. "Tenth and eleventh. Today is the tenth."

"Whatever is at Kronos Plaza, I think we can safely assume Mr. Smythe will not be making the appointment," said Holmes.

But there was something else about the three lines, too. They had clearly been written by Smythe, but they were also different to everything else in the diary. The penmanship was rougher, the handwriting following the same style, yet bigger, looser. Watson voiced her opinion and Holmes nodded in agreement.

With the diary still balanced on one palm, he pulled the latex glove off his other hand with his teeth, then, tilting the diary away from himself, he peered along the edge of the page as he ran a naked fingertip over the last lines. Then he passed the book to Watson, pointing at the lines as she repeated the examination herself.

"The writing is deeper," said Watson. She flipped the page over to look at the previous day. There, at the bottom, the three final lines of text from the next day had very nearly penetrated the paper entirely. "Much more indented. It looks like the ball of the pen was stuck."

Holmes nodded, taking the diary back. He gave it another cursory examination with the pages tilted away from him, then he dropped the diary square on the desk. Looking down at it, he flicked back a couple of pages, and then pointed.

"The angle of the pen, the pressure of the ballpoint, suggests that Smythe usually wrote in this diary while seated, most likely at this desk. Smythe was fastidious in his neatness, which is reflected in his handwriting. Everything about this man is *uniform*."

Then Holmes *hrmmed*, took a step back, and selected one of the bagged pens. Flicking to the back of the diary, he tore a page out, flipped the diary back to the page with the mystery entries, and copied a few lines of text onto the torn-out page. Then he stood tall and nodded, holding up the pen he had chosen. It was silver, the fluting on the barrel less elaborate than all the others.

"This is his favorite pen. Silver, a simple modern design, lacking the baroque ostentation of the others—one suiting the man's personality. The wear on the ball and force required for a smooth flow of solid ink matches the other entries in this diary."

"Which is different to the pen used for those last three lines."

Holmes nodded. "Poor quality ink, excessive force—as you say, the ball of the pen was stuck. And look, the angle of the downward strokes changes partway through the second entry. He most certainly was using a cheap store-bought ballpoint, which proved a most unsatisfactory writing instrument. And he wasn't *sitting* when he made the entries, he was *standing*, like so."

Holmes picked the diary up, balancing it on the palm of his left hand with his fingertips curled around the top of the pages for extra support, tucking the book toward his chest as he positioned his other hand as though he was writing in it.

"He was in hurry," said Watson. "And he didn't have one of his own pens on him for some reason, so he had to use what was at hand." She glanced around the office. "If he didn't have one of his own pens, that means he certainly didn't make the entries here, *or* in his office at Mantis."

"Precisely correct," said Holmes. "But please tell me that you have not abandoned your self-tutoring in the science of graphology. You are still missing an additional factor."

Watson frowned. *Graphology is hardly a science,* she thought, more a spurious Victorian concept, like phrenology—although she had at least read the mountain of literature Holmes had provided her with. However, this was not the time to voice her opinion… and, yes, as she looked over the entries again, she clearly had missed something. The writing was rough, the loops and swirls large and angular. Smythe was in a hurry, they'd already established that, and—

Watson looked up from the page. "He was angry," she said.

"Yes! The groove of the pen strokes is deep—far deeper than required even for the precarious way in which he balanced his diary, or the cheap, unreliable movement of the ballpoint pen he used. The victim was *agitated* when he made these entries."

Holmes laid the diary back down on the desk. Watson took a breath and looked back out to the view of the city.

Their visit to the penthouse had been invaluable—the victim had got himself involved in *something*, something that had got him killed.

But what that something was, they still had no idea.

Watson sighed and planted her hands on her hips. "Kronos Plaza," she said. "Smythe had two appointments for something there, the first of which is tonight."

Holmes took his phone out and tapped at the screen. "It appears that Kronos Plaza is a conference center in downtown Manhattan," he said.

Just then, there was a knock at the door of the office. Two CSU techs stood, waiting expectantly with a uniformed officer. Watson got the message, and gave them a nod.

"I think we should let them finish work here. We can look up Kronos back at the brownstone."

"An excellent suggestion," said Holmes, gesturing to the door. "After you."

9

GREGORY SMYTHE'S MYSTERIOUS APPOINTMENT

It was close to six in the evening by the time Watson and Holmes got back to the brownstone, Holmes calling Gregson en route to update him on what they had discovered at Smythe's penthouse.

Slowly, but surely, Watson felt like they were building up a profile of the victim, and also of his movements. In fact, they had more than just a profile of that—they had his exact location going back six years, for every time point when he was carrying his company cellphone.

Now Watson sat in front of their big computer monitor. On the desk next to the keyboard, her tablet sat upright in its case, a photograph Watson had taken of Smythe's diary page—or more specifically, of the three lines of scribbled text—was on display as she did some research into Kronos Plaza.

As Holmes had said earlier, the Plaza was, in fact, a meeting venue and conference center—nothing particularly upmarket or exclusive, at least judging by the photo gallery on the venue's website, but, Watson imagined, a fairly typical place to hire out for small-to-medium-sized business events. This was confirmed by the venue's FAQ, which said the main auditorium was available for events of up to eight hundred attendees.

The venue's calendar was more informative. It seemed that Kronos Plaza was booked nearly every day of the year, for everything from small medical conferences and annual shareholder meetings of mid-sized corporations, to a few touring church speakers, and even a couple of live author Q&A sessions (the most recent promoting non-fiction titles, neither of which Watson recognized).

Smythe had listed two dates at Kronos—that very night, and the next—and when Watson looked up the events listed, she found they were nothing out of the ordinary, at least compared with the kind of events that the Plaza hosted the rest of the year.

"Here we go," said Watson, turning around in her chair to fill Holmes in on what she had discovered.

The dining room was empty.

Watson listened for a moment, trying to determine whether her colleague was in the kitchen, or perhaps upstairs. She cocked her head, unable to discern any movement anywhere else in the house, and was about to call out when there was a knock on the door. Watson waited a second, but when Holmes failed to materialize, she stood and went to answer the door herself.

Outside she found a young man in a purple uniform and hat standing on the stoop, holding a compact electronic scanner with a stylus dangling from a coiled lead. Down on the sidewalk was a two-wheeled package cart which held a stack of three large, secure document boxes, and parked at the curb one house down was a courier van in the same distinctive purple color and the letters APD stenciled on the side in a large white typeface, under which was the company's full name—Axiom Parcel Delivery. The rear doors of the vehicle were open, and as far as Watson could tell, the entire back was filled with more of the same boxes.

"Gotta package delivery from Mantis Capital for a...

Sheer-luck Holmes?" asked the delivery driver, frowning down at his scanner as he held the device at arm's length, clearly not quite sure if the recipient's name had been entered correctly.

Watson sighed and held out a hand. "It's Sherlock, and yes, this is it," she said, and the driver handed her the scanner. She signed it, and handed it back, glancing toward the van again. "This is obviously some strange usage of the word 'package' that I hadn't previously been aware of."

The driver just laughed, although Watson wasn't sure whether he got the Douglas Adams quote or not. He hopped down the steps, wheeled the cart around, and with surprising speed managed to back the stack of clearly heavy boxes up to the front door.

As he turned around, ready to unload, Watson noticed an ID tag clipped to the man's uniform breast pocket. She recognized it immediately—it was the same ID tag that she, Holmes and the others had been issued when they had visited the Mantis office, complete with the large red V on it to indicate the man was a visitor.

"Wow," said Watson, as the driver dumped the first box over the doorway. "Even couriers can't escape."

The driver stood up and paused, looking more than a little confused—even slightly offended. Watson shook her head.

"Oh, no, I meant the tag," she said, pointing to his pocket. "We were at Mantis earlier and had to go through the same procedure."

"Oh, yeah, yeah," said the driver, picking up the second box. "They're kinda crazy in there. Everyone has to go through it, every day. Even regulars like me. I mean, sure, okay, I get it, they gotta do what they gotta do. But, man, every day, first pick-up. It's like I've never been there before! I get the photo and the fingerprints." He laughed. "Sure as hell glad they don't use ink for *that* anymore."

Watson smiled, and turned her attention to the boxes now

stacked in the doorway. The driver, meanwhile, trotted down the steps, trolley balanced artfully over his back, and headed to load up the next batch from the van.

Holmes wanted paper, and paper was what he got.

A *lot* of paper.

Three trips later, and the delivery was made—twelve huge boxes, each weighing, by Watson's estimation, about the same as the moon. Having shoved all the boxes clear of the front door, she started the laborious process of carrying them from the porch back to the front room. Wheeling around the corner, she staggered under the weight of the first box, and paused to stare at the back of Holmes's red-and-blue checked shirt as he sat at the same computer she had been at just ten minutes before. With a gasp of effort, she let the box drop to the floor with a thud that was as satisfying as it was loud.

Holmes didn't even appear to notice.

"Okay, well, the personnel records from Mantis have arrived," Watson said, dusting her hands off and then brushing her hair out of her eyes. "There are a lot of them."

"Mantis employs just seventy full-time staff," said Holmes, still looking at the computer, still not turning around.

Watson sighed. "I meant *records*. There are more boxes in the hall," she said, walking over to the computer. *Fine*, she thought. *He wanted everything in paper, he can damn well move the boxes himself.*

Holmes had the event calendar from Kronos Plaza still on screen. He clicked the link for tonight's event—the one Watson had been intending to tell him about—and a half-page of information came up.

"Kronos Plaza is a small conference center," said Watson, recapping what she had learned, whether Holmes now knew it or not. "It's used for all sorts of events. Tonight and tomorrow is a lecture from this guy, Dale Vanderpool, some kind of business management guru."

Beside the short column of text was a photo of the Mr. Vanderpool in question. He was either in his early fifties, or had gone prematurely gray, his face looking somewhat more youthful than his hair suggested. In the picture he was turned three-quarters to the camera, the background behind him a towering, soft-focus bookcase. He wore a blue shirt with dark-blue tie under a dark-blue jacket, looking every bit the MBA he undoubtedly was. As Watson looked closer, she could even see his eyebrows were sculpted, along with his cheekbones.

Holmes sat back in the chair, hands clasped in his lap. As he looked at the screen, he tilted his head this way and that as though contemplating a painting by an old master.

"It seems Mr. Vanderpool is a major player in the public-speaking tour business," Holmes said finally. "I suppose people will pay good money to hear what they already know, so long as that information is spouted by someone with a haircut more expensive than their own."

Holmes reached for the mouse and clicked through to Vanderpool's own website, the main page of which was dominated by a slowly changing slider of images, each showing the speaker on a stage, gesticulating with thumb pressed into a closed fist as he leaned forward to what was obviously an imaginary audience, the photos of Vanderpool in action clearly staged publicity shots. Holmes gave a derisive snort at each image as it appeared, then clicked through to the speaker's own tour schedule.

"Kronos Plaza is the final two stops in what appears to be nearly six months of touring, right across the country. Hardly a state has been neglected." Holmes snorted again.

Watson folded her arms. "I take it you don't like management gurus?"

"You underestimate my level of disinterest by some considerable margin," said Holmes. He clicked back to the front page, and gestured with an open palm as he read from the website's main banner.

"'*Unlocking the dimensionality of success for modern business today.*' Never more moribund corporate-speak gobbledygook have I yet laid my eyes on."

Watson sighed and checked her watch. "Well, tonight's event is going to start in an hour. If we're going to find out why Gregory Smythe wrote down the dates, we need to get moving."

Holmes folded his arms and spun around in his chair to look at Watson, the look on his face one of wry bemusement. "If you are going to suggest that I come with you to this, this—" he unfolded one hand to wave at the screen "—*fiesta* of mediocrity, then, my dear Watson, prepare yourself for disappointment." He glanced over at the document box Watson had dumped in the doorway, and nodded at it. "I and my *bees* have a lot of paperwork to study. I suggest you enlist the services of Detective Bell if you desire company."

Watson shook her head. "But don't you want to find out how Smythe is connected to Dale Vanderpool?"

"I have every confidence in your abilities," said Holmes. "We have a lot of work to do, so dividing the tasks seems a better use of time." He paused, and gave another hiss as he shook his head. "Huh!" he muttered. "Dale Vanderpool. How original."

"What's wrong with Dale Vanderpool?"

Holmes looked up at Watson. "That is precisely what I expect you to find out tonight while I hunt for hidden patterns and dark secrets."

Watson glanced back at the document box. "With your *bees*?"

Holmes nodded. "Background noise to help stimulate the powers of observation and insight. I shall take the boxes to the roof and read the paperwork by my hives."

"Don't have too much fun, will you," said Watson. She checked her watch again. "I'll call Marcus, see if he's available. He's going to love the overtime, if nothing else."

Holmes gave Watson a smile that she knew meant he wasn't listening at all, then walked over to the box, hefted it with both hands, and headed toward the stairs.

10

THE LECTURE

Not for the first time that evening, Watson wished she was back at the brownstone leafing through an endless mountain of paper, rather than sitting in the main auditorium at Kronos Plaza, listening to Dale Vanderpool's lecture.

Vanderpool crossed the stage for what had to be the twentieth—thirtieth, *fortieth*?—time, the man never once standing still as he spoke to the packed crowd. He gestured as he spoke, leaning forward as he had been in the photos on his website, his right hand balled into a fist, the thumb pressed firmly down on the top, like he was a politician promising a brighter future.

And in a way, Watson thought, as she shifted to try and get more comfortable on the hard flip-down seat, that was almost what he was. Vanderpool had so far spoken for more than an hour, walking back and forth, back and forth, alone on the stage save for a stool he had not yet sat on and a round table with a glass bottle of mineral water he had not yet touched.

Watson glanced sideways at her companion as Vanderpool completed yet another lap of the stage and headed around for the next run. Slumped next to her, Detective Bell was staring at the stage, his face expressionless. For a moment Watson even wondered if he was still awake, whether the detective had fallen into an open-eyed slumber. But then he blinked, and took a breath that was very, *very* deep.

Watson turned back to the stage and didn't blame him one bit.

She didn't have much corporate experience as such, although there was plenty of that kind of thing—and those kind of people—in the administrative offices back when she worked in a hospital. Exactly the part of the building she had done her best to avoid during her residency.

But what Dale Vanderpool was lecturing on was... well, Watson wasn't entirely sure. It was a strange mix of practical advice on accounting and management, and personal, even *inspirational*, motivation; a discussion of solid matters like return on investment, profit and loss projections, and how to improve turnover, would suddenly swerve off on a tangent featuring armchair philosophy, rallying calls to action, and even the meaning of life itself. And not infrequently, it felt more like the semi-famous management speaker was trying to recruit his audience into some kind of pseudo-religious pyramid scheme. Occasionally, Watson recognized some concepts—Vanderpool seemed very keen on applying various "rules for success" to, well, just about everything, most of which involved the number ten: ten thousand hours to master a skill, ten thousand steps a day to stay healthy, ten thousand miles traveled in a year to maintain your client list.

As Vanderpool droned on, Watson found her mind drifting from the content to the delivery. In person, under the bright stage lights, Vanderpool looked somehow even more artificial than on his website. His too-white teeth shone and his five-hundred-dollar haircut appeared to be a single, solid and quite immobile block as he walked around, waving his hand in his favorite closed-fist gesture. And his suit, although nice, was less well cut than the carefully posed publicity photos suggested, the double-breasted jacket lifting and sagging as he moved around the stage.

Watson slid down slightly in her seat and nudged Bell. Although the auditorium looked nearly full, they'd had no trouble buying two eye-wateringly expensive tickets at the door—tickets that each came with a registration form that had taken a couple of minutes to complete, the pair skipping most of the fields asking for details of the attendee's company, including number of employees, estimated turnover, and a dozen other questions Watson and Bell only gave a cursory glance. Now, sitting at the very back of the auditorium and with a few empty seats around them, it felt safe to talk quietly.

"What do you think?" she whispered.

Bell sighed and lifted an elbow onto the arm of his seat. "He's shorter than I thought he would be."

Watson blinked and looked back at the stage. Actually, Bell had a point. It was a little hard to tell, but Vanderpool was quite a bit shorter than average, perhaps five-two, five-three. Watson thought back to the publicity shots on his website, and realized that they'd all been shot from a low angle, making the somewhat diminutive speaker look a little taller—more *powerful*—than he was in real life.

With a final thrust of his closed fist, Vanderpool took a step back, and the auditorium erupted, not just into applause, but whistles and whoops of delight, like it was a rock concert. A moment later the audience took to their feet to give the speaker a standing ovation. Watson and Bell followed suit, unwilling to be singled out from the crowd.

"I guess I'm the only one in this room who didn't follow a single word that guy said," said Bell, looking around with a frown on his face as he joined in the applause. "Look at this. He just about packed the place full and they lapped it up."

Watson clapped, and like Bell took the opportunity

to look around. Bell was right: the audience had been enthralled by Vanderpool's lecture. They were a curious lot, too: nearly all were male, nearly all a little older than what Watson could safely call middle-aged, nearly all wearing suits in a variety of cuts and quality. Although Watson hated to apply the stereotype, it seemed safe to assume everyone was from the corporate world—managers, VPs, and the like, from companies that were neither large nor small, famous nor insignificant. Just... average.

Which was exactly the kind of audience that would benefit from Vanderpool's management techniques—a touch of good business sense, practical advice, and a boatload of fist-pumping inspiration—and chances are most of the audience would go away re-energized, re-invigorated, ready to take their businesses to the next level.

And hey, good for them. Whatever Watson thought of Vanderpool's cookie-cutter "how to optimize and inspire your workforce" double-talk, there was no doubting he was good at what he did. Sure, Kronos Plaza was hardly Carnegie Hall, but even Watson could recognize the man's talent and strengths.

Which led to the obvious question, one Bell voiced as the applause died and the audience began to sort itself into two groups—one section filing out of the auditorium, the other, probably more than half, forming a loose line down the far right-hand aisle, apparently preparing for a meet and greet with their corporate hero.

"So," said Bell, as he and Watson sank back into their seats, "what would the Chief Financial Officer of an investment outfit worth hundreds of millions of dollars be doing at an event like this? Somehow I don't think Mantis Capital needs advice on how to keep up a positive mental attitude."

Watson nodded. "And even if Mantis saw some value in this," she said, "they wouldn't have sent the CFO."

"Right," said Bell. "He's the wrong type. As CFO he

would have overseen the hedge fund's financial statements and portfolios, along with the company's own finances and internal accounting systems. The most he would do is liaise with their floor traders, not manage them."

Watson smiled. "You seem to know a lot about hedge fund personnel structure."

"Yeah, well, I have an uncle who likes to dabble in stocks and shares and whose chief hobby is to bore the rest of the family to death about it when he comes to visit."

"How often is that?"

"Too often," said Bell with a laugh.

As the pair waited, they watched uniformed venue staff appear and begin setting up an area at the side of the stage, bringing out a table and chair, while a couple of others in more casual clothing—tour staff members, perhaps— appeared from backstage with a couple of boxes, which they unpacked to reveal a healthy supply of books.

Then Vanderpool himself appeared from the side of the stage, to a smattering of applause from the line. He acknowledged it with a wave and smile, then sat himself down behind the table.

"I think you need to buy one of his books for your uncle," said Watson, standing. "Come on, let's go talk to him."

The line for the book signing moved at a good speed, but at Watson's insistence she and Bell hung around at the back, watching the autograph session, their intention being to speak to Vanderpool when it was over without interrupting the time he was spending with his fans. As they discreetly loitered, she used the opportunity to observe him more closely.

And he seemed… nice. His smile might have showed teeth that were too straight and too white, but the smile was a genuine one, the handshake that followed firm and friendly.

Several people got their photographs taken with him, one of his assistants taking charge of cellphones or compact cameras as the owner leaned in over the table, Vanderpool himself remaining resolutely seated. Perhaps, thought Watson, he was a little sensitive about his height?

Watson also took note of the pen he was using to sign the books—a black Sharpie, one he began to shake with greater and greater frequency as he worked through the line. After twenty or so minutes there was just one person left, so Watson motioned to Bell for them to join behind.

The man in front of Bell shared a joke with Vanderpool, but as the speaker went to sign the book, he paused, then hissed in annoyance, shaking the Sharpie again before turning to his assistant at the book stack.

"Do we have another Sharpie in the box? This one's dead." Then he turned to his fan. "Sorry about this. Typical, isn't it, nearly the last book of the night and the damn pen gives up the ghost!"

At this, Bell stepped around the man waiting for his book to be signed and, one hand diving into the breast pocket of his jacket, extracted first his police notebook, then from that the pen that was slotted under the elastic strap that held the book closed.

"Here, will this do?"

Vanderpool barked a laugh and reached up for the pen. Bell handed it over and stepped back with a nod, gesturing for the man at the front of the line to retake his place.

As Vanderpool signed the book with a flourish, he shook his head. "You know," he said, "I normally use a nice fountain pen for book signings. One I've had for, oh, years and years. Best pen I've ever used. And I swear I never go anywhere without it, but what do you know, there's a first time for everything. Must have left it back at the hotel. There you go."

He handed the book to the patient man, who gave

a nervous "thanks" to Vanderpool, before turning and muttering "thanks" to Bell for his timely intervention. Bell murmured a "no problem", and as the man left the stage, Vanderpool offered the pen back. Bell held up a hand and shook his head.

"Hey, keep it," he said, before exchanging a meaningful look with Watson.

Watson knew exactly what the detective was thinking, because she was thinking it too. By his own admission, Vanderpool always used a fountain pen to sign books... one that he had mysteriously forgotten tonight.

Watson and Bell took a step forward. As the last members of the audience remaining, they were now alone with the management guru, his two assistants, and the two venue staffers, who had now moved out into the auditorium, waiting for the event to be officially over.

"Okay, hi there, thanks again for coming!" said Vanderpool, putting on a grin and reaching almost automatically for the next book in the pile, already open and held at the title page by one of his assistants. Vanderpool cast an eye over the empty page, like he was sizing it up, looking for the optimal place to put his signature, even though he had just signed at least a hundred in the last half hour or so.

Then he looked up at the pair, his eyes momentarily flashing between Watson and Bell. His smile flickered for a second, like a light bulb soon to be in need of replacing, then it came back on, bigger, wider, brighter than ever.

"Am I doing a book each, or just the one?"

"Actually," said Bell, reaching back into his coat pocket, now for his detective's badge, "we were wondering if we could have a little word with you?"

As he looked at Bell's badge, Vanderpool's expression seemed to freeze. As with the smile, it was momentary, nothing anyone would possibly notice.

Except Watson, of course. Holmes had taught her well. From his fleeting expression, the minute change in his body language, it appeared that Vanderpool didn't like the police. That in itself was not so uncommon, but, she had to wonder...

What was Dale Vanderpool hiding?

Then Vanderpool lowered the pen Bell had given him, and folded his arms over his still-open book. "Please, ask away. Always happy to help, if I can." His tone was still pleasant but the smile was now tight, forced.

Bell returned his shield to his inside pocket. "I'm Detective Bell, this is Joan Watson. She consults with the department. Do you know this man?"

Flipping open his notebook, Bell lifted out a photograph of the murder victim, Gregory Smythe. Much like Vanderpool's own official publicity photo, Smythe's picture—taken from the Mantis office—was turned three-quarters to the camera, the look on his face stern, commanding. He and Vanderpool were about the same age, Watson noted.

Vanderpool's impressively shaped eyebrows came together over his nose as he took the photo from Bell and squinted at it.

"I definitely do not know who this is."

"Have you ever seen him though?" asked Watson. "Do you recognize him from any of your previous speaker events?"

"Well," said Vanderpool, lowering the photo, "that's more than possible. I meet an awful lot of people on tour. We sell out most nights. Well, as you saw tonight."

Bell frowned. "Nothing ringing anywhere?"

Vanderpool picked up the picture again, and he shrugged, his mouth downturned. "No, I'm sorry, I really am. I'm not good with faces, at all." He laughed, and looked up at the two. "I guess everyone says that." Then he showed the photo to his two nearby assistants, both of whom frowned and just shook their heads, one muttering an apology.

Vanderpool made to hand the photo back to Bell, but then stopped and pulled it back, peering at the picture.

"Do you remember something?" asked Watson.

"Oh, no, no," said Vanderpool. He gestured with the photo to his two assistants. "This is Mike and Jake, they're my roadies, as it were. But maybe one of my other assistants has seen him. Come on, I'll take you backstage. Follow me."

11

THE PUBLICIST AND HER HUSBAND

Watson could hear it as soon as she and Bell followed Vanderpool through a door in the stage wings and into a maze of narrow, black-painted corridors.

A voice, male, speaking loudly, angrily, the sentences ending sharply, incomplete.

Someone arguing—but it was one-sided, only half a fight. Whoever it was, they were arguing on a phone.

Bell glanced over his shoulder at Watson with a raised eyebrow; Vanderpool himself must have been able to hear the voice too, but he didn't show it until the trio reached a door with a sign on it that said GREEN ROOM. There he paused, hand reaching out for the handle before drawing it back a little, then he curled it into a fist, ready to knock on the door instead. The male voice was loud from the other side of the door, but still muffled—Watson could only make out the odd word here and there, but without any context she couldn't ascribe any meaning to what was very clearly half of a very heated discussion indeed.

Vanderpool looked at the door with his lips pursed and his knuckles raised, and he stood there for a second or two longer before clearing his throat. And then he knocked.

Immediately the raised voice went silent. There was a pause, a beat of silence in which Vanderpool reached for the doorknob again. But before he could grab it, the door was pulled open.

Watson blinked as a tall young woman—perhaps late twenties or early thirties—with long black hair poked her head around the doorway, her own eyes wide in surprise. Beyond her, inside the green room, stood an equally tall man with thick black hair slicked back and shiny, his upper lip sporting an elegantly trimmed, deliberately old-fashioned mustache that, to Watson's mind anyway, put him firmly in the hipster camp. He was wearing a checked shirt tucked into narrow black jeans. In his hand he held a cellphone. The man looked a little flushed, his chest rising and falling beneath the checkerboard pattern as if he'd just been running.

The woman looked like she was going to say something to Vanderpool, then she blinked and seemed to realize that Watson and Bell were standing in the hallway too, and her mouth shut. A second later she composed herself, and her mouth opened again, this time in a wide smile.

"Dale, hi," she said.

Vanderpool gestured toward his guests.

"Ah, Sophie, this is Detectives Bell and Watson, from the NYPD."

Watson smiled and held out a hand toward Sophie. "Actually I'm a consultant to the department. Bell is a detective with the Special Crimes Unit."

Sophie looked down at Watson's outstretched hand. "Consultant?" She made no attempt to shake the hand, so Watson dropped it. Beside her she felt Bell bristle.

"We were wondering if we could just ask you a couple of questions," said Bell.

Sophie nodded, quickly, as her companion came out of the

room. His breathing looked about normal but Watson could see he was agitated and trying to hide it.

"Hi, Dale," said the man. He looked at the other two. "Detectives," he said with a nod, then he gestured for them to enter the room. "Come on in!"

Vanderpool grimaced at the pair—both of whom, Watson noted, towered over their boss. "Everything okay?"

The man with the mustache frowned as if Vanderpool was speaking an alien language. "What? Yes, of course. No problem."

It was not a great cover, but Vanderpool didn't seem to notice. Instead, he smiled and motioned for Watson and Bell to enter ahead of him.

The green room was large and spacious, the walls actually painted a bright apple green that Watson wasn't entirely sure was relaxing. There were couches, a TV with a games console attached and a scattered stack of games, a coffee table with a pile of magazines, and an array of food and drink set up along one wall.

Vanderpool clapped his hands and turned to his backstage guests. "May I introduce you to Trent Absolom and his wife, Sophie. Trent here is my tour manager, while Sophie handles publicity and front of house."

Still nervous but slowly calming, Trent offered his hand this time. Watson shook it, and once they had all been introduced, the couple seemed more at ease, although Watson noticed that Sophie remained standing behind her husband's shoulder.

Bell took out the photograph of Gregory Smythe again. "We're looking for this man," he said. "Have either of you seen him before?"

Trent squinted at the photograph, then shook his head; he glanced at Sophie, who shrugged.

"Not that I can recall," said Trent, turning back to Bell. "Why, who is he? Has something happened to him?"

"Well, we're looking into it," said Bell, choosing his words wisely, thought Watson. "His name is Gregory Smythe. He works for a company called Mantis Capital Investment. Would you know if he, or anyone from that company, has been to one of your events?"

Trent shook his head again. "Doesn't ring any bells, sorry. We get a lot of people at these things."

Vanderpool smiled, clutching his hands in front of him. He turned to Watson. "As I said. I'm sorry we can't be more help."

Watson frowned. "We had to fill in a form when we came in. You must keep those records, along with ticket-sale receipts?"

Vanderpool nodded. "That's right. Trent?"

Trent nodded and took a deep breath—whether due to his earlier argument, or the questions now being put to him, Watson couldn't tell.

"Ah, yes, that's right," said Trent. "All attendees need to register, although nearly everything on the online form is optional. Most people put the company they represent down and a contact email, but not all."

"And you don't recall anyone from Mantis Capital signing up?" asked Bell.

"Well, like I said, not everyone puts their company down. But it'll be easy to check."

Bell nodded at Vanderpool. "Okay, we'd like to get a copy of your attendee register, and also the details of your own staff."

Vanderpool looked worried. "What do you think happened to this Mr. Smythe?"

Watson gave the man a reassuring smile. "Like we said, we're looking into it. But your cooperation is much appreciated."

"Of course, of course, anything to help the police." Vanderpool looked at his two staff members. "Isn't that right?"

Ignoring his boss, Trent nodded at Bell. "I'll get you the details. Follow me." He turned and walked out of the green room. Bell exchanged a look with Watson, then followed.

Vanderpool clapped his hands again, and moved over to the table holding his dinner for the evening. He looked over it, selecting a stick of celery, which he dunked into a pot of hummus, then turned back to the two women. He gestured at the spread.

"Please, help yourself. I'm starving!"

12

THE BEES, THEY DO NOTHING

Sherlock Holmes sat on an old wooden school chair on the roof of the brownstone in Brooklyn, leaning forward with his forehead pressed against the glass observation window set into the side of one of his several beehives. On the roof between his feet was one of the folders of information from the Mantis document boxes. In the last two hours he had scanned quite a considerable number of the company personnel files—although not quite as many as he had hoped, his speed-reading technique showing just a little rust—and had found...

Precisely *nothing* of interest.

Every employee—past and present—of Mantis Capital had been screened and screened again, interviewed and tested and vetted before commencing their employment. All were uniformly well qualified and amply rewarded for their contribution to the success of the company.

All were as boring as each other, their details mundane, their lives—to Holmes, anyway—distinctly unmemorable.

And while motive was actually the least important part of the traditional trio of homicidal factors so beloved by the uneducated masses—all a person really needed was the means and opportunity—there was nothing in the Mantis files to suggest that anyone wanted the company's CFO dead.

Even aided by the faint hum of his bees transmitted directly through the frontal bone of his skull, Holmes felt dull, like he was deep underwater, his senses cloudy, his focus drifting.

He made a mental note to himself to conduct a series of experiments correlating concentration with sugar consumption.

And then he pulled himself back to reality—making another note on that particular tangential train of thought and how long he had drifted—and refocused on the document now lying between his feet.

There was, at least, a modicum of interest in the set of files he was currently perusing, a complex set of spreadsheets that represented the GPS data pulled from the phones of every Mantis employee.

As a warm-up, he had reviewed four randomly selected records *not* belonging to Gregory Smythe, and had managed to identify two extra-marital affairs (one between two employees), one terminally ill close family member—possibly an aunt, although that was mere supposition—and an expensive addiction to champagne and a very particular kind of imported Turkish delight.

Perhaps the lives of the staff of Mantis were not as dull as Holmes had at first concluded.

Satisfied with these preliminary results, Holmes had begun a thorough review of Smythe's own movements, and now, staring at the papers laid out on the rooftop, he suddenly found exactly what he was looking for, nearly instantly. That it was so obvious was something of an anticlimax.

Holmes curled his lip, listened to his bees, and decided to recheck his findings. Sitting upright, he pulled his phone from his pocket and brought up Dale Vanderpool's website. He clicked through to the tour schedule, then he carefully placed the phone on the rooftop next to Smythe's printed GPS record.

Vanderpool's website listed the two-night event at Kronos Plaza, New York City. That was the end of the current tour. The stop before the Manhattan double date was in Newark, New Jersey, the previous week.

Newark, New Jersey.

Where Gregory Smythe had also been, also the previous week, for a two-hour period that coincided with Vanderpool's event.

At the exact same location.

Which meant Gregory Smythe had been an attendee.

Holmes frowned at the data, then he picked up his phone and began swiping through the photos he'd taken of the pages of Smythe's diary, back at his plush penthouse apartment.

Smythe was neat to the point of fastidiousness, and this was evident even in his diary—the whole thing was an immaculately recorded journal, countless appointments, notes, jottings all inscribed—aside from those three rushed entries—in his neat, uniform handwriting.

Except... there was nothing at all suggesting he had been at the Vanderpool lecture in Newark. Nothing listed on the diary page for that date in question, and flicking back through another two weeks of pages, no sign of anything that bore even a remote resemblance to the appointment.

Holmes paused. The photos were, of course, limited in their utility—they were a digital record, the phone's screen significantly smaller than the original pages. A better solution would be to call the precinct and get someone to check the real thing, cover to cover and back again. Of course, they were no doubt doing that already, collating Smythe's records to see if they provided any clues to his murder. A standard aspect of the investigation.

Holmes stood and began a circuit of the brownstone

rooftop, the cool night air soothing his nerves. He thought again about Smythe and about Vanderpool... and about how his teeth felt furry and needed brushing.

Far below, the door of the brownstone was unlocked, opened, and slammed closed.

Watson was back. Holmes picked up his phone and very nearly ran from the roof.

Holmes trotted down the stairs as Watson was hanging her coat in the hall.

"I trust your evening was as enjoyable as watching paint dry," said Holmes, standing at the base of the stairs straighter than a toy soldier. "Actually, I take that back. Watching paint dry can be a fascinating exercise, a highly rewarding form of deep meditation."

Watson raised an eyebrow, and moved through into the front room. Holmes bobbed at her heel like an impatient puppy.

"It was okay," said Watson. "Vanderpool just seems like the usual kind of motivational speaker. It was all a bit... I don't know, vague maybe. Part high-school pep rally, part half-baked *Art of War* philosophy." Watson shrugged, then dropped into the art deco armchair by the fireplace, her shoulder bag sliding off onto the floor. "But the place was packed. You should have seen it. People really seem to love him." She shook her head. "I guess they really do find what he says useful. Here."

She reached into the bag by her feet, extracted a book, and held it out. Holmes frowned at it, his hands not moving from his sides, staring at it as though it were about to explode. Watson shook the book, and Holmes finally reached out a tentative hand and took it, his fingers dancing as he grasped it, like it was hot.

"*The Dimensionality of Success,*" he read from the cover.

"Watson, you really shouldn't have." He looked at Watson with an expression somewhere between sucking on a lemon and discovering you've stepped in something unpleasant.

Watson laughed. "He signed it for you."

The expression on Holmes's face became, if it were possible, even more sour. With one finger he lifted the cover and looked at the inscription inside. Then he lifted his eyes to Watson.

"Ballpoint."

Watson rose. She moved to stand in front of Holmes, pointing at the title page he held open. Vanderpool's signature was an elaborate swirl of loops that bore little resemblance to his name, and took up nearly all of the blank space on the page.

"He was using a sharpie to sign the books. It ran out, so Bell gave him his own pen to finish the signing."

"The generosity of the NYPD knows no bounds."

"But, listen, Vanderpool said he normally used a *fountain* pen for his book signings—one he said he'd left back at the hotel that night."

"Curious," said Holmes, "but Vanderpool wasn't the killer."

Watson blinked. "What? You can tell that from his *signature*?"

"Not at all," said Holmes, slamming the book shut in his hand. "I can tell from your body language. You are tired, but with a restlessness that comes from hours of boredom. You met Vanderpool, spoke with him, but your own suspicions were not sufficiently aroused. You do not think he is the killer, and as I was the one who instilled the skills of the detective within you, I trust that judgment implicitly."

Watson felt her shoulders drop. Holmes was right. Perhaps.

She folded her arms and bit her lip. "No, I don't think he is. But it did feel like he was hiding something. He was nervous around Marcus when he found out he was a detective."

Holmes nodded. "Sometimes an understandable reaction."

"We also met Vanderpool's tour staff. He has two assistants, Mike and Jake, whom he called his roadies. And he has a tour manager and a publicist who are married to each other."

Holmes cocked his head. "I sense you have more to report."

"I don't know. Mike and Jake seemed okay—just the hired help, really. Short-term contract as drivers and general workers. But the other two are permanent staff—Trent and Sophie Absolom. Vanderpool took us backstage to meet them. Trent was having an argument with someone on his cellphone. He seemed pretty worked up. They both did."

"And yet?"

Watson sighed. "Like I said, I don't know. There's no reason to connect that conversation with Gregory Smythe. They both denied ever having seen him. Marcus has a list of registered lecture attendees to check though."

"So not a complete waste of time then."

Watson raised an eyebrow. Holmes really seemed to have taken a dislike to Vanderpool and his work, but she was too tired to argue about it now. She returned to the armchair and slumped back into it.

Holmes stood over her in silence. Watson frowned.

"What?"

"Aren't you going to ask me how my evening went?"

"Oh, sorry. How did it go?"

"Progress was made," said Holmes. "Smythe's GPS phone records, kindly supplied by Mantis, show he was in Newark, New Jersey, at precisely the time, date and location of the previous stop on Vanderpool's speaking tour before he arrived in New York."

Holmes pulled the printed GPS records from behind his back and handed them over. Watson took them, then stood and headed over to the big red table in the other room, where she laid the pages out.

"But that date wasn't in his diary, was it?" she asked.

"Indeed not. But its *absence* is in itself an important connection. The kind of pep-talk tripe peddled by a person like Vanderpool is *not* the kind of thing that a person like Smythe would find useful in the slightest. Indeed, Vanderpool's audience is many rungs down the ladder from the lofty heights of a company like Mantis Capital."

"That's true," said Watson. "It felt like everyone in the audience was small business. Middle-management, mostly."

"Accountants of the world, unite and take over," said Holmes. "Smythe hadn't written the appointment down in his diary because he didn't want to leave a record he had been there. He was attending a Vanderpool lecture in *secret*."

Watson shook her head. "But he had noted down the times and dates of the next two stops. And the address of the Athena Hotel. *And*"—she held the printouts up to Holmes—"if he wanted to go there in secret, why not just leave his phone at home? He would have known his location was traceable."

Holmes nodded. "Therein lies a problem. While it is unlikely he would have forgotten about the ability of his employer to track his every move, it is possible he knew that only certain people had access to that record, and if it was generally known that he was otherwise free on that evening, nobody would have any reason to look his location up."

"Unless…"

"Yes?"

Watson pulled out a chair and sat at the table, resting her head in her hands as she stared at the papers laid out before her.

"Unless he was in a hurry. He didn't have his ballpoint pen with him—the one he regularly used. So maybe he'd left his apartment quickly to get to Newark."

"Leaving his pen at home," said Holmes, "but with his phone still in his pocket."

"Right," said Watson. "The first date wasn't in his diary, not because he was trying to keep it a secret, but because he wasn't planning on going. It was a last-minute decision. *Very* last minute."

"And while at the Newark meeting, he discovered something that compelled him to note down the dates of the two New York speaking engagements. And he clearly made contact with someone there, someone who gave him an appointment at a seedy hotel in Washington Heights where he met his end before he was even able to attend the first of the New York dates."

"Yes!" said Watson. "And he was killed with a fountain pen. And Dale Vanderpool's pen is currently missing in action."

"Unless it is currently sitting in the evidence locker back at the precinct."

Watson ran her hands through her hair, then checked her watch. It was late. Very late.

"Okay, so we can go through the lecture register, and I guess start searching for potential suspects from the Newark meeting. But it's been a long day, I need to go to bed." She pushed her chair away from the table and stood. Next to her, Holmes bristled, his lips pursed as he bobbed almost imperceptibly on his heels.

"An excellent suggestion, Watson. Sleep cleanses the synapses, enables new connections to be made." He waved his hand in front of his face, as if miming the restorative qualities of sleep.

Watson headed for the stairs, then paused, one hand on the bannister. Looking behind, she saw Holmes still standing where he was, looking at the documentation.

Of course he wasn't going to go to sleep. Sleep was for mere mortals.

"I will wake you if I discover anything further," said Holmes, not looking in her direction.

Gee, great, thought Watson, and she headed up to her room.

13

THE COURIER'S PHOTOGRAPH

Watson was woken not by Sherlock Holmes, but by sunlight streaming in through her bedroom window. She turned over, rubbing her face, and then saw there was a mug of steaming tea on the nightstand. Watson lifted it, expecting to find a note underneath, but there was nothing.

The tea was hot, and delicious. Then Watson realized she had closed the shutters on her windows the night before. Holmes must have just come in, delivered the tea, and opened the shutters, and then withdrawn as silently as he had entered.

Well, that was an improvement.

Watson took another sip, then, slipping on her robe, headed downstairs, the warm mug cradled in both hands.

She found Holmes in the kitchen, cooking at the stove, spatula in one hand, the other jostling the handle of a pan. He was wearing an apron over a blue shirt with a white, buttoned-up collar, and a waistcoat in a deep, charcoal gray—different clothes than he had been wearing yesterday. Either he had slept, or he had at least freshened up.

"There is a theory," said Holmes, his back to Watson as he worked at whatever it was on the stovetop, "that eating carbohydrates in the morning somehow resets your metabolism, sending your body careening down a dark path where all you can think of for every minute of the day is where the next hit of delicious baked goods and sugar is coming from." He glanced over his shoulder, a playful smirk twitching over his lips. "To avoid this," he continued, turning back to the stove, "a strict morning routine of protein and fat is in fact what is required, as this sets your metabolism up for a day of *vim* and *vigor*, where you will meet success at every turn and all your dreams will become a reality."

Watson pulled out a chair at the kitchen table, but paused, halfway seated, as she processed Holmes's statement.

"Ah… okay," she said, then sat.

Holmes looked over his shoulder again, this time his expression grim. "There is, of course, an alternative theory which states the first is a load of homespun claptrap, and that sometimes what you really need is an enormous pile of pancakes drenched in the finest maple syrup Canada can provide."

Then he turned back to the pan, flipped the pancake in it, then slid it onto the plate on the counter, on which there was already a teetering pile of huge, fluffy pancakes.

Then she saw it. On the kitchen table was Vanderpool's book. It was closed, the page-edge facing toward her.

There were at least two dozen, maybe even more, colored tags sticking out of the pages, marking sections all through the tome. On the cover, four larger Post-it notes were stuck, each covered in dense handwriting.

Holmes deposited the plate of pancakes on the table next to the book.

"You've been doing some reading?" asked Watson.

"I needed something light and fatuous to pass the small hours, yes," said Holmes. "I reviewed the personnel files from

Mantis twice over and failed to find a single item of interest. A blander bunch of stinking-rich investment bankers and traders I have yet to encounter."

Watson grinned. "And did you learn anything from the great Dale Vanderpool?"

Holmes slipped the apron off, then sat himself down at the table. He began serving breakfast for them both.

"If you like Vanderpool's theories about the breakfast of champions, wait until you hear what he thinks about the evils of network television."

Watson enjoyed the pancakes, but she had to admit to herself that after just one she felt it sitting heavily in her stomach. Perhaps Vanderpool's breakfast theory wasn't that outlandish.

She stood to make more tea, dodging past one of the open boxes of Mantis files by the kitchen table. Glancing down, she caught sight of the personnel file on the top. She stopped and stared, moving around the box so she could see the photograph on display the right way around.

Holmes watched her, pointing to the box with his fork.

"Guest pass logs. As we discovered first hand, all office visitors are subject to a rigorous ID check at the door, where they have their digital photograph taken and pass issued. The passes are securely shredded on exit, but the digital records are retained."

"Right," Watson muttered. "Even for couriers."

She lifted the top sheet out of the box. It was the pass details of a delivery person, their name and company details filled out in slanted writing that suggested left-handedness. The photograph on the form showed a young woman with blonde hair, wearing a baseball cap—part of her work uniform—that was a distinctive shade of purple.

Watson stared at the page, reading from it.

"Mantis are positively paranoid about security," said Holmes. "Couriers and other regular contractors are issued day passes so they can come and go, but even so they must go through the same process each and every day."

Watson squinted at the page. "Vicki Summers, driver for… Axiom Parcel Delivery," she said slowly, shaking her head.

Holmes pushed his plate away from him. "You have something?"

Watson wasn't sure. There was something about Vicki Summers, something the subconscious part of her brain was picking up. Watson concentrated, chasing the feeling around her mind like a butterfly. She didn't know who Vicki Summers was, other than what information was presented on the pass sheet. She'd never heard of or seen her before—

No. That wasn't right at all.

And Vicki Summers wasn't Vicki Summers.

Watson moved back to Holmes and thrust the pass sheet at him.

"I've seen this woman before."

Holmes frowned, but he didn't touch the file. "Vicki Summers?"

Watson shook her head. "Her name is Sophie Absolom. She works as Dale Vanderpool's publicist. Marcus and I met her last night at Kronos Plaza. Remember, I told you about her—she's married to a guy called Trent, Vanderpool's tour manager."

Holmes licked his lips, then took the file gingerly. He shoved his plate of pancakes to one side, set the file down on the table and stared at the pass sheet, then placed his hands on his knees. "According to this, *Vicki Summers* was signed in at Mantis Capital no less than *two* months ago." He looked back up at Watson. "Are you certain this is her?"

Watson nodded, gesturing to the photograph. "Well, she wasn't wearing an APD cap last night, and her hair is black now, not blonde, but that's her."

"Then we have our connection." Holmes pursed his lips.

"You said you heard Trent arguing with someone on his phone when you went backstage at Vanderpool's talk. Tell me about it."

Watson sighed and returned to her seat at the kitchen table. "Well, Trent was on the phone. He and Sophie were in the green room. He was talking loud enough to be heard through the closed door, but I couldn't make out much. It was pretty heated, though. When we went in, both Trent and Sophie seemed pretty worked up. They did their best to hide it, but it was obvious. Vanderpool noticed it too, but he didn't bring it up." Watson ran a hand through her hair. "If I didn't know any better, I would have said that Trent and Sophie were both afraid of something."

"Or someone," said Holmes. "And none of Vanderpool's staff, this Trent and Sophie included, said they recognized the photograph of the victim."

"Right," said Watson. "They said they hadn't even heard of Mantis Capital, and according to their register, no attendee has signed up for an event with that company name."

Holmes returned his attention to the photo of Vicki Summers. "A hat and hair dye is an easy disguise." Then he looked back up at his colleague. "Clearly there is far more to Trent and Sophie Absolom than meets the eye."

Watson nodded. "Bell and I got the details of all of Vanderpool's staff last night, the Absoloms included. We should tell him to start running names, see if anything pops up."

"Agreed," said Holmes. "We should update the good captain with our findings. Come on."

He stood from the table, then paused and turned around. He looked Watson up and down. "You might want to put something warmer on."

Watson ignored him as she headed for the stairs.

14

IDENTITIES REVEALED

Captain Gregson tapped a pen on his cheek as he listened to Watson and Holmes relate the discussion they'd had that morning. In front of him on his desk was the pass sheet for the mystery courier driver, Vicki Summers—a woman they now knew was going under the identity of Sophie Absolom, publicist and front-of-house hostess for the Dale Vanderpool roadshow. Whether either identity was the genuine one, it was so far impossible to know.

"Okay," said the captain, once the consultants had finished. "So Sophie Absolom, AKA Vicki Summers, visited the Mantis office months ago, possibly to see Gregory Smythe."

Holmes pursed his lips. "That would be the reasonable assumption."

"We need to start talking to everyone connected to Vanderpool," said Watson. "Sophie Absolom—if that's her real name—her husband, Trent, Vanderpool himself."

"Agreed," said Gregson.

Holmes nodded, his hands clasped in front of him. "I suggest we proceed with not a little haste. If the Absoloms, or indeed Vanderpool himself, are involved in the death of Gregory Smythe, the appearance of a police detective backstage at the lecture last night probably rattled them. They may try and run."

"The final night of Vanderpool's tour is tonight," said Watson. "According to his website and the website of Kronos Plaza, it's still on. There's been no cancellation notice posted."

"Yet," said Holmes.

"Okay," said Gregson. "We'll get things moving." He reached for the phone on his desk, then paused as just then Detective Bell appeared behind the glass door of the captain's office. He knocked once, then opened the door and leaned in around the frame. Watson and Holmes turned in their seats to look at him. On Bell's face was an expression Watson knew very well—something had just happened. Something important.

"We've found something," said the detective, before turning and heading back into the bullpen, without waiting for the others to follow.

Watson, Holmes and Gregson gathered around Bell's desk as Bell took them through his findings on his computer monitor.

They'd been right on the money. There *was* a connection between Mantis and Vanderpool, and it now looked like Sophie and Trent—along with Dale Vanderpool himself— were a part of it.

Gregson folded his arms and stuck his tongue in his cheek as he took in the information. "So they're *all* fake identities?"

Bell nodded, clicking through the files on display. "Yup, all three. Dale Vanderpool, Sophie Absolom, Trent Absolom. The Absoloms only pop up about a year ago, linked to two social security numbers belonging to a real couple from Montana— only the real couple died together in a car accident in 1985."

"A classic method of identity theft," said Holmes, his expression devoid of any humor. "I applaud them for their simplicity."

Watson frowned. "What about Dale Vanderpool?"

"He's a different story—" said Bell, but then Holmes interrupted him.

"Dale Vanderpool is not a stolen identity," said Holmes, "but a *pseudonym*."

Bell turned at his desk to look up at Holmes. "Ah… yes, that's right."

Gregson and Watson looked at Holmes. Holmes turned to them, and he gave a slight nod.

"I knew it was a pseudonym as soon as I discovered what our Mr. Vanderpool did for a living. He has taken a pseudonym from a very apt source—Dale Carnegie."

Watson nodded, recognizing the name. "Of course," she said. "The author of *How to Win Friends and Influence People*."

"Precisely," said Holmes. "And Dale Carnegie's wife was Dorothy Price *Vanderpool*. From that he created a portmanteau, giving himself an entirely new name."

"Except it's more than just a pseudonym," said Bell. "The new ID pops up sixteen years ago as a legal name change in the state of California."

Watson leaned over Bell's chair. "So who was he before?"

Bell smiled. "Oh, wait until you see this." He clicked his mouse, and the scanned forms of Dale Vanderpool's legal name change were replaced by a new page. Watson's eyes went wide at the sight. At Watson's shoulder, Captain Gregson gave a low whistle.

The new page on display was a booking sheet, complete with a mug shot of Vanderpool. He was younger, his chin peppered with a couple of days' worth of stubble, and his hair—a light brown just flecked with the gray that, today, was the predominant color—was longer, looking like it had been messed up and then some effort had been made to straighten it, perhaps for the picture. He certainly looked unhappy with the situation.

"In a past life," said Bell, "Dale Vanderpool was David Hauer, a one-time insurance broker from Chula Vista, California. In 1995 he was convicted of the manslaughter of one of his clients, a guy named Alex Kovalev."

Watson couldn't stop the gasp that escaped her throat as she read, over Bell's shoulder, the next part of the booking sheet. She stood tall, folded her arms, and looked at Holmes, who was still looking at the screen.

"It says he killed Kovalev in self-defense, stabbing him through the eye with—"

Holmes's eyes flicked across to meet Watson's gaze. "A fountain pen," he said.

Bell nodded, turning to the others, exchanging a look with his captain.

"According to the report," said Bell, "there was an altercation in Hauer's insurance office. Kovalev rushed in, confronted Hauer, and the argument became a fight. Apparently the other workers in the office came in to try to break it up, but it was too late. Kovalev went down, and was pronounced dead on arrival at the local emergency room. At the trial, Hauer's self-defense plea got him off the murder charge, but he served five years for manslaughter. He got out in late 2000, and as soon as he was able to he filed for the name change."

"So," said Gregson, rubbing his cheek with the back of one hand as he leaned on the pillar near to Bell's desk, "we have a man who killed someone using the exact same method that killed Gregory Smythe, who then changed both his name and career path, and who has now shown up on the East Coast, employing two other people who have stolen IDs."

"Sophie and Trent will likely have more identities available," said Holmes. "We already know that Sophie Absolom has at least on one other occasion gone by the name of Vicki Summers. Claiming lost identities from the graves of the dearly departed is the easiest way to get a new name and social security number, but it's also the easiest way to get caught. It's possible they have more pilfered identities ready to use, discarding any if they suspect the risk of detection is too high."

"If they're even married, of course," said Watson.

"Oh, that is just one question we're going to get the answer to," said Gregson. "I think it's high time we brought them all in for a little chat."

15

THE BIRDS HAVE FLOWN

The main auditorium at Kronos Plaza was empty when Watson and Holmes arrived with Captain Gregson and Detective Bell, and a small posse of uniformed police officers. Outside, the main entrance was being covered by more cops, as were the stage doors, located on a narrow side street, and the loading dock at the rear of the building.

Inside, the main auditorium space seemed, to Watson, suddenly cavernous, far larger than she remembered it from the previous night. She realized then just how popular Dale Vanderpool was—Kronos Plaza was not an insubstantial venue, and the place really had been filled nearly to capacity.

The auditorium itself may have been empty now, but there was one man on stage as Captain Gregson led the group down the central aisle, between acres of black folded seats.

Dale Vanderpool, his shirtsleeves rolled to the elbows, had his back to them and his head lifted to the ceiling, his arms outstretched and his hands moving in rapid circles like he was doing wrist exercises.

That wasn't all he was exercising. He was in the middle of a vocal warm-up.

"The *rain* in *Spain* falls *mainly* down the *drain*," he said, emphasizing the words like they were an alien language. He repeated the phrase three times, projecting the sounds high into the upper reaches of the auditorium, all the while oblivious to the presence of the police and the consulting detectives. Then Vanderpool switched to making other sounds, limbering up his vocal cords and his lips.

"Ha! Hee! Ho! Hum! Ha! Hee!"

"Mr. Vanderpool," said Gregson.

"Red leather, yellow leather, red leather, yellow leather."

"Dale Vanderpool!"

At once, Vanderpool dropped his arms and spun around, placing one hand over his chest like he'd got a fright. He gulped at the air, then his shoulders slumped and he laughed.

"Oh, I'm sorry!" he said, walking to the front of the stage to look down at the newcomers. "I was just doing some exercises, and I didn't hear you come in. I always do a couple of warm-up sessions before a talk—an early one now, and then one in the green room, just before I go on. I apologize."

He paused, and looked around at the uniformed officers who had fanned out among the empty seats farther back in the auditorium. Another remained right at the rear, next to the main door.

"Uh, what's going on?" asked Vanderpool. "Has something happened? Oh, did you find that missing man?"

Gregson stepped up to the stage, holding his NYPD badge up in one hand so Vanderpool could see it. "My name is Captain Gregson," he said, then he nodded at Holmes. "This is Sherlock Holmes, a consultant to the NYPD. I believe you have met Detective Bell and Ms. Watson."

Vanderpool smiled at the others, but the expression was weak and fleeting, as was the slight nod of greeting that went with it.

"Ah, yes, but…"

"I'm afraid we are going to need to conduct this conversation in a more official capacity," said Gregson, stuffing his hands and shield into the pockets of his coat.

"Official capacity?" The smile reappeared on Vanderpool's face, then vanished just as quickly. "You mean you're... you're *arresting* me?"

"No," said the captain. "Not yet, anyway. But we do want to ask you a few questions in relation to a police matter."

On the stage behind Vanderpool, a uniformed officer appeared, thumbs looped through his belt while Bell, meanwhile, found his way over to the steps at the side of the stage and trotted up. Vanderpool turned and watched Bell approach, but then shook his head and took a step back, his heels now just inches from the edge of the stage.

"But I have a talk to give in—" he checked his watch "—a little over four hours. And I'm behind schedule as it is." He turned around to look back down at Gregson.

On the stage, Bell shook his head. "I'm sorry to say your fans are going to be disappointed."

"Surely there's been some mistake," said Vanderpool, his eyes moving over Gregson, Watson, and Holmes, who had now seated himself in the front row of the auditorium. Vanderpool held his hands up. "I'm happy to cooperate fully with the police. Please, whatever you need to know, all you have to do is ask."

"Thank you for your cooperation, Mr. Vanderpool," said Holmes. "There are indeed plenty of questions we will be asking you in due course." He paused, and cocked his head. "Or should I be thanking Mr. *Hauer*?"

Vanderpool stood with his toes over the edge of the stage, rocking on his heels a little as his lips moved. But no words came out. Watson watched him carefully, noting the quickening of his pulse in his neck and temples, the pallor that had come over his face. Then Vanderpool licked his lips and nodded.

"That's fine, I understand," he said. His shoulders slumped—to Watson he appeared deflated, his fight gone, resigned to his fate.

Vanderpool turned back to Bell, who stood patiently waiting with his hands clasped in front of him. "Can we at least let my staff know? If the lecture is going to be cancelled there are some things that need to be done."

"Actually," said Gregson, "we need to talk to your staff too."

At that moment, a second uniformed officer appeared at the back of the stage. In front of him were the two show roadies, Mike and Jake, both of whom looked a little confused. Bell turned and, apparently seeing the frown on the detective's face, the other officer nodded at the two men in front of him.

"We just found these two out by the loading dock," he said. "There's no sign of anyone else here."

"What?" Watson turned to look up at Vanderpool. "Where are Sophie and Trent, your publicist and manager?"

Vanderpool sighed and flapped his arms against his sides. "That's just what I was going to tell you," he said. "We're so far behind schedule today because Sophie and Trent never showed up to work! Sophie is more than just my publicist, she also handles the front of house. I mean, she's not really supposed to, but she's good at it. I just leave her to it. I mean, Trent isn't really needed at night, but he lends a hand—"

Holmes leapt out of his seat and, without a word, rushed for the door leading to the backstage area.

Watson exchanged a look with Gregson, then they went after him.

In the maze of corridors backstage, Watson raced to catch up Holmes, his back disappearing around corners as he somehow found his own way to the green room.

Once there, he waited for Watson and the captain, his expression firm and grim. Then he gave the other two a nod, and flung the door open.

The room was empty, save for a cleaner in her Kronos Plaza uniform, running a vacuum cleaner over the carpet. Save for the lack of food and drink laid out on the table, nothing seemed to have changed since Watson had last been in the room. There was a small wheeled suitcase—the kind designed to fit into an airplane's overhead locker—by one of the sofas, Vanderpool's monogrammed name tag clearly visible on the handle. But, that aside, there was no indication that anyone else had been in the room.

"We have to find them," said Watson, turning to the others.

Holmes stood in the center of the room, staring at nothing, and saying even less.

16

THE DEATH OF ALEX KOVALEV

Captain Gregson stepped into the precinct interrogation room, file folder under one arm, Detective Bell at his heels. From the neighboring observation room, Watson watched both men quietly take a seat in front of Dale Vanderpool, who sat with his hands hidden under the interview-room table, his eyes searching for something invisible on its surface.

Holmes stood by Watson's side, silent, chewing on a thumbnail as he stared through the two-way glass.

Vanderpool had seemed calm, at least up until now—not exactly what Watson would have called *relaxed*, but he had been true to his word, coming quietly and without protest— or the need for handcuffs—back to the precinct, where he had waited without complaint in the interrogation room, politely accepting an offer of coffee from one of the uniformed officers on duty.

As Captain Gregson unbuttoned his jacket and pulled the right side of it away from his body as he got comfortable in his chair, Vanderpool looked up and met the detective's eye. Then he straightened in his own seat, and the faint, slightly uncertain smile played over his lips again. His half-full polystyrene coffee cup was on the table in front of him, and he turned it around, and around, and around, absently with the fingers of his left hand, as he waited for whatever it was the police had in store for him.

Gregson flipped open the file and cast an eye down the sheet, nodding to himself. Without looking up, he asked: "You want to tell us what happened back in Chula Vista?"

Vanderpool cleared his throat and stretched his neck out. Watson could see that, clearly, this was not a topic he was particularly keen on discussing. He cleared his throat again, his subsequent comment confirming her deduction.

"I'm sure you have everything you need in that file, sir."

Detective Bell, meanwhile, had placed a manila folder of his own on the table, but it remained closed as he leaned forward, hands clasped, toward their suspect.

"We know that you were born David Hauer, and that you were a modestly successful Californian insurance agent. You never quite made it to running your own brokerage, but you had a strong client list. Things were looking good, weren't they?"

Vanderpool pursed his lips and shrugged. "Well, all this was a very long time ago…"

Gregson's eyes remained on the sheet inside the folder. "You could have made something of yourself if it hadn't been for the drink, right?" he asked. Then his eyes finally rose to meet Vanderpool's.

As Watson watched, Vanderpool seemed to hold his breath for a moment, then he sighed and his shoulders sagged. He nodded, his smile flickered on again then went out almost at once, and he looked back down at his lap.

"I'm afraid that is quite true," he said. "I was a drunk. Every drawer in my office had a bottle. There wasn't even any room left in my filing cabinet for case folders, I had to keep shifting them around the bottles of Scotch. I couldn't get up in the morning without a drink. I couldn't get to sleep at night without it. During the day, forget about it. But I told myself it wasn't a problem. I managed at work for, oh, a long time, a long time. I don't think anybody knew, unless they were looking through my drawers and found the bottles. Or maybe that was exactly what they did. If they knew, nobody said anything, or did anything. I was bringing in enough money and clients. If it's not broken, don't fix it, right?"

His eyes lifted, the smile reappeared, fleetingly.

Watson felt very sad for him.

"Except you did break, eventually," said Bell. "You broke when Alex Kovalev came in to your office on the morning of September 14, 1995."

"Ah yes," said Vanderpool. He lifted the cup of coffee and took a sip, and even from the observation room, Watson could see his hand was now shaking quite badly, although his voice, while quiet, sounded strong.

Vanderpool put the cup down, and without further prompting, began to talk.

"Alex Kovalev. You know, he came in that morning, and he was angry. I mean, he was in a *rage*. I don't blame him for that, not at all. He'd just lost it all in a house fire—the whole place had gone up, taking... well, taking everything with it. Electrical short, as I recall. But it could have been much worse, of course, although he didn't quite see it that way. He and his family were safe, but, well, they'd have to start over, start again."

Vanderpool paused. Gregson and Bell glanced at each other before Vanderpool continued, his own eyes fixed firmly on the table.

"Kovalev was insured to the hilt. Full coverage, full payout. They'd have to start over, but they had a head start. Everything was in order."

Vanderpool paused again and ran his fingers along the edge of the table. He lifted his chin, but his eyes were still firmly downcast.

"Until the claim was declined. Now *that*... that was my fault. I'd mismanaged the account—his wasn't actually the first, either, but I'd managed to catch my own mistakes. Or at least I thought I had. Kovalev's case had slipped through. I mean, maybe we could have fixed it eventually, done something, I don't know. But at that moment, he was going to get absolutely nothing, and it was all my fault."

A heavy silence fell over the interview room. Watson glanced at Holmes. He now had both hands by his sides, curled into fists, and he was watching the interview with narrow eyes, his lips pursed.

"So you killed him?" asked Gregson.

Vanderpool's eyes snapped up. "No!" he said, affronted, then he sat back and seemed to calm down. "I mean... that wasn't how it happened."

"So how *did* it happen?" asked Bell.

"Well..." Vanderpool stopped, and he sighed. "He came into the office, angry, like I said. His life was ruined, and it was my fault. And he was right, it *was* my fault."

A pause, a beat.

"I... well, I don't actually remember what I tried to do. Apologize perhaps. I don't know. I don't remember. My blood must have been 100-proof in those days. But what I do remember is that he came into my office and launched himself at me, went for my throat. I was standing in front of my desk. I stepped back, tripped over my own feet. I reached behind me, to stop myself falling. By that point it was, well, it was chaos. My office had glass walls, everyone could see. I think there was screaming, there was shouting. There were some people behind Alex, I think anyway. Others from the office, I think they were trying to see if they could maybe jump him or something.

"But when I fell against the desk, my hand landed on my fountain pen. It was... it was just right there. So I grabbed it,

I didn't even really think about it. And I swung. I don't know, I was drunk, I was off balance.

"I was… afraid.

"So I swung, and I fell forward."

Vanderpool had his hands up in front of him now, his left held palm-out, the right curled as though wrapped around the pen from his memory. He was staring at that hand, his forehead creased in confusion.

Then he dropped both hands and looked directly at Captain Gregson.

"I remember that much," Vanderpool continued. "Then Kovalev, he just went down, backwards. It was like a tree falling. And I fell with him. We hit the deck, and I remember the air coming out of him, like he was… I don't know, like he was deflating, like a popped balloon. I can't describe it any other way. I remember his breath in my face, the way it blew the hair out of my eyes.

"That's when I realized what had happened. It was probably the adrenaline, the shock, pulling me out of it. My hand, it was covered in blood. I was holding onto something and it didn't move, and my hand slid off and all I could do was lie there, on top of the man I'd just killed, staring at my hand covered in all that blood. And I remember the blood… I remember how warm it was."

Watson watched as Vanderpool held his hand out again, and turned it over in front of himself, first staring at the palm, then the back, then the palm again.

Reliving the memory, the moment.

Reliving the horror.

Gregson ran his tongue along his teeth, then turned the report around in the folder in front of him, so Vanderpool could see. But Vanderpool was still staring at his own hand.

"You struck Alex Kovalev in the left eye with the fountain pen," said the captain. He tapped the report, and finally

Vanderpool's eyes moved down to it, although his hand stayed exactly where it was in the air between himself and the two policemen.

"Kovalev died instantly," said Bell, picking up the thread.

There was silence in the interview room, Vanderpool's hand in the air, his lips moving as he looked at the report.

Gregson cocked his head. "I'm sorry, you'll have to speak up a little," he said, his words dripping with sarcasm. In the observation room, Watson shifted uncomfortably on her feet. Beside her, Holmes remained impassive and unmoved as he watched the proceedings.

Vanderpool cleared his throat and dropped his hand. Regaining composure, he lifted his chin and winced, like he was stretching out a stiff muscle, then he placed both hands flat on the table, next to the report. He gave it one more glance, then nodded. When he next spoke, his voice was loud and level.

"It was an accident. I was acting in self-defense, but I had no intention of harming that man. Only protecting my own life."

"Right," said Bell, the smile on his face decidedly unpleasant. "Your defense team managed to get you a voluntary manslaughter conviction rather than homicide."

Vanderpool smiled sadly, and nodded slowly. "There were plenty of witnesses."

"You were sentenced to seven years in San Quentin, you served out five."

Vanderpool cleared his throat. "Yes, and you may not believe it, but I'm truly thankful for my time there. Prison changed my life."

Bell frowned. "That's what you *say*, but now, all these years later, you turn up in New York City and someone else has another little 'accident' with a fountain pen."

Now Bell opened his folder and turned it around. Within were crime scene photos from the Athena Hotel, showing

Gregory Smythe splayed on the floor, staring at the ceiling, fountain pen *in situ* in his right orbit.

Vanderpool gasped, visibly jolting in his chair as he looked at the image. Then he looked up at the detectives.

"But… this is the man you were looking for! You didn't say he was *dead*!"

"Gregory Smythe," said Gregson, "was murdered at the Athena Hotel in Washington Heights two nights ago. Look at the pictures. He was stabbed through the right eye with a fountain pen. That sound familiar?"

"I never met the man," said Vanderpool, with a shake of the head. "I hadn't even *heard* of him until your colleagues came asking. Nor his company, either… what was it, Mentis Capital?"

"*Mantis*," said Bell. "We have reason to believe Gregory Smythe had been to at least one of your speaker events."

Vanderpool shrugged. He shook his head again. Watson observed him closely—he was thrown, flustered, nervous… but there was something about his body language that she felt was genuine.

Exactly the kind of reaction someone would have when thrown into a situation like this. To be confronted with your past, one that you were running from, one that was full of shame and guilt, full of *pain*—that would have been difficult. Very difficult.

Watson grimaced, unsure whether her reaction was logical or emotional—probably a bit of both. But she turned to Holmes and voiced her concerns anyway. To her relief, he nodded, his eyes still fixed on the view through the observation room window.

"If we take his word that he killed Alex Kovalev by *accident*," he said quietly, "and that the act was fuelled by an addiction, in his case to alcohol, then there is nothing to suggest Mr. Vanderpool, *né* Hauer is likely to repeat that act, using the exact same methods and tool."

Watson nodded. "Right. Otherwise he's just framed *himself*. He's innocent, he has to be."

"Absolutely and categorically," Holmes said, "the answer is *yes*."

Watson frowned and returned her attention to the questioning in the other room.

"Listen, I don't dispute my past," Vanderpool was saying. "What I am disputing is that I killed this man. Like I said, prison changed me, in a *good* way. It taught me an awful lot."

"About what, exactly?" asked Bell.

"Life, Detective!" Vanderpool leaned forward, suddenly animated. "And about myself. I could see what I'd become, where that had taken me. I may have killed Alex Kovalev accidentally, but I was in prison because of my own actions. Everything I had done in my life had led to that moment, Detective. Everything! It took the death of that poor man for me to realize that. Prison *changed* me—completely. I became a new person."

Captain Gregson raised an eyebrow. "Literally, right? I mean, once you got out, you changed your name and magically discovered this new career path of yours?"

Vanderpool smiled, this time showing a little teeth, clearly more comfortable talking about his new life.

"Nothing magical about it, sir. In prison I'd learned so much about human nature, about what drives us, our desires, wants, needs. Fantasies, even. I saw it all, firsthand, with my own eyes. With my head clear for the first time in, well, *years*, I realized I could help others. I was good at my job, I knew that, but I also knew that selling insurance was only a part of it. I knew *people*. I knew what made them tick, what made them work, what motivated them, what made... well, what made everything worthwhile.

"While I was inside my job was prison librarian, so I took the opportunity to do some research. I developed a set of training techniques for management. I started making notes. I ran a couple of groups at the prison, and it went well—my fellow inmates thanked me for my help. The guards, too. I'd finally found I could do something useful, something I could give back to the world. Then, once I was out, I created a blog, started doing little videos on the Internet. It worked. And, look, the rest is history. Here I am. I made a new life for myself. A life that I love. I'm making a real difference to a lot of people—and never *once*, not *once*, have I used my own past as an example."

Vanderpool licked his lips, nodding, perhaps more to himself than the others.

"David Hauer died that day in 1995, along with Alex Kovalev. My name is Dale Vanderpool. That's who I am. That's who I was supposed to be, only I never knew it until it was almost too late."

Gregson and Bell looked at each other. Neither of them were giving much away, but Watson wondered what they made of Vanderpool's story. He *seemed* genuine, but there was still an outside chance he was just a very good actor. And, yes, killing someone using the exact same method that had killed Alex Kovalev twenty-plus years ago was a very good way to frame yourself—but it was also, Watson thought, perhaps the ideal cover, a double-bluff that maybe he thought he could get away with.

In the interview room, Gregson turned back to Vanderpool.

"Can you tell us where you were three nights ago, between the hours of nine P.M. and midnight?"

Vanderpool sighed and smiled, relaxing. "Oh, of course. We'd just arrived in town, and I had a book signing from seven until about eight-thirty. Then we had a quick dinner, took about an hour, I guess."

Bell raised an eyebrow. "You guess? That only takes you to nine-thirty."

"Ah, yes," said Vanderpool. "Well, after that, I got back to the hotel at about, oh, ten. Might have been ten-thirty. I was with Trent, my tour manager. We had some drinks in my room until at least eleven-thirty, twelve. First night in a new town, and it's the first time we've been booked in New York City. So, you know, it was something worth toasting."

"Don't tell me, you stuck to the soda?" asked Gregson.

"Well, of course, I don't drink anymore, sir, I think we've already—"

"The one problem with your alibi, Mr. Hauer—"

"It's *Vanderpool*."

"Mr. *Vanderpool*," the captain continued, "is that Trent Absolom isn't around to confirm it."

"Surely you can check with the hotel. Someone will have seen us, there must be security-camera footage—"

"Oh, don't worry," said Bell, "we're looking into it."

Vanderpool fell silent.

"Tell me, Mr. Vanderpool," said Gregson, "have you found your fancy fountain pen yet? You know, the one you normally sign books with. The one you say you lost."

"Ah… no, actually." Vanderpool ran a finger along his bottom lip. "To be honest, I haven't really had much chance to look properly."

"Maybe we can save you the trouble."

At that, Gregson reached into his jacket pocket and brought out the weapon used to kill Gregory Smythe. The pen, still crusted with dried blood and other fluids, was sealed in a plastic evidence bag. Gregson dropped it onto the folder in front of Vanderpool, the heavy pen making a surprisingly loud thud.

The suspect frowned, peering at the pen but not making any move to touch the bag or examine the contents.

"Look familiar?" asked Bell.

Vanderpool looked up at the detective. "Well, no." He

pointed to the evidence bag. "That pen isn't mine."

Gregson smiled. "Take a closer look. It's a LeFevre. A good brand, so I'm told. A little above my tax bracket unfortunately."

Vanderpool's eyes went from the captain to the bag and back again. He wet his lips again.

"A LeFevre?"

Gregson nodded. "And what kind of pen do you use, Mr. Vanderpool?"

"Well, I…"

"A LeFevre?"

"Well… yes. Yes I do. But I'm telling you, this pen isn't mine."

Bell's eyebrow went up again. "Are you sure about that?"

Vanderpool barked a short, nervous laugh. "Look, I lost mine in my hotel room. Surely you can just go and search the place and find it?"

Then he sat back and folded his arms, his expression, his whole demeanor, settling into a steely, controlled calmness. Perhaps he was falling back on his own techniques, Watson thought: shutting the interview down.

"I think I'd like to call my attorney now, gentlemen," he said.

Captain Gregson and Detective Bell exchanged a look, then they stood and left Vanderpool alone at the table.

17

THE SECOND MURDER

Gregson and Bell, along with Watson and Holmes, reconvened in the hallway of the precinct bullpen, just outside the closed interview room door.

The captain shook his head, his hands on his hips. "He's lawyering up. *And* we don't have enough evidence to charge him with anything—all we've got so far are some very loose and *very* circumstantial connections." Gregson sighed. "He's not the only rich person with a taste for expensive LeFevre fountain pens, but he says the pen used to kill Smythe isn't his."

"And yet," said Holmes, "his own missing pen has yet to be located."

Detective Bell frowned. "But surely the link between Mantis Capital and Vanderpool's speaking tour can't be a coincidence?" he asked.

Holmes nodded. "Indeed not, Detective. The world has many wonderful and strange things within it, but I am sorry to say that *coincidences* are not among them."

Watson considered Holmes's words, then folded her arms, looking at her colleague. "But Vanderpool is innocent," she said, recalling their conversation from the observation room. As she spoke, Holmes's eyes flicked over to hers, but he kept quiet.

"Wait, Vanderpool is innocent?" asked Bell.

"He is innocent, yes," said Holmes. "Why would he murder someone with a fountain pen, replicating nearly exactly the death of Alex Kovalev? You saw his reactions in the interview room, his body language, inflections of speech—you were sitting right in front of him, able to observe with even greater clarity than I was. That period of his life is clearly still a trauma for him, and he truly believes that having done his time, he was born anew." Holmes waved his arms, sculpting a circle in the air between himself and the others. "And he can't very well frame *himself*. Nor would he have any obvious desire to throw away what appears to be a highly successful and, if I may say, *lucrative* new career."

Just then, Bell's phone buzzed in his pocket. He walked away to take the call, and when he returned his face was grave. "That was the team at Vanderpool's hotel. They've searched every room booked for his tour staff—there's no sign of Trent or Sophie Absolom, but their room looks like it has been turned over, and in a hurry too."

Holmes frowned. "As we suspected, the Absoloms—or whatever their real names are—have been spooked, and are in the wind."

"But was it because of our visit," said Watson, glancing at Bell, "or because of that argument we overheard?"

"Well," said Bell, "whatever the reason, guess what the team found when they searched Vanderpool's room?"

Watson's eyes widened. "A fountain pen?"

Bell nodded. "They're sending a photo over," he said, and right on cue, his phone buzzed again. "Here we go."

He thumbed the screen, studying the image for a moment, then turned it around so the others could see. Holmes snatched it out of his hand and peered closely at the screen, his lips pursed. Then he nodded.

"A LeFevre. Nearly identical to the one used to kill Smythe, too. *But*—" he paused, then pinched the screen to zoom in, then he turned the phone back around to the others "—it has a cap, with an engraved serial number. With this information we should be able to trace the pen's history right back to the workshop in Switzerland."

"Okay," said Bell, taking his phone back, giving Holmes a look that Watson recognized as a mix of mild annoyance at Holmes's apparent rudeness, and quiet resignation that nothing about that was ever going to change. "So we're back at square one."

"Well, we have a BOLO out for Trent and Sophie," said Gregson. "Nothing so far, but there's a chance they haven't got that far yet."

"They will, of course, now be traveling under different names," said Holmes, "and, most likely, new appearances."

At this, the captain frowned. "We'll do our best."

Holmes glanced back toward the interview room. Beyond that door, Watson knew, Vanderpool would be patiently waiting for his lawyer. So far, the investigation was not panning out as she expected, and they were pretty much in the dark. Watson wondered if, really, Dale Vanderpool knew any more about recent events than they did.

Holmes turned back to Gregson. "Dale Vanderpool's arrest in 1995 and subsequent trial took place in California," he said. "I need you to contact the Chula Vista police department and the relevant courts and/or district attorney's office, and get all the paperwork and evidence records from the case sent over."

Gregson nodded and cocked his head at the consultant. "Okay. You think there's something Vanderpool isn't telling us?"

"On the contrary, I think Vanderpool is being entirely open and honest, Captain."

"But," said Watson, the connection coming together in her own mind, "there has to be someone else involved. Someone who knew the details of the original case."

"Which presumably is Trent or Sophie," said Gregson, "or perhaps both."

"Except they are only recent employees of Mr. Vanderpool," said Holmes. "I think a thorough review of the Kovalev killing is in order."

"We'll get on it," said Gregson. He nodded at Bell, and the two of them turned and walked toward the bullpen.

Watson watched them go, lost in her own thoughts, before seeing the pair get stopped by a uniformed officer halfway down the hallway. The trio of policemen stood in conference for a few seconds, then Gregson turned on his heel and marched sharply back toward Holmes and Watson while Bell and the uniform rushed on into the bullpen.

Holmes lifted an eyebrow as the captain rejoined them.

"Well," said Gregson, "now we know it's definitely not Vanderpool."

Watson frowned. "What?"

Holmes nodded, his hands in his pockets. He bounced on his heels a few times. "There's been another murder," he said.

It was a statement, not a question.

Gregson nodded. "There has. And this time the victim is Trent Absolom. His body was found in Brooklyn, in a parking lot."

"Oh no," said Watson, as she felt a sinking feeling in her stomach. "He was stabbed, wasn't he?"

"Through the *eye*," said Gregson, his expression grim. "But there's no sign of the weapon this time."

Holmes looked at the other two. "Come on, we need to see the scene of the crime. There is not a moment to lose."

18

THE NOBLE ART OF TRIGONOMETRY

I t was late afternoon by the time they arrived at the crime scene. As the police pool car pulled up in the street, Watson surveyed the area from the backseat window.

They were in Brooklyn—not far from the brownstone she shared with Sherlock—but in an area where the steady, insidious spread of gentrification had yet to sink its claws. The crime scene—a parking lot—was like any of the hundreds of other small lots in each of the five boroughs, a roughly rectangular open space sandwiched between tall, narrow brick buildings, which looked like a mix of light industrial warehouses, cheap apartments and a few stores. In the lot itself were spaces for perhaps fifty cars, maybe more if the rear of the site hadn't been covered with bricks from a semi-collapsed small wall, a relic of a past building demolition that hadn't been entirely completed. In the same vicinity several black trash bags had been dumped, and some small attempt had been made to cover the fallen brickwork with a tarpaulin, but clearly a long, long time ago, Watson suspected, given the rotten state of the blue canvas.

There were two police cars and an unmarked van in the lot. CSU techs were already setting up underneath a small, portable marquee erected in the back corner of the parking lot.

Gregson led the way, Holmes and Watson close behind. As they approached the marquee, one of the CSU techs in blue disposable overalls turned around and offered a greeting.

Watson recognized him immediately: Eugene Hawes, the medical examiner befriended by Holmes, who indulged the pathologist in late-night chess matches at the morgue in exchange for free and unfettered access to the facilities—and to the bodies stored within.

"Well now," said Eugene, a broad smile crossing his face. "Sherlock Holmes, the one and only. Not often we cross paths out in the big bad city, eh? Haven't seen you around the morgue either recently. Still smarting from that last game, I'll bet?" Eugene chuckled and shook his head. "Mate in eight. I could hardly believe it."

Watson saw Holmes's nostrils flare. He kept his hands in the pockets of his pea coat; Watson could see him curl his fists just that little bit tighter. "It was mate in *nine*, and it was sheer luck."

Eugene's smile got ever wider. "I thought you didn't believe in luck, Sherlock?"

"Don't you have a dead body to tell us about?"

Holmes turned away and made a point of moving closer to the crime scene itself, extracting a hand from his pocket to gesture to the body, which lay face up by the collapsed brick wall, surrounded by the black plastic trash bags.

Eugene cleared his throat and joined his friend. "The deceased is one male, in his mid-thirties—"

"The late Trent Absolom, yes," said Holmes. "Feel free to skip ahead."

Eugene bristled slightly. "Well, the victim was killed in the early hours of the morning, that much is obvious."

"Was he killed here, in the parking lot?" asked Watson.

Holmes lifted a single finger and pointed it at Watson,

indicating to her that her question was a good one, one he was most likely just about to ask.

Eugene cocked his head. "In the parking lot, yes, but not where he is lying now. He was killed then dragged a few yards—you can see the trail. He was dumped here, by the wall, and the killer, or their accomplice, pulled the garbage bags over the body to hide it. The body was found when the manager of the lot called the city to report the trash and get someone to come out and collect it."

Watson joined Holmes by the body. It was Trent, no doubt about it, the hipster mustache and beard framing a mouth open in what looked like surprise. His eyes—his *eye*—was open, the other nothing but a reddish-black stain.

Holmes bent down to examine the wound closely, taking his phone and the lens attachment from his inside pocket to get a magnified view. Watson couldn't help grimacing as Holmes's own face came within an inch of the victim's.

Gregson walked over from where he had been talking to the officers on the scene. He shook his head at Watson. "No sign of any weapon here," he said. "The uniforms have done one sweep of the lot, but they'll do another. There's a lot of trash and rubble to pick through, but so far, no joy." The captain sighed and turned to watch Holmes poring over the body. "The killer must have taken it with them."

"That seems likely," said Holmes, not interrupting his own examination.

Watson turned to Eugene. "Was there anything on the body?"

The examiner nodded, and, stepping past Gregson, clicked his fingers at the uniformed officer by the back of the open CSU van. The officer nodded, grabbed something from inside the vehicle, and jogged over.

Eugene took the item and, as Holmes stood up, pocketing his phone and lens, handed it to Watson.

The item was a clear plastic evidence bag. Inside it was a cellphone.

"Okay," said Gregson, watching. "So perhaps with that we can find out a bit more about who Trent Absolom really was."

Holmes nodded, then he looked at the others, the expression on his face frozen. "I wonder," he muttered. He leaned over to the table underneath the marquee and pulled a fresh pair of blue latex gloves from the box that sat among the other items from the CSU toolkit. With the gloves on, Holmes took the evidence bag from Watson, opened it, took the phone out, and turned it on. After fiddling for a few minutes, Holmes nodded.

"Interesting," he said.

"What is?" asked Watson.

"There is but a single text message saved on this phone," said Holmes. Watson moved to his side to get a look, and he angled the screen for her to read.

She read the message twice, just to make sure, then she looked up at her colleague.

"It's this address."

"Place *and* time," said Holmes, nodding. He turned the phone to Eugene so the examiner could get a good look. "I would say with some certainty that the time of death was sometime shortly after three A.M," he said. "Not only *that*, but he was killed by the same person who killed Gregory Smythe, and that person most *certainly* wasn't Dale Vanderpool."

Gregson frowned. "How do you know the killer was the same person?"

Holmes stepped up to the captain and showed him the phone. Gregson looked at the screen, but from the look on his face, it was clear to Watson that he wasn't entirely sure what Holmes was referring to.

Watson pointed over the top of the screen. "The number," she said.

"Indeed," said Holmes. "Trent Absolom received a text from the same number that summoned Gregory Smythe to his demise in Washington Heights."

"But that phone was a burner," said Gregson. "We tried to trace it. The number is completely dead."

"Then someone, Captain," said Holmes. "Has brought it back to life."

It was dark by the time the CSU techs were ready to move Trent Absolom's body to the NYPD morgue, an ambulance now having arrived and parked up at the scene. Holmes spent the time studying the crime scene, watching as uniformed officers and more CSU techs pulled the trash and rubble apart to search for any sign of the murder weapon, or some other piece of physical evidence. Watson helped as best she could, but it had been a long day and she was in dire need of coffee. She stopped and leaned back on the police pool car, watching the others.

She checked her watch, then pushed off the car and walked over to Holmes. At this point he was standing in the center of the parking lot, looking around, his hands firmly in the pockets of his pea coat.

"What do you think?" she asked. "Smythe was killed by someone who knew about Vanderpool's past. Then Trent was killed the same way. Did he know about Vanderpool as well?"

"Neither Vanderpool nor Trent killed Smythe," said Holmes, "but perhaps Trent found out the truth, or knew too much. He and his wife had secrets of their own, after all. He may have been a loose end in need of tying."

"What about Sophie? It's possible that she could have killed Smythe, and then her husband."

"If Trent really was her husband."

Watson watched the techs load Trent's body into a bag,

and the bag onto a wheeled stretcher.

"The killer knew both victims," said Watson, musing aloud. "He—or *she*—texted them, and on both occasions the victim followed the instructions, apparently without question or concern for their own safety."

"Indeed," said Holmes. "Both victims were most likely taken by surprise. There was no struggle, no fight. Just a well-aimed blow when the victim least expected it. The size and strength differential between the killer and the victims—if the killer was, as you suggest, Sophie Absolom—would matter little."

Watson pulled the collar of her coat up against the gathering cold of the evening. Everything they considered made sense—which was exactly the problem. There were too many connections, too many possibilities. All theories, all a collection of circumstances that seemed, on the face of it, to follow a logical order.

In her own mind, two opposing trains of thought fought for dominance.

On the one hand was the principle of Occam's razor, which said that the simplest explanation was the most likely. Events ran from A, to B, to C, following the path of least resistance.

But on the other was the advice that Holmes was fond of reminding her of: the nature of the human brain to find patterns where none exist. Perhaps the events surrounding the murders of Gregory Smythe and now Trent Absolom fit a pattern simply because her brain was telling her they did.

The ambulance was ready to leave. Watson turned to watch the vehicle and the two police cars start up and roll out of the parking lot.

Gregson, the collar of his own trench coat high, marched back over to the two consultants.

"I'm heading back to the precinct. We should have the preliminary results of the post-mortem in a few hours. I'll call when we find out more."

"Thanks," said Watson. She turned to Holmes. "You know, we can walk home from here."

Holmes nodded, but he was looking elsewhere. Watson could sense something was up. As she watched, Holmes frowned, then snapped his head around the other way, quickly.

Gregson and Watson exchanged a look, and then she asked: "What's up?"

Holmes shushed his colleague with a raised hand, then fell into a crouch, fingertips pressed against the wet asphalt of the parking lot. A second later, his feet shot out from under him and he fell into a perfect push-up position. Then, balanced only on his toes and fingertips, he slowly lowered himself to the ground until his cheek was on the blacktop, his face turned toward the crime scene.

"You want to share something with us, Holmes?" asked Gregson, looking down at the consultant, with his hands firmly buried in the pockets of his coat.

Holmes moved his head, dragging his cheek on the rough ground as he craned around to look out of the parking lot entrance. Watson turned, followed his gaze. There was nothing much there—just the street—and on the opposite side a somewhat dilapidated high-rise that probably went up in the late 1980s, the first floor of which was some kind of budget furniture shop. Watson could see sofas and a reclining easy chair on display through the wide glass frontage of the dark showroom.

Holmes leapt to his feet, apparently oblivious to the scree adhering to his face and the front of his pea coat. He looked at the other two, a smile on his face, a sparkle in his eyes.

"How's your trigonometry, Captain?"

"My *trigonometry*?"

"You know," said Holmes. "Angles, distances, triangles." He looked at Watson. "I have often said there is no finer geometric shape than an equilateral triangle."

"I'll take your word for it," said Watson, her eyes narrowing. "And this relates to Trent Absolom how, exactly?"

"I think I can show you just who the killer is," said Holmes. "Follow me."

19

THE SECRET OF THE PIZZA PARLOR

Holmes led Watson and Captain Gregson out of the parking lot and onto the sidewalk. Then he stopped at the entrance, looked first right, then left, then up at the eighties office block opposite. Then he turned on his heel to look back at the parking lot, peering up at the buildings that framed it, and then, finally up at the darkening, cloudy sky.

Then Holmes turned to Watson. "This way," he said, and, with his hands deep in his pockets, he walked briskly to the right, along the sidewalk.

Watson and Gregson exchanged a look, and followed. Holmes was on to something, and whatever it was, he was going to let them in on it in his own sweet time.

Just farther along the sidewalk, Holmes stopped at the premises adjacent to the parking lot. Watson came up to his side and looked up at the signage.

"*Rio's Gio's Pizza and Kebabs*," she read from the old neon sign suspended nearly directly above them from the overhang of the building. Glancing at the frontage, she saw that Rio's Gio's was a typical small greasy joint of dubious quality and hygiene that, given the quiet, backstreet location, probably did most of its business through takeout orders and delivery. Its front windows were mostly covered from the inside with posters and placards advertising special offers and combo deals, and if there was a city-mandated health rating on display, Watson couldn't see it.

Holmes nodded, mostly to himself, and headed inside.

The store interior was brightly lit, making Watson realize just how dark it had gotten outside. The place smelled more of kebab meat than pizza, and at the back of the store, behind the counter, three rotating columns of uniformly gray meat were grilling. The kitchen itself was out of sight, no doubt located beyond the door at the back, through which appeared a male in his late teens, Rio's Gio's-branded apron over a black t-shirt and jeans.

The young man's eyes lingered a little over his supposed patrons, before he pulled a large pad of cheap newsprint paper out onto the counter and reached for a pen.

"Okay, what can I get you?" he asked.

Holmes looked up at the menus, set high on the back wall above the kebab grills. "How about all of the footage from the last twenty-four hours from the security camera installed outside?" he said, still apparently reading the list of pizza and kebab combo meals.

The teen behind the counter grimaced, pulling his head back like he'd just got a whiff of something very strong and very unpleasant. "Say what now?"

"Oh, that's fine, I can get it myself," said Holmes, and without making eye contact with the kid, he went to the other end of the counter and lifted the partition to step through. The teen ran over at once.

"Hey, pal, what the hell is this? We've had enough trouble with you guys already, so get the hell out, okay, or I'll get the old man out here!"

Holmes stopped halfway through the counter. He smiled at the teen.

"Yes, I'm sure you have."

The kid shook his head, his hands curling in frustration. "Have what, you freak? Get the hell out!"

"Trouble, recently," said Holmes, politely. "That's why you installed the security camera outside and angled it so you could record any activity, not immediately outside the store, but on the sidewalk just down the street."

The teen sighed and flapped his arms. He looked at Watson and Captain Gregson, and shook his head.

"Okay, you know what? I'm calling the cops. You freak shows can wait around and get arrested or get the hell out, entirely up to you."

Gregson stepped forward. "We *are* the cops," he said, holding out his badge. "I apologize for my colleague, but if you could help us out…?"

The teen looked at the badge and took a step back, the grimace returning to his face, like he was sucking on a leaky battery.

"What the hell is this about? We call the cops and they never come, so what, now you're just visiting for the hell of it?"

Watson laid a hand on the countertop, and immediately regretted it; her skin stuck to the surface. "We're looking into something that happened in the parking lot next door," she said. "Around three A.M. Are you open then?"

The teen seemed to calm at Watson's manner, and shook his head. "Some nights, but not always. And not last night. We closed up around one-thirty, I think. So what happened next door?"

"A man was murdered," said Holmes.

At this, the teen went pale. "What? Murdered? The *hell*?" He rubbed his face, then ran a hand through his hair. "What happened?"

"That's what we're trying to find out," said Gregson. "Now, if you don't mind? I think my colleague here wants to see the footage from your security camera. Is that right?"

Holmes nodded, then turned back to the teenager. "If you please," he said, giving a slight bow.

The kid looked at the three of them in turn, then he spent a few moments smoothing down the front of his Rio's Gio's apron. *A nervous gesture*, thought Watson. She didn't blame him.

Then the teen nodded to the door at the back of the store.

"It's this way."

The teen from Rio's Gio's—Peter, the eponymous Rio's nephew, apparently—fiddled with an old portable ten-inch television set that sat on a high shelf at the back of the pizza parlor's kitchen. The only other person working was a Mexican cook introduced by Peter as Mario. The man seemed to speak little English, and he continued to work, sorting bags of frozen pizza toppings in preparation for the night ahead, while the others gathered around the set in the corner.

"We checked all the nearby surveillance feeds as standard, Holmes," said Gregson. "But this is a quiet street. There's not much out there of any use that actually *has* a camera— just a hair salon, that furniture place across the street, couple of others farther down. But they're all either pointed in the wrong direction, or the cameras weren't even on."

"But you didn't check this one, did you?" asked Holmes, glancing sideways at the captain, the corner of his mouth curling up.

"No, we didn't," said Gregson, "because it's on the same side of the street as the parking lot, and the camera is pointing in the completely opposite direction. What makes you so sure there's something worth seeing here?"

Holmes's earlier words came back to Watson, and she clicked her fingers. "Trigonometry, right?"

"Indeed," said Holmes. "I said earlier there was no such thing as a coincidence, but in this instance, I am happy to stand corrected." He pointed back through the kitchen, toward the front of the takeout joint. "This pizza parlor *stroke* kebab joint is adjacent to the parking lot. In front of the parking lot, on the opposite side of the street, is a furniture warehouse with an expansive plate glass frontage. To my eye, the angle of the camera outside this establishment may be just *so*, allowing us to get a view into the parking lot itself via the *reflection* in the window of the furniture store."

Gregson whistled and looked at Watson. She just folded her arms and shrugged. The captain turned back to Holmes. "That's a long shot, even for you."

"On the contrary, Captain," said Holmes, "that's trigonometry."

Peter stepped back, a small wand-like remote control in his hand, which he handed to Holmes. "Okay, here we go."

Holmes pressed play, and the four of them peered at the small black-and-white screen.

The surveillance footage was rough, the camera slightly out of focus and overexposed, the whole image shimmering slightly. The field of view was mostly the sidewalk in front of and just a few yards down from Rio's Gio's. As Holmes fast-forwarded, the timestamp spinning on toward the period in the early hours of the last morning that was, according to the text message retrieved from Trent's phone, the time of his murder, not much happened. A small handful of people came and went. A car pulled up, was loaded with takeout, then took off. This was repeated twice. A little while later, a group of four youths came and lingered outside the joint for a while, only to be chased off by an older, irate Asian man who came out of the store, waving his arms. He had the same apron on as Peter, and was wearing an old-fashioned garrison cap featuring the store logo.

"That's my uncle, Rio," said Peter. "We've had a little trouble outside the place in the last few months. Tussles, mostly. One time they fell against the window and cracked it. Like I said, the cops, they don't want to know."

"Which is why your uncle installed the security camera in the first place," said Holmes.

"Right."

"And," Holmes continued, "thanks to Mr. Rio's diligence in documenting his difficulties, we may have a lead in a very different kind of crime."

With that, Holmes released the fast-forward button. On the screen, the front of the furniture store diagonally opposite Rio's Gio's—but directly across the street from the parking lot—suddenly lit up in a flare of white. As it faded, Watson could see the faint yet distinctive outline of the rear of a car, tail lights blazing, in the window.

To her own amazement, it seemed that Holmes's theory might have been right.

Holmes paused, peered at the screen, then handed Watson the remote. She took it, and was about to ask Holmes what he was thinking, when he moved to the corner of the kitchen, beyond where Mario was unloading frozen goods from the walk-in freezer. There was a small, greasy chair in the corner. Holmes picked it up, deposited it in front of the desk, then clambered first up onto the chair, then the desk itself. Order receipts and paperwork toppled over, to the protests of Peter, as Holmes got his nose right up to the television set on the high shelf.

"Can you make anything out in the reflection?" asked Watson.

Holmes *hrmmed* loudly, then shook his head. He turned to look down at the others and nodded at Gregson.

"Captain, we'll need to analyze this footage back at the precinct, see if we can enhance the view."

Holmes hopped off the desk while Gregson spoke to Peter about getting a copy of the footage. Watson sidled up to Holmes, and the two of them stared at the wavering, still image.

Watson shook her head. "It's going to be tough getting anything useful out of that. The picture is terrible and the reflection is very indistinct."

Holmes nodded, but he took a step forward and pointed. "Look at the bottom of the car, that bright rectangle. The license plate. We have a clear shot of it."

Watson stared at it. He was right, it was the license plate, but it was completely bleached out in the distorted, flaring reflection. She frowned. "I guess we might be able to run it through forensic enhancement. But it's not much to go on."

"Small steps, Watson," said Holmes, turning to his companion. "Small steps."

20

CLARITY GAINED

Back at the precinct, Watson left Holmes in one of the big meeting rooms, where he and a department computer tech worked on the footage recovered from the security feed at Rio's Gio's. She wandered into the hallway, where the department's hot beverage machine was, dispensing the NYPD's famously awful coffee. As she waited for her cup of barely drinkable yet scalding liquid to be prepared, Detective Bell came over and began eyeing up the snacks in the vending machine alongside.

"And now we wait, and wait, and wait," said Bell. He picked his candy bar of choice and began depositing quarters.

"Right," said Watson, laughing. "The default state of the police detective. Nothing has come in on anything else then?"

"Nope," said Bell, watching as his snack clunked into the tray at the bottom of the vending machine. He bent down to extract it. "No hits on the BOLO we have out for Sophie Absolom. We're still canvassing stores that sell fountain pens. Vanderpool's lawyer told us where we could put our theories and took his client away, but not before we told him not to leave town. Nothing yet from the hotel Vanderpool was staying at. They've got good security footage but it doesn't show much—people coming and going, Trent, Sophie, Vanderpool included. And it confirms his alibi for the night Gregory Smythe was killed." He sighed, his fingers busy working the wrapper of his candy bar open. "Feels like we're treading water here, you know?"

"Believe me, I know." Watson nodded, taking a tentative sip of her coffee. Perhaps it was the long hours and the frustrating nature of the case, but somehow the coffee actually tasted pretty good for once.

"You really think Holmes can pull something out of the footage from that pizza joint?" asked Bell, nodding toward the meeting room. "He's been in there for a couple of hours now. I could hardly make anything out on the *sidewalk*, let alone reflected in the window across the street."

"Well," said Watson, "there was definitely something there. Maybe if the image can be enhanced just enough. It doesn't need to be perfect, only—"

Holmes rushed toward them down the hallway, his face lighting up as he saw Watson and Bell.

"I have something!" he said, then began waving at them frantically. "Quickly now, quickly!" Then he turned and dashed away.

Watson and Bell looked at each other, then went after Holmes.

Holmes led them back to the meeting room, where he had been working. At the far end was a large television, at least sixty inches across, and on the long table that filled most of the room were two laptops. Seated in front of one was a young woman with her hair tied up in a ponytail. She was wearing what looked like running gear. Watson noticed that an armband holding a music player, headphones wrapped around it, was sitting on the table behind the laptops.

Holmes pulled up a chair at the other laptop and gestured to the woman. "Sally Eastman here is the best forensic image technician the New York Police Department has," he said. "She has kindly agreed to curtail her regular evening run to come and help with the analysis."

"Oh, thanks," said Watson. "We appreciate it. We need all the help we can get on this one."

Sally shrugged with a smile. "Duty calls. And now Sherlock owes me three big favors."

Holmes looked up from his computer. "I do believe it was *two* favors."

Sally turned to Holmes, the smile on her face suddenly very fixed, and very cold.

"Three."

Holmes gulped, his eyes locked with Sally's, then he jerked his head away, returning his attention to his laptop.

"Very well. Three."

Bell sighed. He took a bite from his candy bar, then used the remainder to gesture to the TV. On it, paused, was the security footage from Rio's Gio's. If anything, it looked even worse to Watson now, enlarged from the tiny, cheap TV at the pizza joint's kitchen to the giant department OLED display.

"So what have you got?" asked Bell, his jaw working on his chocolate.

"*This*," said Holmes. He tapped at his keyboard, and the footage on the screen rolled on. It was the same section they'd seen back at the pizza joint, the window of the furniture store flaring as it caught the lights of the mystery car entering the parking lot. As the light faded, Holmes paused the image, then leapt out of his seat. Moving to the side of the TV, he pointed at the reflection.

"Now, if Ms. Eastman will work her magic."

Watson watched as, back at the table, Sally worked at the laptop, her fingers flying over the keyboard and trackpad.

On the TV, the section of reflected image was outlined and cropped out of the picture, then zoomed in to fill the whole screen. A diagonal line then ran over the image from top left to bottom right again and again as, Watson guessed, Sally passed a series of pre-set filters over the image. With each pass, the image became grainier and grainer, until it was hard to tell that the distorted picture was the reflected back end of a car at all.

But the bright rectangle that was the car's license plate stood center stage. It was blurred, most of the letters and numbers still completely bleached out. There was a *T*... maybe a *5*...

Holmes got out his phone from one pocket and its magnifying lens from another, slipped it over the phone's camera, and used it to examine the TV screen. Curiously, he wasn't looking at the license plate, but at a small, fuzzy area just a little higher up.

Watson frowned. "Surely all you're seeing is pixels."

"Pixels are all we need," said Holmes, moving back around to her and Bell. "Look."

He showed them his phone. On it was an enlarged, pixelated shot of a tiny square from the TV screen. It showed a white circle, in the middle of which were two angled vertical lines, forming a V shape.

Bell tugged at his chin. "Hey, that looks familiar."

Watson stared at it. "What is that... a logo?"

"Indeed it is," said Holmes, nodding. He moved back to his laptop and turned it around for the other two to see. The web browser was open, the main page of the site showing a photo of a family of four dressed in bathing suits, the youngest member holding a huge inflatable beach ball, posing by a large people-mover.

Overlaid on the bottom right of the banner photo was a logo: a light yellow circle, with a dark blue V in the center.

"I knew it," said Bell. "Voyager Car Rentals. I've used them on vacation a couple of times in the last year or so."

"So the mystery car was a *rental*?" asked Watson.

"It was," said Holmes, "and I would like to put it to you that it was a rental car hired by the killer himself. Observe."

With a wave at Sally, the TV screen cleared and returned to the raw footage from the pizza joint. They watched as the reflected image of the Voyager rental car disappeared from the furniture-store window, then the footage began to fast-forward as Holmes gave a running commentary.

"The rental car enters the parking lot at three-twelve in the morning, and then there is no movement on the street until six minutes later, three-eighteen *precisely*, when another car arrives."

Right on cue, the footage returned to playback, and the familiar form of a yellow cab pulled up, sliding alongside the front of Rio's Gio's before coming to a stop with its tail lights just within range of the camera. A passenger got out on the sidewalk side and almost immediately moved out of camera view. Then the cab lurched off.

There was no movement for about twenty seconds, then, across the street, a shadow flickered in the furniture-store window.

"The cab deposited Trent Absolom," said Holmes, "who was apparently quite happy to make the secret rendezvous." He pointed at the reflection. "It's difficult to make out, but he walks along the sidewalk from Rio's Gio's, then into the parking lot."

Watson nodded. "Where he was killed by the driver of the rental."

Holmes stared at the screen. He waved again, and with a click of Sally's trackpad, the footage rolled on at double speed. A moment later, Holmes held up a hand and the playback continued normally.

"Another eight minutes elapse, and then the killer departs."

The furniture-store window flared again as it was hit by lights that were much brighter than before—this time the headlights of the rental car, as it drove directly out of the parking lot.

"The driver turned *right*," said Holmes, "returning via the same route by which they arrived. And, unfortunately, not passing by the front of Rio's, denying us a good look at not only the license plate, but possibly the driver."

Bell had his notebook out already. He pointed at the screen with his pen, then began jotting something down.

"We have the time and place, so we should be able to pull traffic cams from nearby. The parking lot may not be well covered, but the driver had to have hit a thoroughfare sooner or later. ALPR should be able to get a clear read at some point. If we can get a fix farther away, we might even be able to grab another feed and see who was in the driver's seat."

Holmes nodded. "An excellent suggestion. The car should be fairly easy to identify by the Voyager Rentals stickers on it—I believe they are on both front and rear windshields."

"On it," said Bell. He flipped his notebook closed, and headed for the door just as Gregson appeared through it. He was carrying two folders: one thin, a regular manila folder, the other a bulging file in a folder that was a mottled red-brown color. He hefted them up and handed both to Holmes.

"Overnighted from Chula Vista PD," he said, tapping the thin file. "The file on the Kovalev manslaughter case. And," he said, now indicating the red folder, "the erstwhile David Hauer's prison jacket from San Quentin."

"Thank you, Captain," said Holmes. He took the folders to the table and set them down side by side with enough room to open both, which he then did, simultaneously. Watson moved around to peer over his shoulder, and saw David Hauer—now known as Dale Vanderpool—as he was back in 1995, staring back at her from his prison photograph. She could clearly see the damage both his alcoholism and the events surrounding the death of Alex Kovalev had done to the man. He looked old—in a strange way, older than he did now, twenty years later—and tired, his hair neatly parted, but with huge bags under his eyes and deep lines carved into his face.

Holmes began to flip through the pages in both folders, turning each page simultaneously and sequentially, at a rate of about one per second. The Chula Vista PD file was finished first, so he pushed that aside, and focused instead on the prison jacket. Watson watched, but soon gave up on trying to follow the contents.

Gregson glanced at Watson. "What's he—?"

"Quiet!" said Holmes, and then he closed the prison jacket and handed both folders back to the captain.

"Thank you, Captain," he said. "That settles it."

"Ah, settles what?"

"Dale Vanderpool—the once and former *David Hauer*—is entirely innocent. The two murders are a setup, a rather unconvincing and, dare I say, amateurish attempt at framing a man who has clearly moved on from his past, quite literally, starting a new life."

"Which is what we already thought," said Watson, frowning. Gregson meanwhile, glanced down at the folders.

"Are you saying you read *all* of his files?"

Holmes gave a non-committal shrug. "I will admit my speed-reading has slipped a little. I'm probably down to only eighty-three or eighty-four percent retention, but I gleaned the salient facts."

Gregson sighed. "Which are what, exactly?"

"Something has been under our noses this whole time."

Then for Watson, the penny dropped. She sighed and shook her head. Gregson looked at her, still none the wiser.

"There's something else going on," said Watson. "There's *another* crime, hidden underneath this one."

Holmes looked at her, his expression dark. "The act of murder is one of the most heinous a human being is capable of," he said, his voice low, quiet. "What is possibly worse is that, in this case, a *double* homicide is merely a cover, two acts of brutal violence carried out as a sideshow, distracting us while the *real* crime is carried out."

Watson felt her stomach heave. A distraction? Two men were dead, their lives snuffed out with gruesome violence. But to say that this was a... a what? A *secondary* act? A distraction to throw suspicion elsewhere, to send the police chasing their tail while the killer or killers got away with something else entirely?

That was a very particular kind of cold. To consider humans to be so... *disposable*.

"If that's the case," said Gregson, "it sounds like we're dealing with a real psychopath. I mean, if they staged two murders just as a distraction."

"You may be right, Captain. The killer is cold, calculating, emotionally disconnected," said Holmes. "*But*, in this instance, we are lucky."

"Lucky how?"

"Our killer may be a psychopath," Holmes continued, "but the one typical characteristic of that criminal type which he seems to lack is *intelligence*. The murders are a facade, but a sloppy one. As I said, window-dressing."

Watson shuddered. Holmes must have noticed, because he glanced at her and she saw it in his eyes, that peculiar mix of concern and excitement and *impatience*.

The game was afoot. And time was very possibly running out. They had to catch the killer.

And stop whatever else it was they were doing.

"Watson," said Holmes, "I suggest we go to the morgue."

She nodded, seeing where his thoughts were going. "I can examine the wounds on both victims—Gregory and Trent," she said, then she turned and laid a hand on the thick prison jacket that recorded Dale Vanderpool's conviction and time in San Quentin. "And I can compare the two new victims with the examination and autopsy records from the original case."

She picked up the folder and headed for the door, then she stopped and looked over her shoulder. Behind her, Gregson gave Sally the nod that she could go home, while Holmes himself was busy again with his phone.

"What are you doing?" she asked.

"Calling ahead," said Holmes, "to tell Eugene to get the chessboard ready."

21

WATSON'S EXAMINATION

Watson found working in a morgue to be strangely comforting yet oddly disconcerting. The environment was cool, and quiet, and well lit—artificially. It was peaceful, a place of cold, emotionless science, yet also a place that stirred one's feelings.

When she'd entered medical school, progressing from scientific study and laboratory work to practical clinical education, she had thought those kind of feelings would fade away as her experience grew. But they didn't, and she now knew they never would—not for her. While she'd spent many hours in pathology labs during her training, she'd spent less once she was actually in practice at the hospital. And as a surgeon, the morgue was the sort of place you *didn't* want to be visiting very often at all.

The other thing about being in a morgue is that you could easily lose track of time. The even, artificial lighting, the controlled temperature. You could lose *hours*.

Watson caught herself yawning, then checked her watch, and checked it again.

Yes, you sure could lose hours in a place like this.

Laid out on the slab in front of her was the body of

Gregory Smythe. A sheet covered him to the chest, the top of the thick stitches sewing up his chest cavity after the autopsy only just visible. His face had been cleaned of blood and debris from the left eye, which had been totally destroyed in the attack that had killed him. The fountain pen used had entered the cranial cavity to a depth of at least four inches, taking out the optical nerve entirely.

On the slab behind her was the body of Trent Absolom. He had been stripped, and was likewise covered with a sheet, but a full autopsy was not scheduled until early the following morning.

No, scratch that... later that *same* morning.

Peeling off her latex gloves, Watson sighed and turned around. On the other side of the morgue was another row of examination tables—*slabs*, in pathology parlance—all of which were empty save for the one in the middle of the row. On this slab was a chess set. Dr. Eugene Hawes and Sherlock Holmes were seated on stools on opposite sides of it, both completely motionless as they studied the board. There was no clock running—their games often took months—and it felt like it had been just as long since somebody had made their last move. Watson wondered if the players even remembered whose turn was next.

"So how did I do?" asked Eugene, not turning around. Watson joined them at the table.

"I'm not sure I'm qualified to pass judgment on your pathology skills," said Watson, "but I agree. The wounds to Gregory Smythe and Trent Absolom are both angled from the right, the trajectory fairly sharp, entering downwards toward the orbit."

"In complete contrast," said Holmes, "to the injuries sustained by Alex Kovalev in 1995." He finally tore his eyes from the board to look at Watson. "Correct?"

"Correct," she said, running the case file over in her mind. "Kovalev's fatal injury was to the same eye, but the angle and direction was from below, to the left."

"Consistent with someone of a smaller stature—such as Mr. Vanderpool—making the attack," said Holmes. "Whoever killed the other two men was much taller and right-handed."

Watson shrugged. "Perhaps. Vanderpool struggled with Kovalev in the insurance office. It's possible their fight obscured the angle and trajectory."

"But Vanderpool *is* left-handed."

"Yes," said Watson. "He drank his coffee back at the precinct with his left hand." She turned back to look at the two bodies on the slabs opposite. "There's another difference between the wound inflicted on Gregory Smythe and the one on Trent Absolom."

Holmes lifted a hand and hovered it over a bishop on the chessboard; as he did Eugene leaned forward, his eyes widening. He sucked in a breath with a loud hiss, clearly in anticipation of the long-awaited next move.

Then Holmes dropped his hand and slid off the stool to join Watson. Eugene exhaled loudly and said something under his breath, then he moved off his own stool and joined them.

Watson pulled the big overhead light which hung on a spring arm from the ceiling down low over Trent's face and turned it on, illuminating his ruined left eye cavity clearly. She pointed with her gloveless little finger, making sure to avoid any inadvertent contact.

"Trent's orbital wound is much larger than Smythe's," she said. "Trent's eye was destroyed entirely, and according to the X-ray, the orbit itself has a hairline fracture. You can see bruising around the socket and upper cheek too."

Holmes peered closely at the face of the dead man. "A greater force and greater violence was applied," he said. He curled his fingers and mimed a stabbing motion at Trent's face. "The killer's fist made contact with the victim's face.

If Trent had survived the attack, he would have developed a rather large black eye by now."

"Right," said Watson. "But here's the interesting thing." She moved over to the neighboring slab and Gregory Smythe's body. "The damage inflicted on Smythe is smaller and cleaner. No facial bruising, and no fractures, but—"

"But," said Eugene; picking up from Watson he headed over to a nearby free-standing wheeled trolley, from which he extracted a set of X-rays which he then clipped into the light box over on the wall, "there is bone damage. Take a look." He flicked the light box, then indicated the relevant area with a pencil extracted from his lab-coat pocket.

The X-ray showed it very clearly—Smythe's skull, looking from the front to the back. Inside the socket of his left eye there was a minuscule wedge of opaque matter floating at the seven o'clock position. "The orbital bone was chipped at the back," said the examiner.

Holmes peered at the X-ray image. "Indicating a *deeper* wound inflicted with a *sharper* object."

"Which," said Watson, "is consistent with Smythe being stabbed through the eye with the LeFevre pen."

Eugene nodded. "The nib of that pen is an indium-iridium alloy. It's very strong, but not very brittle. The nib connected to the back of the orbit with enough force to chip the bone."

Holmes turned away from the X-rays. "You therefore suggest that Trent's injury was more severe because it was not inflicted with a fountain pen with a sharp, strong nib."

Eugene pursed his lips. "That's exactly what I suggest. Trent's killer used a different weapon. Maybe it wasn't even a pen. It could have been a screwdriver. Could even have been a stick."

"And that's also why it wasn't left at the scene," said Watson. "The LeFevre was left in Smythe's eye at the Athena Hotel as a sign—the killer wanted all the attention focused on incriminating Vanderpool."

Holmes nodded. "But in a crumbling Brooklyn parking lot, with nothing quite so lethal as a fountain pen with an indium-iridium nib at hand, the killer had to use more force when attacking Trent to ensure the strike was a fatal one. He or she then took the weapon with them, hoping that the method of Trent's demise would be enough for the light of suspicion to remain fixed upon Vanderpool."

"Okay," said Watson. "Smythe's murder was, clearly, carefully planned. But, in comparison, Trent's murder is sloppy—there's a lack of preparation. So what if Trent had nothing to do with Smythe's murder…"

"*But*," said Holmes, "had found something out about it."

Watson nodded. "And he needed to be silenced."

"Quickly."

There was a beat, then Eugene laughed. "You guys are so cute when you work together," he said, and then he frowned as both Watson and Holmes glared at him. He held up a hand in apology. "Sorry," he said. "So who was this Trent guy anyway? The report that came in with the body says he was using a fake ID."

"A *stolen* ID, yes," said Holmes. "His supposed wife too, who we know variously as Sophie Absolom or Vicki Summers."

"Whom we have yet to locate," said Watson.

"Huh," said Eugene, scratching his chin. "You think she could be it—the killer?"

Watson shrugged and folded her arms. "It's possible. She's about the right height. Strength might be an issue, but desperation can make people do remarkable things when they need to."

Holmes shook his head. "On the contrary," he said, "Sophie Absolom, or whatever her real name is, is *not* in fact the killer. In fact, I firmly believe that she will be the next *victim*."

"What?" Watson dropped her arms. She gaped at Holmes,

wondering where the hell that particular deductive leap had come from.

"There is a third party at work here, Watson," said Holmes. "And his work is not yet complete."

22

LATE NIGHT PUZZLE PLAY

The 11th Precinct of the NYPD was quiet, the night shift having taken over long ago. Watson trailed in after Holmes, walking past the coffee machine in the hallway. Whatever the flavor—whatever the *ingredients*—caffeine was something she was in desperate need of. She let Holmes go ahead as she stopped to get herself a cup. She suspected that their long day—and night—of work was not yet done. How Holmes managed to keep going, Watson didn't think she would ever know.

Five minutes later, she found Holmes in Captain Gregson's office, both Gregson and Bell pulling a double shift as they waited for news from their two consultants. Both of the policemen had fresh coffee steaming in NYPD mugs, surrendering, like Watson, to the mercy of the evil machine in the hallway.

Holmes waited until Watson had closed the office door behind her and sat down before speaking. He turned back to the two detectives.

"The medical evidence clearly suggests that Dale Vanderpool was not in fact responsible for the murders of

Gregory Smythe and Trent Absolom," said Holmes. "There are a number of significant differences between those two recent killings and the one he was convicted of in 1995."

Bell frowned. "You might be right on that one, but we're still keeping an eye on him. We need to cover all our bases."

"I assure you, Detective," said Holmes, linking his fingers together over one knee, "Dale Vanderpool has been set up, and in a particularly clumsy manner."

"Well, hold on," said Gregson. "While you were poking around in the morgue, we got Vanderpool back in for another interview with his lawyer. His alibi for Trent Absolom's murder is that he was asleep in his new hotel."

Holmes shrugged. "Easy enough to substantiate, I would think. A hotel of the caliber Mr. Vanderpool is likely to stay in will be a considerably more salubrious—and secure—establishment than the Athena in Washington Heights, where we found Gregory Smythe. There should be a wealth of documentary evidence readily available to corroborate his claim."

"Yes, it is," said Gregson, "and don't worry, we're going to check everything."

Watson stifled a yawn. "Still nothing on Sophie Absolom?"

"Not a thing," said Bell, sipping his coffee. "But we did ID the rental car from Voyager. We picked it up heading north into Queens. Didn't manage to get a good shot of the driver but we got the plates. It was hired from a small out-of-town branch in New Jersey."

"We're liaising with the local PD there," said Gregson, "but it's too late to follow up now. We'll send a detective over first thing in the morning to check it out and get an ID for the person or persons who rented the car."

"Speaking of it being late," said Watson, trying again to stifle a yawn, but this time failing in spectacular fashion, "I need to sleep. Are you coming back to the brownstone, Sherlock?"

Holmes nodded. The two consultants said goodnight and

left the precinct. On the way home in a cab, Holmes said not a word, and a thousand different thoughts about the case spun around and around in Watson's exhausted mind.

As soon as they got home, Watson headed straight for the stairs, but she paused, one hand on the bannister, as Holmes bustled past her into the main room. With a sigh—and another yawn, and a longing look up the stairs toward her bedroom—she turned back and followed him. That Holmes was going to pull an all-nighter was obvious. She only hoped he didn't expect her to join him.

Watson collapsed onto the art deco sofa as Holmes began shuffling files around—he had brought the Chula Vista police file, Vanderpool's San Quentin prison jacket, and stacked on the floor by the fireplace were some of the personnel files from Mantis—including the pass sheet for Vicki Summers, the courier who was most definitely another fake ID for Sophie Absolom.

Holmes began selecting papers, files, and photographs, and started pinning them up on the wall.

Watson checked her watch. It was nearly three—a full twenty-four hours since Trent had been killed, and more than seventy-two since the death of Gregory Smythe in Washington Heights. They had a wealth of data, and that was exactly the problem—too much. Too many leads, too many connections that were obvious, too many suspects that were anything but.

If the attempt to frame Vanderpool had been a poor effort, then it had at least succeeded in something else—confusing the case.

Which, as Holmes had already pointed out, was most likely the real reason for the crimes. Not to frame Vanderpool, even circumstantially, in a vain effort to have him sent down for a crime he didn't commit, but to hide something else that was going on.

But what?

Watson yawned. She kicked her shoes off and curled her legs up onto the sofa as she watched Holmes work in silence.

The killer knew Vanderpool's true identity—David Hauer. The killer knew what David Hauer had done, and how he had done it.

So why did Gregory Smythe need to die? What had he found out, ostensibly at the Vanderpool speaker roadshow? Why had he gone to that one date in the first place, and why had he not recorded it, like he recorded all the other minutiae of his schedule, in his personal diary? How had the killer gotten his contact details, and why did Smythe agree to trek all the way up to Washington Heights—an appointment he was eager to keep, given the way he had rushed into the hotel lobby when he realized the meeting had been brought forward and he was now running late.

Holmes pinned Smythe's photograph on the wall, the personnel shot from Mantis. Next to him, he pinned a photograph of Trent Absolom. This one was a printout, taken perhaps from the Vanderpool speaking tour website. Trent Absolom—a man Watson had met for just ten minutes, maybe even less—stared back at her.

Why was Trent killed? He and Smythe shared one thing in common—a connection to Vanderpool's speaking tour. Smythe was a secret attendee. Trent worked as the tour manager.

Except Trent wasn't even his real name.

So what had *he* discovered at—or perhaps about—the tour? The same thing Smythe had? He was contacted by the killer too, from the very same burner cellphone number.

And he was killed in the same way, but in a hurry, his murder rushed, unplanned, taking place in a crummy Brooklyn parking lot in the middle of the night.

Why did Trent have to die?

What was the killer hiding?

Holmes pinned a third picture to the wall, centered underneath the images of the two victims.

Sophie Absolom. Trent's wife. Vanderpool's publicist and front-of-house manager.

Except the photo wasn't of Sophie Absolom. It was of Vicki Summers, the courier, her blonde hair—a wig? Dyed?—poking out from under the purple APD cap. She'd been to Mantis weeks before the Vanderpool tour had even hit town.

And now the CFO of Mantis was dead, and Sophie was missing.

Holmes stood back and scratched his chin as he considered her photograph. Watson blinked her drowsiness away.

"There are three options," said Holmes, without turning around. "That Sophie Absolom knows the identity of the person who killed Gregory Smythe and her fake husband, and has fled in fear for her life."

"Or that she's already dead and we just haven't found her body yet," said Watson. The grim thought sent a cold ball turning in her stomach.

"Quite so, Watson, quite so," said Holmes, glancing over his shoulder at his colleague. "Or thirdly," he said, returning his attention to the wall, "that she *is* the killer, and is laying low awaiting the next play. You said yourself she was tall—far taller, in fact, than Dale Vanderpool. Tall enough to be responsible for the angle and trajectory of the fatal blows on both Trent and Gregory Smythe. Although this theory, I believe, we can discount. I do not believe Sophie Absolom is the killer."

Watson rubbed her face. Holmes was right, because there was one piece of evidence they had yet to fit into the puzzle. One single event that was apparently enough for Sherlock Holmes to exclude Sophie from the currently non-existent pool of suspects.

"The phone argument," said Watson, recalling her first

meeting with Sophie and Trent. "You think Trent was arguing with his own killer."

Holmes turned around, rocked on his heels, his lips pursed. He lifted his chin.

"The third party," he said. "The same person, calling from the same number that first texted Gregory Smythe, and that then texted Trent later, inviting him to his own death."

Watson shook her head and sank back into the couch. "A burner phone," she said, and she yawned.

"The wonders of the modern world," said Holmes. Then his gaze shifted, coming to focus somewhere in the middle distance.

Watson yawned again, and when she opened her eyes Holmes was back by the fireplace, staring at the photographs he had arranged on the wall.

He said something about "going back to the source" and "reviewing the evidence" but Watson was sure of neither, and when she opened her eyes again the room was empty and the only light came from the paper dragon lamp on the mantelpiece.

And then she closed her eyes again and she fell into a deep and warm sleep on the couch.

23

WITH A LITTLE HELP FROM SOME FRIENDS

Watson awoke with a jolt. She was warm—there was a blanket covering her, placed by Holmes, she assumed—but her neck was stiff and sore and her shoulders were practically immobile from resting on the low, rounded arm of the sofa.

The front room of the brownstone was still empty and the dragon lamp on the mantel was still on, but the room was now lit by sunlight streaming in through the main windows. It was morning.

Watson closed her eyes. Just for a moment. Just for a—

She woke with a jolt again, the memory of a dream fading quickly, a dream in which Holmes had been shouting something about the mighty Scots pine.

From somewhere above her came the sound of stomping feet, followed by a fanfare, and then Holmes started…

Watson sat up.

Holmes had started singing?

Watson cocked her head, listening, unsure if she really was awake or not. She couldn't actually make out the lyrics save for the odd snatch of words, but there was something very familiar about it.

Something about… lumberjacks. And… going to the *lavatory*?

Watson got to her feet, rubbing the sleep from her eyes. She listened a little more, then headed for the stairs.

Sherlock Holmes was in the media room, standing in front of the bank of TVs, although they were all off or on standby. Positioned in front of them was a small folding table, on which sat Holmes's laptop. The laptop was plugged into the home theatre system the TVs usually ran through, and it was playing the music to which Holmes was now singing. The green light on the top of the laptop's screen told Watson that the computer's webcam was on.

Watson focused on all of this, intently, as she tried very hard not to pay any attention to Holmes himself. Because Holmes was standing in the middle of the room, naked except for a fur trapper's hat jammed on his head.

It was far, far too early in the morning for this.

Chest puffed out, hands apparently held in a position where suspenders would perhaps cross his chest, Holmes took a breath to sing the next line, but stopped and glanced over his shoulder at Watson standing in the doorway.

"Not now, Watson, I'm just getting to the chorus," he said, then he lowered his voice to a ridiculous stage whisper. "I've been building up to this moment for quite some time."

Watson took a half-step backwards and turned away.

Tea. She needed tea. Lots of tea. Strong, black, hot tea.

A moment later the music stopped.

She turned back around, carefully. Holmes was now wearing what looked like the dress trousers from a tuxedo. The trapper's hat was still on his head.

He nodded at her. "You can come in now," he said, then he gestured to the laptop. "I have explained to all and sundry that

I need to take a momentary intermission in my performance."

Watson just stood there with her arms folded, dreaming of tea and of starting the day over, wishing that her neck didn't hurt and that she'd slept in her own bed.

"Explained to who?" she asked, not really caring much for the answer.

Holmes bent over the laptop and tapped at the keyboard.

"My personal selection of musical highlights from episodes of *Monty Python's Flying Circus* is being live-streamed to… one hundred and ten thousand viewers. Give or take."

He gave Watson a grin she would have called sheepish if her sleep-addled brain was capable, and he stood there with his arms by his sides, bouncing on his bare feet.

"I have made a bargain with *Everyone*," he said. Watson glanced at the laptop; the green light was still on, indicating he was still streaming. She sighed and took a step toward the wall, just to make sure that she was out of sight.

"My performance was linked to a number of forums on the dark net," Holmes continued, "and it appears to have gone somewhat viral."

He beamed at Watson, clearly delighted.

She just sighed. "You're enjoying this, aren't you?"

He nodded. "I am concealing this fact from Everyone, of course. Their challenges are calculated to cause maximum embarrassment and I don't want them to be disappointed."

"And singing Monty Python songs naked isn't embarrassing?"

"Oh," said Holmes, glancing down like he was surprised to find himself suddenly wearing pants. "A minor sacrifice for my art."

Watson rolled her head and began massaging the back of her own neck. She was still fully dressed, her clothes creased from her night on the couch. She was also still wearing her watch, which she checked. It was just after six in the morning.

She'd had about three hours' sleep.

Well, isn't that just great.

"Okay, fine," said Watson, "so what's the deal with Everyone?"

"Ah," said Holmes. He reached forward and lowered the laptop's lid halfway, then he stepped over to where Watson was standing by the wall. "I'm eliciting their help in revealing the true identities of Trent and Sophie Absolom."

Watson frowned. "Can't the police do that through the normal channels? Why get Everyone involved?"

"Because Everyone has means and methods the police don't have," said Holmes, his tone brusque. "Besides which, I have already spoken to Detective Bell, and so far they have hit nothing but dead ends. The method by which the Absoloms selected their new identities is as old as it is simple, but it works, and clearly they are professionals." He gestured to the laptop with an open palm. "*Hence.*"

"Everyone," said Watson. She really wished she knew more about them—and that Holmes was less quick to turn to their help when needed. But, she had to admit, the anonymous group of hacktivists had come through for them in the past.

"*Everyone* is a tool," said Holmes, as though reading Watson's thoughts. "And if you have a tool, then it is stupid not to use it." He turned back to look at the half-closed laptop. "We find out who the Absoloms are, we find the killer."

"How can you be so sure of that?"

Holmes sighed, then he moved back to the laptop and pulled the lid back up.

"I apologize for the delay and I beg your indulgence," he said, peering into the webcam. "The second half of our musical journey will commence presently."

Then he closed the laptop completely and grabbed a remote control from the easy chair that had been moved to the side of the media room to make space for Holmes's performance. With a press of the button, the array of TV sets all sprang into life at once.

Watson stepped toward them, casting her eye over the displays. They each showed what looked, more or less, to be the same thing—a freeze-frame of some kind of event, crowded with people sitting in rows. There was a stage at the front in most of the images, but two TVs showed events much smaller in scale in which the speaker merely stood at the front of a room as he addressed his audience.

The speaker being Dale Vanderpool.

Holmes pressed another button on the remote, and the video footage started simultaneously, the sound of multiple Vanderpools talking, overlaid with applause and laughter. Some of the footage was superb quality—full HD, Watson thought, with high-fidelity sound to match. But two TVs showed footage at a much lower resolution, one of which was not widescreen but in the tall, thin pillar-box format characteristic of filming with a mobile phone held portrait rather than landscape. The footage was rock steady in a couple of displays, and wobbled to a varying degree in others.

"As I said just last night," said Holmes, gesturing with an expansive wave of the remote to the televisions, "the wonders of the modern world. Thanks to the almost pathological desire our culture has developed to record and document the minutiae of everyday life, there are available online nearly full video recordings of every lecture in Dale Vanderpool's most recent tour, all shot by members of the audience, with varying degrees of success."

"Wow," said Watson, but in reality, it wasn't that surprising. As Holmes said, people would record anything. A business lecture—one at which the secrets to success were being revealed? Of course there would be videos online. "So you've watched all this?"

Holmes nodded. "While you were asleep downstairs, I

watched recordings of all fifteen tour dates."

"Fifteen? But I was only asleep for a couple of hours."

"Indeed, Watson. But I viewed them simultaneously, thus expediting review of the data by quite some margin. And I found something rather interesting—"

He lifted the remote and seemed about to show Watson something, when his phone buzzed from the floor. Holmes scooped it up, remote still pointing in the direction of the TV sets, and read the text message, then he put the phone back down.

"But it will have to wait," he said. "It seems my audience grows ever more impatient, and if I am to secure Everyone's help in identifying the Absoloms I must fulfill my part of the bargain."

With that, he lowered the remote, and began undoing his dress pants.

Watson held up a hand and turned away.

"Okay, knock yourself out. I'm taking a shower and I need breakfast," she said, heading for the door. Holmes paused, pants still *in situ*.

"Ah, actually," he said, "I could use a female singer for this next part." He rolled his hand in the air. "It may expedite matters if you, well, joined me in—"

Watson closed the door very firmly behind her.

24

HOLMES MAKES A REQUEST

Holmes was still deep in his performance for Everyone when Watson checked in an hour later—she only hoped the time and effort was worth it.

Rather than wait for him to finish, she headed over to the precinct, where she found Detective Bell on the phone at his desk. He nodded a greeting, murmured something into the receiver, then hung up.

"Hey," he said. "I was about to call you."

"Any updates?"

"Yes and no," he said, shuffling the papers in front of him. "I was just getting a status update on the BOLO—still no hits on Sophie Absolom. Wherever she is, she's keeping a low profile."

"Or she's taken a new identity and has a new look already," said Watson, remembering the photograph of Vicki Summers, the blonde-haired courier identity Sophie Absolom had assumed at Mantis. Of course, Sophie—and Trent—would have been masters at keeping off the radar. Holmes must have realized that too, which was why he'd recruited Everyone. If they could find her true identity, perhaps that would make her easier to trace? Watson wasn't sure, but she knew that what they really needed now was a break in the case, and a big one at that.

"Could be," said Bell, breaking Watson's trail of thought. He clicked his computer mouse to wake the monitor. "But we've got a little further on the rental car that was at the second crime scene."

Watson moved around Bell's desk so she could get a better look. Bell pointed at the screen with his pen. A video was paused in a small window.

"Voyager Car Rentals released their security-cam tapes from their office in New Jersey where the car was rented."

He hit the spacebar and the footage began to roll. It showed a tiny office, apparently little more than a prefab with two desks and a tiny counter, and a small coffee table scattered with magazines in front of two small armchairs. The office had big windows looking out onto a very large parking lot, row upon row of rental vehicles of all sizes gleaming in the bright morning sun.

The Voyager rep was at the counter, pointing out some paperwork details to the two customers, a man and a woman, on the other side.

Well, that confirms one thing, Watson thought. She pointed at the screen. "That's Sophie," she said. The woman in the footage was wearing a baseball cap, but her hair was long and black, and while she was only shown in profile, she was standing close to the security camera, which was of much higher quality than the one installed outside Rio's Gio's. Watson recognized her immediately.

"But that isn't her husband," said Bell. And he was right. The man with Sophie was large, stocky, his t-shirt stretched over a bulky frame that wasn't fat but *muscular*. He had blonde hair and a blonde goatee, and like Sophie, he was wearing a baseball cap. He was farther away from the camera and was leaning over the desk, which made his face a little harder to see.

But one thing was very clear. Trent Absolom, he was not.

Watson folded her arms and stepped back, narrowing her eyes as she watched the silent footage.

"The third party," she muttered under her breath. Bell turned in his chair to look up at her.

"The what?"

Watson pointed at the screen. "We think there's a third party involved, and I'm going to guess that's him."

Bell lifted a sheet from the stack on his desk and handed it to Watson. It was a duplicate of the car rental form from Voyager, and stapled on the underside was the angled photocopy of two Oregon state driver's licenses. Sophie Absolom and the mystery man stared back at Watson as she read their details.

"Josephine Banks, Harold Banks." Watson lowered the papers. "The same names they used to book the room at the Athena Hotel." She frowned. "That seems a little careless, to use the same IDs."

Bell shrugged. "Well, Harold Banks matches the description of the male from the hotel too." Bell cracked a grin. "I think we've found your third party."

"I'll call Sherlock," said Watson, pulling her phone from her bag. As she unlocked it, the device buzzed in her hand. She blinked—there on the screen was a text message from her partner. "Oh," she said.

"What's up?"

"It's from Sherlock," she said, her forehead creasing in confusion as she read over the message. "He wants us to go to an address in the Bronx, and he says to… bring a crowbar and a jar of kosher hamburger dill pickles?"

She looked at Bell. Bell just sighed, already unhooking the jacket hung over the back of his chair. "Ours is not to reason why," he said.

"Wait a minute, I'll call him," said Watson. Then her phone buzzed again.

Another text.

Bell stood and read over her shoulder.

NO QS NOW PLS WILL XPLAIN ALL
JUST BRING ITEMS

Watson sighed. Bell was right—if Holmes had found something, then it would pay just to follow his directions. But would it hurt if, just once, he wasn't so damn cryptic?

"I'll let the captain know—"

There was a buzzing from Bell's desk. He froze, jacket almost but not quite on. He slipped his remaining shoulder in, then reached over and grabbed his phone.

He sighed.

"What is it?" asked Watson.

"It's from Holmes," he said. "He's sent me a list of recommendations for the best delis in midtown to get the pickles from."

Watson tried very hard not to laugh, and she almost succeeded.

Almost.

25

THE WAREHOUSE

Watson and Bell approached the address Holmes had sent them on foot, having parked farther down the street, out of sight. Bell carried a brown paper bag containing a jar of the finest—and most expensive—kosher dill pickles available in the Five Boroughs, while Watson hefted a silver crowbar with red-tipped ends that they had borrowed from the rescue-equipment store back at the precinct.

The address in question was in an industrial estate at the northern limits of the Bronx, a zone of deserted crisscrossing streets, nothing but hulking warehouses and small factories, the majority of which had real-estate signs posted outside, talking up the remarkable low lease rates per square footage should anyone, thought Watson, require a boatload of cheap floor space in precisely the back end of nowhere.

They saw Holmes long before they reached him. He was silhouetted against the bright sky, standing in the middle of the empty street that wove between two warehouses, hands in the pockets of his pea coat, feet planted firmly in a wide V as he faced them. As they got closer, he nodded, not in greeting but in apparent satisfaction that his strange request had been fulfilled to the letter, and then he disappeared out of sight around the corner of the building.

Watson and Bell merely glanced at each other, sharing a common thought about their colleague, before following.

Around the corner of the building they found a door and a window, which seemed tiny in the side of the huge warehouse. Holmes was crouched next to the door, apparently examining the lock.

Watson approached, holding out the crowbar.

"Here," she said. "Now are you going to tell us what we're doing way out here—wherever 'here' is?"

Holmes glanced up first at Watson, then at the proffered crowbar. He said nothing, then looked at Bell.

"You procured the items I requested, I see."

Bell nodded. "One crowbar, one jar of pickles," he said. He lifted the brown paper bag. Holmes stood, and, stepping around the crowbar, took the bag.

As Watson watched, he opened the bag and extracted the jar, leaving Bell to hold the crumpled paper. He unscrewed the jar, grimacing with effort until there was a sharp click. He looked up, his face a picture of delight.

Flipping the lid off, he extracted a pickle, waggled it a little, sending droplets of brine flying, and began to eat. As he crunched on the pickle he looked at the other two, nodding, but not speaking.

"Did you call us out here just so you could eat pickles for breakfast?" asked Bell. He looked at Watson. "And who has pickles for breakfast? Oh, right," he turned back to Holmes. "Sherlock Holmes does!"

If Holmes detected the sarcasm in Bell's voice, he didn't show it. Instead, he licked the brine off his fingers and screwed the jar shut before handing it back. Bell took the jar, one eyebrow raised as high as it would go.

"You'll have to excuse me, Detective," said Holmes.

"Pickles are a particularly good source of vitamin K. As Watson here will attest, I had a rather exhausting night watching endless hours of video footage online before giving, if I may say so myself, a rather grand musical performance."

Bell just gave a disinterested shrug, and put the pickle jar on the ground. And although she was hardly an expert, Watson wasn't entirely sure about the vitamin K claim.

Then she realized where he had most likely gleaned that doubtful fact from.

"You've been reading Vanderpool's book again, haven't you?" she asked, her tone—to her own surprise—more accusatory than she had expected. "I thought you disagreed with his dietary theories?"

Holmes nodded. "I am cautiously skeptical, Watson, but, as you should know, any theory is worthy of a test. Now, aren't you going to ask me what's inside this otherwise unremarkable building?"

Bell looked up at the vast frontage of the warehouse. It was corrugated sheet iron, and it had clearly seen better days. Even the asphalt of the road underneath them was cracked, and there was a vigorous growth of weeds from between the splits.

"Wait," he said, frowning and rolling his shoulders, "is this something we need back-up for? I can get more units here if we need them."

Holmes shook his head. "In this case, what we need is the upmost discretion. Cars, sirens, rigmarole, will only exacerbate what is a very delicate situation."

"What delicate situation?" asked Watson. "Sherlock, what are we doing here?"

Holmes glanced down at the crowbar dangling from her hand, the tip resting on the cracked roadway.

"Thanks to the efforts of Everyone," said Holmes, "not only have I discovered Sophie Absolom's true identity, but I have discovered her current location."

He casually hooked a thumb over his shoulder, indicating the warehouse.

"Now," he continued, "I suggest you stop looking so surprised and get to work on the door. The lock is rusted shut and while there is another, less neglected entrance around on the main street, I'd rather not just walk in the front door."

The inside of the warehouse was damp and dark, and the floor was scattered with trash—newspaper, plastic straps from packing crates, bits of wood broken off from the same and from the pallets that the crates would have sat on. There were plenty of the latter, towering piles of them, forming a dense maze that seemed to fill the entire building. It was also cold, and while it had been rather still outside, the cavernous, skeletal structure of the warehouse seemed to catch what little breeze there was and amplify it, the sound howling somewhere around the decaying corrugated iron high above them.

Whatever the warehouse had stored, whoever owned the building, it clearly hadn't been used in quite some time.

Once Bell had jimmied the stuck door with the crowbar, the detective had insisted they split up—the warehouse was huge and they stood more chance of finding Sophie that way. Holmes, so keen to secure a crowbar and jar of pickles, had neglected to suggest they bring a third useful item: flashlights. Bell had a small pocket light, carried as a matter of course in his inside jacket pocket, and Holmes had extracted a larger model of the same from his coat. This left Watson with the light on her phone—which, actually, was remarkably effective.

If the battery lasted. As she shone it over a stack of abandoned pallets, she noted she had forty percent charge remaining. The LED light was going to drain that quickly. If Sophie was in the building, they had to find her, and fast.

Watson crept onwards. The warehouse wasn't quite in *total* darkness—there were windows set high, near to the ceiling, and while they were partially boarded, pale light filtered in well enough through the dirty glass. Although this, in combination with the light on her phone, meant Watson was tiptoeing around deep, angled shadows.

Bell had been right. They needed back-up. Creeping around the warehouse was stupid—if Sophie was even here in the first place. Watson had no idea how Holmes and Everyone had determined Sophie was here, but she would make sure she extracted an answer to that question once they were out. But, in the meantime, the chances of finding Sophie seemed very slim indeed.

Watson walked on, then stopped. There was a sound ahead, like someone tripping on a pallet fragment and sending it skidding across the dirty cement floor. Watson listened for a moment, then killed her light. Allowing her eyes to adjust for a moment, she made her way toward one of the outer walls of the warehouse and, once she had reached it, started crabbing along it. The sound had come from ahead, somewhere...

Another sound, the same, this time from behind her. She wasn't sure which direction Holmes and Bell had gone in, but the intention was to cover different quadrants of the building. But with no real plan and with only three people covering the huge space, the chances were that they were simply chasing each other.

There was no further sound. Watson continued onwards, thinking how ridiculous this was. There were times when Holmes just needed to follow standard police procedure, and this was definitely one of them—

Then she stopped. Was that somebody ahead of her, behind a stack of crates? It was hard to tell, her brain playing tricks as it formed shapes and patterns out of nothing but shadows and dust.

And then the shape moved. Yes, it was a person, someone getting into a more comfortable position.

Watson edged farther. She pushed off the warehouse wall, heading toward a line of tall industrial shelving, all of which was empty, but which nevertheless provided good cover. She laid a hand on it to help guide herself. The metal was cold and greasy, covered with a layer of thick dust. Just ahead, at the end of the row, was another stack of crates, then an empty aisle, before more rows of shelving with another stack of crates at the near end. The figure was crouching behind those crates, and had his or her—it was impossible to tell—side turned to Watson.

What should she do? Watson ducked down and took a breath. She had her collapsible single stick in her shoulder bag. In the dim light of the warehouse, she might be able to sneak around and... what? Knock their suspect unconscious? That was nonsense, a fiction propagated through a diet of film and television. To knock someone out required quite a lot of force, more than most people thought. It also ran the risk of serious brain injury. The last thing she wanted to do was send Sophie Absolom to the hospital.

But what choice did she have? Cursing inwardly, she dropped farther down behind the crates and reached into her bag, trying her best not to make any sound whatsoever.

Then she had another idea.

Instead of her single stick, she pulled out her phone, and, shielding it as best she could in her hiding place in case the light of the screen gave her away, she thumbed the device on, slid the brightness to nearly nothing, then brought up the message app. She knew both Holmes and Bell had a tendency—like a lot of people these days, actually—to keep their phones on silent. Hopefully if she messaged them, they would feel the vibration, and she wouldn't inadvertently give away their positions.

"You can come out, Nancy."

Watson froze, and looked up. Holmes's voice echoed around the warehouse. He could have been standing right by Watson, or equally on the other side of the building. It was impossible to tell. *Nancy?* Of course. Everyone had uncovered her true identity. Nancy was her real name.

Where was Holmes? Watson figured it out soon enough. Holmes was close. Very close. As she watched from her vantage point, the crouching figure hiding on the other side of the aisle stiffened, adjusting her footing, and seemed to glance down at her hands, like she was fiddling with something Watson couldn't see. But the figure—Nancy, apparently—didn't come out of her hiding place.

Not yet.

"I can assure you, I am here only to help," said Holmes, his voice louder. Watson peered over the crate, down the aisle to her right.

There he was. Sherlock Holmes stood in the middle of the aisle, lit by a beam of light stabbing down from the windows high above, almost like a spotlight, dust dancing in the beam. He had his hands by his side.

Of Bell, there was no sign, but Watson thought he must have heard Holmes too. Right now the detective would be making his way over, trying not to make any sound himself. Or perhaps he was doing the sensible thing, heading out the warehouse to call for back-up.

"I can take you somewhere safe, I promise," said Holmes. He began walking forward, slowly, toward where the woman Watson knew as Sophie Absolom was crouched. Then she stood.

Holmes stopped where he was. He smiled, and held out a hand.

"Please, come with me, I promise you'll be safe."

That was when Sophie lifted her hand and Watson saw what she had been fiddling with in the shadows.

It was a gun, and it was pointed right at Sherlock Holmes.

26

THE STANDOFF

"Don't move!" yelled Sophie, her voice high and cracking. "Stay where you are! Don't come any closer!" The words tumbled out, tripping over each other. Her gun arm was straight, the elbow locked, and Watson could see it wobble in the air as Sophie fought to control herself.

She was afraid.

"Who the hell are you? How did you find me?"

She was also *surprised*—clearly she hadn't been expecting to meet Holmes.

Holmes held both hands up, like he was surrendering to the enemy. With a gentle smile, eyes wide and glittering in the dim light, he took a slow step toward her. The gun in Sophie's hand didn't move any more than it had already, but in her nervous state Watson knew that something bad could happen at any moment, whether Sophie intended it or not. Holmes was apparently confident he could talk her down, figuratively speaking, but it was a risk.

Watson had to do something. Slipping the strap of her bag off her shoulder, she reached inside and took out her collapsible single stick. It was light, black, small, and expanded to full size at just the touch of a button.

Watson crabbed sideways, heading along the shelves. Soon she was at the aisle, and diagonally behind Sophie. The woman had all her attention on Holmes.

Which was exactly what Watson needed.

She backed up a little, out of the weak light from the high window, and stood up, slow enough to make herself known to Holmes. To his credit, he didn't even glance in her direction, his gaze entirely fixed on Sophie. But he *had* to have seen her.

Watson crossed the aisle quickly, padding on the balls of her feet in total silence. Now she was at the other shelves, just one row behind Sophie.

"Nancy, you don't need the gun," said Holmes. "I'm only here to help you."

"How do you know my name?"

Holmes took another step closer.

And so did Watson.

"I'm here as your *friend*," said Holmes. "I can get you out. You want to get out, don't you? Look at what's happened. You've been abandoned by the others. First sign of trouble, they scarpered, throwing you to the lions."

Another step closer.

"You can help us catch them. We can find who did all of this."

Another step.

"Stop!" Sophie's voice was now a screech of terror. The gun was held high.

Holmes reached out, and Watson could hear Sophie take a gulp of air as she leaned forward with her gun hand.

It was now or never.

Watson sprinted forward, thumbing the button on the truncheon. It telescoped to full length in less than a second, and Watson swung. The stick connected with Sophie's locked elbow, which flexed, Sophie crying out as she released the gun and drew her arm reflexively toward her body. Watson swung again and caught Sophie flat across the stomach, driving the air out of her lungs. Sophie pitched forwards and fell onto her side, gasping for breath. Watson stood over her, stick ready for another blow, but it wasn't needed. Sophie Absolom was down and would not be getting up again in a hurry.

As Watson puffed for breath, relieved that her plan had worked, Holmes came up to her.

"Excellent work."

Watson shook her head. "You took a risk there."

"I must admit I didn't think she would have a gun."

Footsteps approached from down one of the aisles of shelving, and Bell jogged to the scene. He came up short and took in the situation, his own service weapon held in a high, safe position. Apparently satisfied, he holstered his gun and then took his handcuffs from his belt.

On the warehouse floor, Sophie coughed and spluttered, heaving for breath, as Bell gently rolled her onto her back and slipped the cuffs on.

Watson collapsed her single stick and slid it back into her bag. Then she turned to Holmes.

"How did you know Sophie was here?"

"I arranged to meet her," said Holmes. "First Everyone managed to discover her real identity, and then with my assistance we dug up an email address that she and her accomplice have been using. All I had to do was spoof the address and contact her to arrange a meet-up."

On the floor, Bell helped Sophie up into a sitting position. The woman's face was red, one side covered in dust. She looked up at Watson and Holmes with wet eyes, but she didn't say anything.

"As I suspected," said Holmes quietly, "things have not gone according to their grand plan. Sophie here was most eager to meet with her accomplice to hash things out, as it were."

Bell stood and walked over to the packing crates. He looked around for a moment, shining his torch into the shadows, and then he flicked it off and took a handkerchief from his pocket. He bent down and disappeared from sight, and a moment later stood and walked back to the others.

"Yeah, I'll bet she was eager," he said, holding her gun carefully by the grip, the barrel pointing down. He nodded at Holmes. "I'll call for a wagon to take her back to the precinct. You two want to ride along?"

Watson opened her mouth to confirm that they did, but Holmes cut her off before she spoke.

"You go ahead, Watson. I need to retrieve something from the brownstone first."

Then he strolled away, hands in his pockets, across the dark warehouse. "See you there," he said, and he didn't turn around.

27

SOPHIE'S CHOICE

Another day at the 11th Precinct, another suspect to interview. They were back in the dingy interview room. Watson thought the slightly worn, depressed look of the room was all part of the design, something to make the suspect uncomfortable, anxious, a not-so-subtle hint that if you were in that room, like Sophie Absolom was now, then you were probably in a lot of trouble, and it was in your best interest to talk.

That was also evident in the body language of the two police officers who were carrying out the interview, and in their very deliberate positions in the room. Captain Gregson sat at the table, folders of paperwork in front of him—containing, Watson thought, files relating not just to this case but to others, or perhaps even a blank notepad or a stack of paper taken from the photocopier to bulk the folders out. It was an old police trick. For the suspect, the volume of paperwork on proud display would only make them more nervous as they wondered what the hell the cops *really* had on them.

Detective Bell, meanwhile, stood in the corner, one thumb looped through his belt, his jacket pulled back just enough to show the strap of his body holster and the top edge of his gun. If Gregson was the good cop, then Bell was the bad one.

Not that Sophie—or Nancy, as Watson now knew her real name to be, although she still found herself thinking of the woman by her previous alias—seemed to need much intimidation. She was afraid, that much was clear as Watson watched, alone, from the observation room. The suspect remained handcuffed—she had, after all, pulled a loaded weapon on Holmes—and her hands were clasped together on the table in front of her. They'd let her clean up a little, but her clothes were still a little rumpled and dusty from the tussle in the warehouse.

But there was something else, too. Watson tilted her head, her eyes narrowed as she watched the suspect. Sure, Sophie was afraid. She shook even as she sat there in the interview room, her fear barely controlled, simmering just beneath the surface.

But she was also not talking.

Not. A. Word.

If she was afraid now, she had been worse at the warehouse in the Bronx. After the confrontation with Holmes, she had become nearly inconsolable, wailing and kicking enough to need two burly members of New York's Finest to bundle her in the back of the police car that Bell had called for. Once the door had slammed shut, Sophie calmed down, and Watson had watched her look around, like she couldn't quite figure out what she was doing locked in the back of a police car. Shock, perhaps, as events finally caught up with her. But then Watson thought she saw something else. Sophie... well, she didn't *relax*, as such, but a certain tension had gone, the screaming edge of her fear replaced with something less electric. If there had been pure panic in the warehouse, here at the precinct it was now just a cold, steady nervousness.

And Watson thought she knew why.

Sophie Absolom was afraid. But she also felt... safe. Here

she was, in police custody, in a locked room in the center of a large precinct house.

She was *safe*. Nobody and nothing could get to her.

And that included Holmes's *third party*—the man calling himself Harold Banks. The man Sophie was working with—and a man she was scared of, too.

Scared enough to take a loaded gun to the rendezvous Holmes had arranged.

And Harold Banks was dangerous, because Sophie knew what he was capable of—and what he had done. Which so far included murdering Gregory Smythe and Trent Absolom, Sophie's supposed husband.

The question was, to what extent was Sophie involved? How much did she know? Was she truly Harold's accomplice? Was this all planned, and did she plan it with him? Or was she an innocent—the third party's associate, yes, but one with no knowledge of what her partner had done?

Watson wasn't sure that that was really any different in the eyes of the law. Sophie was at the very least an accessory after the fact.

In the interview room, Gregson was trying again, but Sophie wasn't listening, wasn't even looking at him. In the corner, Bell shifted on his feet and, perhaps tired of the tough guy routine, straightened and did the buttons of his jacket up.

So Sophie was afraid of Harold, and she felt safer in police custody. Which was fine—and, in most cases, a good bargaining chip for the police. They could offer protection in exchange for information. In situations like this, suspects usually cracked.

But not Sophie. She wasn't talking, because while she was fearful of her former partner in crime, she also didn't want to give him up.

Watson sighed and contemplated another cup of bad coffee. So far there had been little learned from the interview, and this didn't seem like it was about to change anytime soon. So she headed out into the bullpen, then turned down the corridor. The coffee and snack machines were halfway down, and at the end stood the main elevator doors.

As she approached, the elevator dinged and its doors opened. Holmes marched out, carrying under his arm a manila folder stuffed with enough papers to make it as thick as an old-fashioned New York City telephone directory.

"Hey," said Watson, gesturing at the folder. "Where have you been? And what's all that?"

Holmes stopped and extracted the folder from under his arm. He held it in both hands, then tapped the top with the fingers of one hand.

"Data," he said, "which I think will help shed quite a light on our mystery." He glanced down the corridor. "Has she said anything yet?"

"Ah, no, not yet," said Watson, folding her arms. "She's clearly protecting her accomplice, this Harold Banks. Or whoever he really is. She hasn't said a single thing since we took her in. The captain and Marcus are still in there with her."

Holmes nodded and headed for the observation room, Watson at his heel, her need for caffeine temporarily forgotten. Once inside, Watson could see the situation had changed little in the interview room. Both Gregson and Bell were now seated, and while Sophie had changed position—her cuffed wrists now on her lap—she was still not even meeting the gaze of her interrogators.

Holmes watched the scene for a few moments, Gregson and Bell going over the same information, the same questions, that Watson had heard a dozen times now. She shrugged.

"It's strange. She's clearly afraid of Harold, but she just doesn't want to give him up. Surely she can't think this will go on forever."

"Indeed," said Holmes. "She thinks she has protection

here. I wonder what would happen if we threatened to throw her to the wolves, as it were?"

Then he reached forward and rapped sharply on the observation-room window. In the interview room, Sophie jumped in her seat, her eyes crawling over what was, from her perspective, just a big mirror. Gregson and Bell, somewhat more accustomed to such interruptions, merely exchanged a look, then stood and left, Gregson gathering up his folders. As soon as the interview-room door closed behind them, Holmes darted back out into the bullpen hallway.

Watson stayed to watch Sophie for a moment. Her even temperament had been shattered by Holmes's interruption—the fear that had been crawling under her skin had now erupted in full force. Her gentle shivering had turned into full-on shakes, and she wrung her hands, her eyes scanning every corner of the interview room.

Watson headed out and found Holmes, Gregson and Bell in conference outside the interview-room door. Holmes saw her coming and lifted his chin at her. He held out a thin folder. Watson took it and glanced inside. She recognized the contents, and looked back up at Holmes.

He nodded.

Gregson took a seat at the table, Holmes next to him. Bell and Watson stood by the door to observe.

The captain cleared his throat. "Ms. Absolom, this is Sherlock Holmes and Joan Watson. They consult with the department and would like to put some—"

Holmes dumped his heavy folder onto the table with a thud. Sophie jumped in her seat again, her eyes moving between the folder and Holmes.

"Nancy," he said, and she flinched. Holmes smiled. "Can I call you Nancy? Or do you prefer Vicki? Or Sarah-Jane?

Or maybe even Ludmila?" He chuckled, perhaps to himself, and turned to Gregson. "I must admit, that one threw me a bit. Didn't fit the pattern, as it were." He turned back to the suspect. "But then that was why that particular name was selected for that particular job, wasn't it? How's your Russian accent these days?"

With Sophie watching with wet eyes wide open, Holmes opened the thick folder. Watson pushed off the wall and stepped around his chair to get a better look at the contents.

The first papers Holmes picked out were printed screenshots—a little fuzzy, a little low-resolution, but clear enough. Images taken from the online videos of the Vanderpool speaking tour. Each printout had the time, date and location written in Holmes's rough hand across the top.

"Dale Vanderpool, management guru and motivational speaker *extra-ordinaire*," said Holmes, and as he spoke he shifted the papers around like it was one of those magic tricks where you had to guess which cup the pea was under, until the screenshots—seven in total—were arranged in the correct chronological order. Happy with this, Holmes gave a little self-satisfied hum, then dropped his hands under the table and leaned forward toward the suspect.

"The Vanderpool speaking tour is a highly successful enterprise, not only for Mr. Vanderpool himself, but for a large proportion of his attendees. I have to say that whatever snake oil that man is peddling, for some it appears to have quite the desired effect."

Sophie stared at the images, her eyes moving from one, to the next, to the next. Watson saw her brow crease in confusion, the corners of her mouth twitching. Whatever Holmes was showing her—and the rest of them—she didn't quite get it.

But... she suspected.

Holmes reached into his pocket and pulled out a pen.

"Mr. Vanderpool has been running his business with quite some success for a number of years now," he continued. "Successful enough for you—or your associates—to take notice. You didn't start attending the lectures because you wanted a change of career. Quite the contrary."

With the pen, Holmes circled two people seated in the audience in the first image—a screenshot dated over a year ago, from a date in Austin, Texas.

Sophie stiffened.

"Sophie and Trent, a young couple just starting out with an exciting business venture of their very own," said Holmes. "Is that how you pitched yourselves?" Then he turned to the captain.

"According to social security records, the identities of Sophie and Trent Absolom first appeared eighteen months ago. Shortly thereafter, the pair started attending Vanderpool's talks. After attending one in Austin—" at this he glanced at Sophie "—a trial run, perhaps, testing the water, getting the lay of the land, et cetera"—and then he turned back to face Gregson—"there was a gap of two months, and then they started appearing at every single one of Vanderpool's tour dates, following him from city to city."

Holmes turned back to his printouts, and circled a few more people in the audience. "Not only that, but you got progressively more involved, edging farther and farther forward. You weren't trying to go *unseen* at the meetings. Indeed, you *wanted* to be noticed. There's even video of you and your partner having a discussion with Mr. Vanderpool as he was signing books for you." He rotated the image in question, which showed Sophie and Trent at the table, Vanderpool seated, stack of books at his elbow. "On this occasion you spoke for a full four minutes, and then you and Trent and the unsuspecting Dale Vanderpool went backstage."

Another still, this time showing Trent halfway through

a door being held open by Vanderpool, who was smiling at Sophie.

"And then another month later, and you are no longer in the audience. No! You are front of house, you taking the role of tour publicist while Trent is the new tour manager."

The last still showed Trent and Sophie—she in a smart suit and jacket, he dressed more casually in his hipster style, but still far more formally than he had been as a regular attendee, his hair now slicked and beard trimmed into a precise Van Dyke.

Holmes tilted his head at Sophie. "It was lucky you were both available and qualified for the positions, able to step in so quickly to fill the breach left by the suspiciously sudden resignation of Vanderpool's two previous employees. Of course, Mr. Vanderpool didn't make any connection—he was too busy trying to salvage his tour, and you came in and saved his bacon. He was too busy being thankful to suspect there was anything untoward bubbling just beneath the surface."

Gregson, who had been following Holmes's summary, sat back and folded his arms, the smile spreading across his face just a little on the smug side. But Watson didn't blame him. What Holmes had found, even with the help of Everyone, was nothing short of remarkable.

Holmes returned to the folder. All eyes in the room were on him as he pulled two more printouts from his prodigious stack of papers.

Gregson glanced down at the sheet, then rocked a little in his chair as he suppressed a chuckle. Holmes handed it to him. The captain cast an eye over it, then turned it around and slid it toward Sophie.

They were driver's licenses, two of them, the photos showing a man and a woman, respectively. There were also copies of multiple IDs—state cards, even a gym membership form.

"Nancy Brennan," said Gregson, reading from the sheet,

tracing the name on the license with his finger, like he was teaching a slow child how to read. "And, let's see now, Trent Absolom's real name is… Carl Warren. And it doesn't look like you were actually married, but you have faked it a few times." Gregson shuffled through the papers, then raised an eyebrow and gave a low whistle. "And you have quite the rap sheet too."

Holmes, his eyes on Sophie, a smile on his face, drew out another sheet from the folder and handed it to Gregson. The captain pursed his lips as he cast an eye over it.

"Carl Warren," he muttered. "One-time trader at a large Chicago-based Fortune 500 company. And doing rather well too, at least until he lost that cushy job when he was charged with insider trading." Gregson clicked his tongue. "What, giant annual bonuses and ski holidays to France not enough for him?"

Sophie bit her bottom lip. She still hadn't spoken. Watson wasn't sure if she was showing stoic willpower, or had been rendered speechless by the flood of evidence Holmes had managed to gather on her and her "husband".

"And Nancy Brennan," said Holmes, "a serial confidence trickster and identity thief from Corpus Christi, Texas."

Gregson dropped the sheet with a dramatic flourish and sat back in his chair.

Holmes glanced up at Watson, then gestured with an open palm toward the table.

Her turn.

She took the folder she had been carrying and placed it on the table. "But the Dale Vanderpool roadshow wasn't actually the target for a new scam, was it? It was Mantis Capital. In fact, they were targeted six months ago. It was a long game you were playing, but one where the rewards were worth it."

Watson flipped open the folder. Inside was the guest pass from Mantis, identifying Sophie as Vicki Summers, the delivery driver.

"We know another of your identities, too," said Watson. "Josephine Banks. It was the name you and your partner— your *other* partner—used to book the room at the Athena Hotel in Washington Heights. The hotel room in which you killed Gregory Smythe."

"And," said Bell, pushing off from the wall to stand on the other side of the table, the quartet now almost surrounding Sophie, "the ID used to book the rental car in New Jersey. The car you planned to use for the getaway. Only that didn't happen, did it?"

Sophie licked her lips.

"Something went wrong," said Holmes, linking his fingers and gesturing with his clasped hands to emphasize his words. "Your accomplice. He had other ideas."

He pulled another sheet from the folder, this one showing on one side a still from the security footage from Voyager Car Rentals, showing Sophie and "Harold", and on the other side, a shot from the Athena Hotel lobby. Sophie's accomplice couldn't quite be seen, but there was enough of his side to show, at least in comparison to the image from Voyager, that it was likely the same man.

Holmes sat back. "I understand your reluctance to cooperate. You are afraid. Of course you are. This man, *Harold*—he's dangerous. You know he's dangerous, maybe you've always known. Why else would you be ready with a loaded gun when you agreed to meet him at the warehouse? You had no choice. You had to take precautions. You needed to defend yourself. Because, who knows what he is capable of? After all, he's already killed twice—including one man with whom he was working. Who is to say he won't kill again in order to cover his tracks, to make his escape?"

Sophie shifted in her seat and leaned forward, bringing her hands up onto the table again. She looked at Holmes and her lips parted a little. Something he'd said, Watson thought, had caught her attention. His deductions had been right on the mark so far, but there was something new.

Then Watson got it.

"You don't know, do you?" Watson leaned on the table, her voice low. "He didn't just kill Gregory Smythe. He killed Trent too."

Sophie stared at Watson, her mouth now falling open even more. She worked her jaw, like she was trying to find something to say, but no sound came out.

Gregson leaned in, the experienced cop reading the situation, taking the opportunity that had suddenly presented itself. "We can help you," he said, and he said it quietly and with emphasis, the good cop, the cop who wants to help, who can offer protection, safety, a deal.

A way out of a big, hot mess.

"Because," he continued, "he's going to come after you. You know he will. He's killed at least twice and he's prepared to do it again, and again, and again. Anything and everything that is required to cover his tracks."

He paused and he sat back. Sophie's gaze moved around the room, from Gregson, to Bell, to Watson, and finally to Holmes. The two looked at each other in silence for a long, long time.

Then Sophie closed her eyes and when she opened them again she was looking at the captain.

"Okay," she said. "I'll talk."

28

THE CONFESSION

Sophie drew a deep, shuddering breath. And then she spoke.

"His name isn't Harold. It's Vinnie. Vinnie Talben. Or at least that's what he calls himself. I don't know if that's his real name. I assume it is, but, well, maybe it isn't. *Probably* isn't. He's one of us, a con artist, like me and Trent… like me and *Carl*. He's a hacker. A forger. From somewhere, I'm not sure. The Midwest. Indiana or Idaho. Somewhere anyway. Or maybe not. Maybe that was a lie too.

"He hired us. He's the boss. He came and found us and he hired us for this job, because he knew we had the skills. I don't know how he knew where to find us. I guess word gets around. You do some jobs. You get caught. You do some time then you get out and you get back to work. Sooner or later people are going to figure out who you are, what you are, where you are. And Vinnie, he's good. Good at information. That's the key, that's what he keeps saying. *Information*. You know more than other people, then you're ahead of the game. You're winning. Information is everything.

"The job seemed pretty simple at first. He gave us new IDs—they were good, too, some of the best we'd ever seen.

Social security numbers, licenses. Everything was *real*, they checked out. We were *married*. He said it was good for the brand, because that's what we were. A brand. We practiced for a long time, too. Working everything out, everything we might come across, what people might ask us.

"Vinnie sent us out to these meetings run by Vanderpool. We didn't know why, Vinnie kept it all to himself—information, right? That was how he worked. He only told us what we needed to know, only fed us a little, enough to keep going, and going. We were Sophie and Trent, a young couple, newly married, setting out in the wide world of business. Entrepreneurs, or wannabes anyway. That fit too—we were figuring it out, working on a plan, learning how it all came together.

"For this thing to work, we really had to know about Vanderpool, his whole philosophy of business. So we had to read it all, the both of us. He's written a lot, you know, and damn, there was so much. Trent and I tested each other until we knew it all back to front. But that was all part of the plan. Play the part, take the role. We were being paid by Vinnie and he promised us that something big was coming. The biggest play of our lives, in fact. But he wouldn't tell us what it was. He was in control—not just of the play, but of *us*.

"So we kept working at it, slowly, slowly, and Vinnie began feeding us a little more, telling us to go deeper, start getting in with Vanderpool. So we did, and then one day his tour manager and publicist quit—and we were in the perfect place to take over. That was Vinnie. He told us later how he did it. All he had to do was hack their emails, send in their resignations. I'm not sure what story he made up, but it didn't matter. They were gone, I don't know what happened to them and—

"Wait… do *you* know what happened to them? You don't think… oh my *God*, do you think he killed them too? I mean… I'd never thought he was capable of something like that, but then I guess I never really knew him, did I?

"Oh God. Anyway... we were there. We took over. Vanderpool knew us and he knew his tour was sunk without us. It was easy enough, we'd been planning so long. I was better at the con than Trent, but he had the numbers know-how. He looked after the logistics while I liaised with the booking agents, the venues. I guess I just have the knack of working people. The tour kept on going without a hitch. Dale was thankful, too. So thankful.

"Can I get a water, please?

"Thanks.

"So the tour went on. Then Vinnie gave us the next set of instructions. We were in charge and we had access to everything—Dale just left us to it. He didn't want to know anything about what we did or how we did it. So long as each night was a sell-out, he didn't care. And they were, for the most part. Tickets for the tour were booked well in advance—months and months sometimes. So as we went from city to city, I'd take the attendee lists and feed them back to Vinnie. Then he'd send me back a list of names. It wasn't many, just a few at each lecture. I was the tour publicist but it didn't take much to make it as the front-of-house supervisor too. Vanderpool didn't have one, so it looked like I was just helping out. He liked that. But it was all part of the play, too.

"I'd identify the target from Vinnie's list—they were all middle managers, supervisors, that kind of thing. And I'd offer personal services, one-on-one courses, management focus groups and training sessions back at their offices. Even personal styling and publicity—all under the Vanderpool brand.

"He didn't know anything about it, of course. Dale, I mean. He gave the lectures, he signed the books.

"We did the rest and he didn't even know.

"Of course it worked. Every time. I told you, we probably knew Dale Vanderpool's theories and practices better than he did. Plus I had a little advantage. What, you think I don't know how to turn on the charm, give men of a certain age a little bit of attention, little bit of a thrill? I've been doing this a long time, trust me. And I've done worse. This... this was nothing.

"I mean, I'm not saying it was *easy*. But I actually went through with it all. I'd go to the offices, run through a few sessions. People loved it. Nobody ever realized they were just getting the same thing they'd seen at the lectures spoon-fed back to them. But it was the personal touch, like they were investing in some real quality services.

"And while I was there, I'd get to work. Vinnie had it all worked out. He was an engineer originally, I think. Computers. That kind of thing. He used to talk about white hats and black hats. I didn't always follow his conversations, but I knew enough to guess which color he'd been on the side of.

"I don't know how he started. Or why. I mean, how did any of us end up where we are? Do we really know or even care?

"So Vinnie had it all worked out. With me at the companies, turning it on for the executives. You wouldn't believe what grown men will do. What they'll let you get away with if you just smile in a certain way and wear a certain kind of skirt. It was embarrassing, in a way, how it didn't even take that much effort. Once I was in the office, all I needed was access to a computer.

"Vinnie did the rest.

"There was a computer program—a Trojan horse, I think that's what he called it. I had it on a USB stick, and when I plugged the stick in it got to work. I didn't need to do anything. I think Vinnie called it a brute force attack. But it worked. It installed itself onto the computer and then it spread, infecting the whole network. It could break down walls, Vinnie said. I guess that's what it did and I guess it worked because once a company was infected, Vinnie was *in*. I could even watch him work. He was somewhere else, remotely accessing the servers, looking for the goods while the little program copied as much data from the company as would fit on the stick. That's so I could take that away with me. It was faster and safer than copying stuff over the net. That's what Vinnie said.

"That was all we had to do. That was the whole job.

"Now are you going to offer me protection or what? Because you're right. Vinnie's a dangerous man. I...

"I didn't know about Trent. I knew about Smythe and I'll tell you about it, but look, this is all on him, on Vinnie, not me.

"Yes, I had a gun.

"I know.

"But I don't know if I could have used it.

"But yes, Vinnie is dangerous. And once he finds out where I am, I won't be safe.

"So please.

"Please, help me."

29

LINKS UNCOVERED

Watson stretched her arms over her head as she waited for the coffee machine to complete its diabolical task.

Sophie's story was filling in a lot of blanks, but there was still plenty missing. She'd been talking for what felt like hours—a marked change from her original attitude. She was still fearful of Harold Banks—or Vinnie Talben as they now knew him—but at least she was talking.

As Watson listened to the coffee machine whir and spit, she ran over Sophie's story in her mind. There was something she kept coming back to, something unexpected.

It was about Trent. The news of his death had startled Sophie, for sure, although it hadn't had quite the devastating punch Watson was expecting. But the more she thought about it, the more she wondered whether it had actually been reasonable to expect Sophie to act in any way that Watson could fathom.

To understand Sophie, she had to understand how her mind operated. Criminology, as Holmes had taught her, was as much of an art as it was a science, a complex blend of philosophy and psychology, as well as forensics.

All of which was to say, Watson thought, that maybe Sophie wasn't quite the kind of person she appeared to be. She was young and beautiful. Smart too. Very smart. But whatever spark was there, whatever "untapped potential" Sophie possessed had taken her in another direction. Holmes might have called it "the dark path" in one of his more melodramatic moments, but Watson saw it a little differently.

Because, she realized, Sophie was a professional. She was working, and she was good at her job. It just so happened that her job—her chosen career—was on the *other* side of the law. That intelligence, the skills and abilities she clearly had, had been directed toward a life of crime.

Which brought Watson's thoughts back around to the murder of Trent Absolom—or rather Carl Warren. Sophie had been shaken, but having absorbed the news, she was already looking for an angle that would benefit her. She was in danger, and she knew it—Trent himself, her fake husband, was proof of that.

But... was she really a psychopath, by its technical definition? To do what she did, to take advantage of others and use them for her own personal gain, it took a certain... perspective on life. Sophie, Watson realized, couldn't relate to people, not in the same way that Watson and Gregson and Bell and Holmes—

Well, okay, maybe not Holmes. He was a classification all of his own.

So while the news of Trent's murder hadn't been the sucker-punch everyone wanted, it had been enough to change Sophie's perspective, shift the angle around enough for her to cooperate for, as she saw it, her own survival.

But that wasn't enough for her. Not yet. She still had other crimes to wriggle out of, and at the moment, she was playing the innocent. She was merely a pawn, an employee of Vinnie Talben. The same with Trent. They were villains for hire, two crooks following the money. Sophie had emphasized that point several times in her story, even through the tears and choked confession.

The problem remained: how much use was Sophie, anyway? She wasn't the killer. She hadn't murdered Gregory Smythe and she hadn't murdered Trent Absolom. She claimed not to really know what Vinnie was up to.

Vinnie Talben. It all came back to him. What was he doing? What was *his* plan, the one he hadn't told his two minions? The plan to target the speaking tour was clever, but… how had Vinnie even come up with the scheme? And what was the end goal? What was the big payout he had promised the others?

Maybe it didn't all come back to Vinnie. Maybe there was another keystone, a fulcrum on which the whole mystery pivoted.

Dale Vanderpool.

Vinnie Talben knew who Dale Vanderpool was—who he *really* was. He knew about David Hauer and, most importantly, he knew what Hauer had done and *how* he had done it, all those years ago in California.

The coffee machine had been finished for several minutes by the time Watson snapped out of her reverie. She grabbed her drink, a fresh set of questions forming in her mind.

Questions like how Talben knew Vanderpool. How Mantis Capital had been identified as a target by the group.

And how Gregory Smythe got involved—discovering something which had gotten him killed.

It was time for some answers.

They reconvened in the interview room, this time Detective Bell leading the trio of Gregson, Holmes and Watson in. Sophie's water had been refilled and she played with the cup on the tabletop as she watched Watson walk in and take a seat. Holmes stood in the opposite corner regarding the suspect, hands deep in the pockets of his steel-gray jacket. Gregson sat next to Watson, and Bell remained standing by the two-way mirror.

"Do I need a lawyer for this?" Sophie directed the question at Captain Gregson. All the captain did was shrug.

"For what?"

"For a deal," she said. "For protection." She looked around the room. "You said I would get protection."

Gregson linked his fingers on the table, and twiddled his thumbs as he watched the suspect. Then he gave another shrug, like he couldn't have cared less.

"We're going to need a whole lot more from you before we get around to discussing any kind of *protection*, Ms. Absolom. Or should I call you Ms. Brennan?"

"What? You said—" Sophie lifted both cuffed hands and rubbed her forehead, exhaling hotly as she calmed herself. "You said I could get protection," she said, her voice a low whisper. "Vinnie is still out there—"

"Exactly," said Gregson. "He's still out there, and so far you've given us nothing that will help us bring him in."

Watson saw the moment had come to reopen the line of questioning.

"What was Vinnie accessing from the companies?"

Sophie sighed, her shoulders slumping as she leaned on the table on her elbows. Her eyes remained downcast.

"I don't know. Honestly, I have no idea. He just paid us to play our roles and our roles *only*. He never explained what he was doing, what he was taking. We did what he said." She sat back, upright in her chair, a knowing smile on her face. "Information, remember? Information was everything to him."

Holmes pursed his lips. "Knowledge is power. Yes, you did mention it. Vinnie has the knowledge, and therefore has the power—over you and your associate."

Sophie looked up at Holmes, but she didn't bother saying anything.

"Vinnie also knows Dale Vanderpool," said Holmes. "Knows who he *really* is."

At this, Sophie leaned forward, her brows knitting together in confusion.

"What do you mean, who he really is?"

"Like you and your late *husband*," said Holmes, pronouncing the final word with exaggerated elocution, as if it were two words, not one, "Mr. Vanderpool had a secret past and another life. Originally he was David Hauer, a drunk who killed a man with a fountain pen through the eye in 1995."

Sophie's mouth opened in surprise.

"I don't know anything about that," she said, then she looked around the room, leaning forward, her eyes getting wider and wider. "You have to believe me! I didn't know anything about *that*!"

Holmes merely smiled. "Perhaps not. But the fact is that Vinnie Talben *did*. I understand his methodology—using the tour to inveigle his minions into the cogs and wheels of mid-sized businesses. Ingenious, really. So the question is, did he know who Dale Vanderpool was before, or after? And in either case, how did he get that information?"

"I'm telling you," said Sophie, "I don't know anything."

"So you didn't know your boss, Vinnie, was planning on killing Gregory Smythe?" asked Gregson.

"No, I did not."

"But you know that he did. You were at the Athena Hotel."

Sophie dropped her head, and then nodded.

Watson leaned forward. "You want protection? You want to be safe from Vinnie? Then you have to help us bring him in. He's out there right now. He's killed two people. Maybe you're not connected. Maybe we can do a deal. But our priority has to be to bring Vinnie in before he kills someone else."

Sophie took a deep, shuddering breath, and then she looked up.

"I don't think Vinnie is at the top," she said.

Gregson and Watson looked at each other. Holmes just frowned. "Explain."

Sophie sighed again. "Vinnie keeps a low profile. He doesn't like to get involved, not in person. Everything was by phone." She frowned. "Or email."

Holmes snorted.

"But," she continued, "sometimes he came to the meetings— we just signed him in under different names, it didn't matter. We controlled the attendee lists. But when he came he never spoke to us. He stayed at the back, and he was always on his phone. Like he was, I don't know, relaying what was going on at the meeting to someone else. And then he would leave. He never stayed for the whole lecture, and he always left early, slipping out. He never spoke to *anyone*. And he never hung around. He came in, and then he was gone. Neither of us ever saw him leave."

Gregson shifted in his seat. "His boss wouldn't happen to be someone at Mantis Capital, would it?"

Sophie frowned.

"Gregory Smythe, perhaps? Maybe he and Vinnie had a disagreement, something went south, Vinnie had to kill him and fix the blame on Vanderpool?"

Sophie grinned, and barked out a short, loud laugh before rubbing her forehead again.

"It wasn't Gregory."

"But you knew him," said Watson. "And you knew Mantis Capital. You were there weeks ago, signing in as Vicki Summers, a courier driver for APD. Just a temporary cover, with a stolen uniform, another fake ID. We have your details from the Mantis security files."

Watson flipped open the folder she had brought in earlier, and showed Sophie the record from Mantis. Sophie stared at the sheet and nodded.

"I presume," said Holmes, "you are now going to try and tell us that you were not, in fact, there to meet Gregory Smythe."

Sophie looked at him. She didn't answer. Holmes pressed her again.

"So who was it?"

"Nobody."

Gregson smiled. "Oh, you'll have to do better than that."

"I'm telling the truth," said Sophie. "Listen."

30

ONCE UPON A TIME IN NEW YORK CITY

*S*ophie waited in her van, a monster vehicle that was a pig to drive, more like a small truck than a delivery van. She'd rented it just a couple of hours before. It was white, and unmarked. Sitting on the dash in the window was a long rectangular card that said APD ON DELIVERY DO NOT TOW in big black handwritten block letters.

The van was entirely empty, save for Sophie sitting in the driver's seat, dressed in the weird purple uniform that Axiom Parcel Delivery forced their staff to wear, and the small package sitting on the passenger seat.

The van was the perfect cover. Nobody would suspect anything or question why the van wasn't the same color as the driver's clothes. It happened often enough—a courier or delivery van has a fender-bender, gets put out of action for a while. But the deliveries have to get made and the driver needs to earn his paycheck, so you go to plan B.

A rental. A big one, big enough to fill with all the packages to deliver, laboriously transferred from the original, liveried vehicle. Then make up a quick sign to stick in the window and the day's work goes on. Probably half of the delivery vans in Manhattan were unmarked rentals.

But Sophie only had one delivery to make. She glanced at her watch, then glanced at the package sitting next to her. It was a large yellow bubble envelope, sealed. It bulged in the middle, but it was light.

Sophie didn't know what the package contained. She didn't know anything, only where to go for a photo and to pick up the prepared ID and stolen uniform, where the rental yard was from which to hire the van, and the time and place to make the delivery. All of that information had been given to her by Vinnie, because Vinnie was the boss and because she did what she was told to do, no questions asked, and he paid her to do it. She trusted Vinnie and so far, things were going just fine. There was a payday on the horizon, a big one, for her and for Trent. Vinnie had promised.

Okay, so, true, this was a little out of the ordinary. She'd been in New York for a few days now, not as—she checked the fake driver's license sitting in the well between the driver and passenger seats—Vicki Summers, but as Sophie Absolom, the name she'd had for months and months. In fact, Sophie Absolom was a real record-breaker. She'd used it for so long that it almost felt real.

Almost.

Vicki Summers. She was a cutie-pie. Blonde hair, long enough to hide her own black locks. Her eyebrows were still dark, but that was fine. So were a lot of blondes'. The photograph on the license might have only been taken yesterday, but the license, it was a real piece of work. It not only looked real but it looked old, used, slid in and out of a wallet or purse for a few years.

Vinnie was good. In fact, he was the best—neither Sophie nor Trent had seen IDs of comparable quality, not for a long, long time.

All in all, it was a good gig. Vinnie paid them money and they did the work and that was that.

And then there was that something on the horizon, the big thing coming. And once they'd collected their payout, it would be time to depart from the service of Dale Vanderpool and his little traveling roadshow, and Sophie and Trent Absolom would cease to exist, like so many names they had taken over the years.

That time was soon. Vinnie said so. Soon. The tour was ending in New York City and the roadshow would be over for another year. Dale Vanderpool would use the break to write another of his stupid books, and then it would probably all start up again. A new book, a new theme, a new tour. Yawn.

Only it would be a new tour without Sophie or Trent. Vanderpool would have to do a spot of re-staffing.

Sophie checked her watch again. Time was passing, but it was quiet in the alley and cool in the van. At the appointed moment she would nose the vehicle out onto the street, fight the Manhattan traffic and the stick shift, and park up outside the offices of...

She frowned and, from underneath the package on the passenger seat, she slid an old-fashioned clipboard to read the destination.

Mantis Capital Investments.

Sophie had to admit, the name caught her eye. Two words in particular: Capital. Investments. They were a financial firm, and that sounded just fine to Sophie. A ripe target for the team.

Except...

Except they weren't likely to send anyone to Vanderpool's talks, now were they? His shtick was targeted at a lower demographic, a mix of middle-income, small-staff businesses with an annual turnover up to the low millions, and entrepreneurs just starting out, whether they were young and excited about the brave new world of business, or older, jaded, executives on the out or looking for an escape.

Mantis? Neh. Mantis were off the table.

But still, it was nice to dream.

Another check of the watch. Nearly time.

The delivery was a pain, but hey, what Vinnie wanted, Vinnie got. She was in NYC finalizing the details with Kronos Plaza anyway. It was a bigger venue than they normally used, and the manager was being a bit difficult, like he didn't believe they could pay for the booking, despite the sizeable deposit. So it required the personal touch, and that was what she was here to give. The tour wasn't due to arrive for another two months.

And while she was in town, just another little job. Easy. Get yourself suited up. Drop off a package, pick up another. Get in, get out.

Easy.

She glanced at the padded envelope on the passenger seat. She picked it up, squeezed it. Whatever was inside, there were lots of them—small, hard oblongs, plastic perhaps. A bunch of USB sticks, most likely, and most likely the very same ones she'd used to siphon corporate data from a dozen firms in the last six months. She didn't know what Vinnie wanted the information for—but he was paying them, and that money was coming from somewhere. The USB sticks were probably the source. A little corporate espionage, a little money laundering, a little insider trading.

Who the hell knew. That was Vinnie's department, not hers.

What Sophie did know was that it was time to roll, so she started the white van, drove it slowly out into the main street, and slipped into the traffic.

31

A LITTLE PROBLEM IN NEWARK, NEW JERSEY

*S*ophie checked her phone, then checked it again, reading from the list of attendees for tonight's lecture. She wasn't sure, but she had a feeling the man standing at the back of the venue's lobby wasn't on the guest list, nor was he a ticket holder. He was wearing a suit, a three-piece no less, blue pinstripe, with peaked lapels that wouldn't have looked out of place sometime just after the Great Depression, and he was very tall and fairly old, his silver hair immaculately parted, forming two wedge-shaped blocks on his head. All he seemed to be doing was...

Well, he wasn't doing anything, exactly. He was keeping out of the way, apparently ignoring the not insignificant spread of finger food, coffee, tea, water and juice that the other attendees had descended on like a swarm of locusts as soon as the lecture had broken for its twenty-minute intermission. He just stood there, casting his eye around, looking down a long nose at the other attendees, his lips tightly squeezed together. He didn't look like he was having much fun. In fact, he didn't look like he wanted to be there at all.

And, according to the information Sophie had—or didn't have, technically speaking—he wasn't supposed to *be, anyway. Whoever he was, he must have come in after the lecture had started, because she sure as hell hadn't greeted him at the door, as she greeted every attendee each and every night on tour. True enough, she didn't remember everybody, but her whole job, the whole reason she had to stand there as the front-of-house host, was to keep an eye out for their marks, the unwitting targets that Vinnie had identified. So everyone was greeted, their names and affiliations cross-checked against Vinnie's list until Sophie knew who was who.*

This guy, he wasn't on any list. He hadn't come in with the rest. There was something about him, the way he stood, the way he looked around.

He was different.

He was also looking right at her.

Sophie adjusted her posture, put on a smile, and walked over to him, nodding a greeting to a few attendees as she passed them, weaving her way through a constellation of men (it was always men) in suits drinking coffee and eating donuts in small, tight circles.

The man in the blue pinstripe suit didn't take his eyes off of her as she approached, didn't take his hands out of his pockets. He looked at her with big blue eyes and as she got closer a smile appeared on those tight, thin lips. It was almost like he recognized—

Sophie nearly missed a step. She couldn't help it, but she caught herself, and she kept walking. Her heart thudded in her chest.

But... yes, he'd seen it. The man in the blue pinstripe suit. He was still watching her, the smile still on his face. The smile that said:

I know who you are.

It was impossible. Couldn't be. She put the thought out of her mind and she came up to the man, holding out a hand in greeting.

"Hi!" she said, like a cheerleader about to start a pep rally. "It's so great you could make it!"

The man continued to smile, but he didn't shake her hand. He simply extracted one of his own hands from his pocket and scratched the side of his nose.

And then he said: "I know what you're doing." He grabbed Sophie's wrist. Hard. Fast. He pulled her toward him, turning as he did so, leading them farther back against the wall of the lobby area, to where a column and curtains provided ample cover from the rest of the crowd.

A bell chimed. Just five minutes of intermission left. The attendees crowded around the tables of free food for their second hurried helping.

Sophie pulled herself out of the man's grip, but while he relented, the smile didn't leave his face. It was cruel, and small, just like the look he gave her.

"I don't know who you think you are," Sophie whispered, "but if you would like to take your seat, perhaps we can continue this conversation later."

Yes, *she thought*. Later, with Trent by my side. Maybe Vinnie too. I'll have to call Vinnie.

"You were in New York City two months ago," said the man, and he looked her up and down. "Don't they pay you enough here? Or is moonlighting as a delivery driver more of a hobby for people like you?"

Sophie's breath caught in her throat. The man continued.

"You were at the office of Mantis Capital. Don't deny it. I saw you. And when I get back to the office I'll check our security logs. And then you will be hearing from me again."

When in doubt, feign ignorance. It was a standard tactic. The risk of recognition came with this kind of life, and this wasn't the first time Sophie had found herself in this type of situation. So, all you had to do was pretend the other party was mistaken, then get away and stay away. That *actually worked, most of the time.*

But this guy... he had, what did he say, security logs? Some kind of records?

Of course. *Mantis Capital. The delivery. She'd been photographed—even fingerprinted—when she'd gone in. Vinnie hadn't told her anything about that part, but again, sometimes things happened and sometimes you just had to roll with it.*

And sure, her fingerprints were on file with not just a half dozen local police departments, but federal law enforcement too, able to be called up by any authority in the country. Her photograph too—she could count at least three mug shots she'd posed for.

But she also knew that the information she had had to part with at Mantis would just be kept on file and not shared with any other parties—and that included law enforcement. At Mantis she had signed in as Vicki Summers, and nobody would be any the wiser.

Except, it seemed, this guy in the fancy suit.

"I know who you delivered the package to," said the man. "How many more are in on it, eh? How many more are participating in this, this... charade?"

"Look, I don't know what you're talking about—" not true "—and I certainly don't know who you think I was delivering something to—" that bit was true, she really had no idea; she just went in, went through the security rigmarole and got the package signed off, and picked up the one that was waiting for her, and then got the hell out "—but I'm afraid I'm going to have to ask you to leave now, sir."

The man cleared his throat and the intermission bell sounded again. From across the lobby, one of the uniformed ushers from the venue was heading toward them, on a no-doubt-helpful mission to ensure nobody missed the start of the second part of the lecture. As the usher approached, the man in the blue pinstripe suit straightened the front of his jacket and gave the usher a nod, then looped his arm around Sophie's, pulling her as tight as the smile on his face.

Together they headed back toward the auditorium, but at the door, the man released Sophie from his grip. He nodded to the usher near them. "Thank you," he said, as the door was held open, and then he turned to Sophie. "I'll speak to you later, my dear," he said, and he gave a cheery wave before stepping through into the auditorium.

Sophie smiled and waved back, for the benefit of the usher. Then she gave the man a nod and the auditorium door was closed. As soon as it was, Sophie spun around and marched back across the lobby, already bringing up a contact on her phone and thumbing the call button.

"Trent," she said, as soon as it was answered. "Listen, we have a problem here."

32

THE BEST LAID PLANS

In the interview room, Watson took a sip of her coffee as she listened to Sophie relate the phone conversation she had had with Trent. Behind her, Watson could hear Holmes pacing back and forth, as he had been nearly the whole time Sophie had been telling her story.

"He was so calm," she said. "He just said, it's fine, we can handle it. I was angry, I think I asked him what the hell was going on with Mantis Capital, and who the guy was. Of course, Trent knew as much as I did. He said he'd called Vinnie, and then he asked me to describe the guy. So I did, and then Trent said I should just stick to the plan and to the schedule and he'd see what Vinnie said."

Holmes's footsteps stopped. Watson glanced over her shoulder and saw he was facing away from them, toward the door. A moment later he spun on his heel, glancing at Watson before fixing his gaze on Sophie.

"A problem had arisen," said Holmes, "but one that your boss, Vinnie Talben, could easily solve. Or at least that was what you and Trent both hoped."

Gregson nodded. "A problem solved by killing the man in the blue pinstripe suit—Gregory Smythe."

Sophie frowned. "I told you, I don't know who he was. I only ever spoke to him twice—both times on that night in Newark."

"Gregory Smythe was the Chief Financial Officer of Mantis Capital," said Watson. "He'd seen you when you visited the office to make the package delivery two months earlier."

"*But*," said Holmes, bouncing on his heels, "meeting *you* in New Jersey"—he stabbed a finger at Sophie—"now *that* was a surprise for him. Because he was there for another reason altogether."

Sophie shrugged. "Look, I don't know who he was, only that it sounded like he was on to us. Which meant then we either had to get rid of him, somehow, or get out."

"And you chose the first option," said Gregson.

"*No!*" said Sophie. "I didn't choose anything! *Vinnie* did. After I spoke to Trent, I stayed out in the lobby for a few minutes. Then Vinnie himself called. He gave me more instructions—he said Trent was right, I just had to go back into the auditorium, act like nothing had happened, but to pull the man out. It was easy enough. He was sitting at the back, and it was like he wasn't watching the lecture, he was watching the audience. I remember, he had his arms folded, and he was smiling the whole time, like he knew exactly what the hell was going on. More than me, even.

"So I grabbed his arm, and I didn't even need to say anything—he just took one look at me and followed me out. We stood in the lobby and he didn't say anything—maybe he was expecting a confession, or something, I don't know what.

"But I had my instructions. I asked for his phone number and I got it. And then I said what Vinnie told me to say— that we were coming to New York City, that we should meet again, and that we'd be in touch. I said it would be worth his while, that we could come to some kind of arrangement. I was just repeating what Vinnie had said, but it seemed to work. He looked at me, that smile still there, but it was... I don't know. It was... quizzical, maybe? Like he was trying to read my thoughts, figure out if I was lying or if I was telling the truth. Whatever, I guess he bought it. He left straight away.

"So a couple days later I met Vinnie. He came by the hotel we were at, the one in New Jersey. Trent stayed away. He and Vinnie didn't like each other much, but Trent knew that business was business and being friends was strictly optional. Vinnie said he had it all worked out. We went to New York. We went to the Athena Hotel—he'd found it somehow, and he seemed to think it was the best place to arrange our meeting. It was out of the way, hard to get to. Not the kind of place the guy in the suit would ever visit. No one would see him. Then I called the number that the guy had given me. He said he'd been waiting. I gave him the time and place for a meeting. He seemed... well, he seemed pretty pleased. Like he knew he was on the winning side. That worried me. I told Vinnie, but Vinnie, he was just so calm. I asked him who this guy was and what Vinnie was going to tell him, but Vinnie just told me to shut up and trust him. Everything was going to be fine. So I didn't think about it."

Gregson raised an eyebrow. "You didn't *think* about it?"

Sophie met the captain's gaze. "No, I didn't. Look, Vinnie was the boss. He did everything. I just did what I was told."

"Just following orders," said Holmes. "You do realize that hasn't been a valid defense in more than half a century?"

"What was I supposed to do? Vinnie... he had a hold on us. He knew who we were. The job was coming to an end— it was a long con, and he said it was worth it. We'd been working for months. We couldn't just throw that away."

Sophie gave a shuddering sigh and reached for her water. The cup was empty so she put it down again and tried to fold her arms as best she could with the handcuffs on.

"I came back to the hotel in time for the meeting, only..."

She paused. Wet her lips and chewed on the bottom one for a bit.

"He was already dead?" asked Watson.

Sophie nodded and closed her eyes. "Vinnie answered the door—he was standing there, cleaning his hands with wet wipes. I didn't know what to do—I remember standing in the doorway and behind Vinnie I could see the man in the suit, just lying there, on the floor. Then Vinnie moved aside to let me in, and I saw...

"I saw what he'd done."

Sophie cleared her throat before she continued.

"Vinnie closed the door and then he wiped down the handle. The first thing he said was, 'Don't touch a damn thing.'

"I didn't know what to do. I asked what had happened, I said that the meeting was for later. Vinnie said yeah, well, he changed the time, brought it forward."

Sophie looked at Watson, at Gregson, at Bell. Her eyes finally settled on Holmes.

"He planned it," she said. "From the beginning, he'd planned it. He wasn't going to talk to the guy, offer him a deal or something to shut him up. He had always planned on killing him. I remember I asked him who the man was, and Vinnie said it didn't matter. I told him I didn't want any part of this, and he said it was too late, I was already part of it. All I had to do was stick with it, see it through.

"But... he killed him."

Sophie held back a sob. Watson shifted in her seat as the suspect's tears appeared, and glancing sideways she saw Holmes watching her, his own expression impassive, emotionless.

To Holmes, Sophie had long ceased to be a person. She was now a *case*, a study in the criminal. And for Sherlock Holmes, this was what it was *all* about—not just his job, his hobby, his passion... this was his entire life. Now, on the cusp of a breakthrough, when all the long hours of work and chasing their own tails finally started to come together—this, *this* was the moment Holmes strived for. To solve the case, catch the perpetrator, protect the innocent—yes, these were all part of it. That was why he did it, because he had a talent, and he knew he had a duty to put that talent to good use.

But there was something else, too. Above all else, Holmes wanted to *understand*. Not just the criminal mind, but the mind in general—what made people tick, what made them *human*.

He was seeing it now. As Sophie's facade, her mask, began to disintegrate, Holmes got his moment, now, the chance to see the *real* person, and to try and understand.

Sophie glanced up at the group seated in front of her, then sniffed and continued.

"It was a mess. Vinnie was so calm, that was the worst part—it was like... I don't know. The world was falling apart and there he was, wiping his hands, looking down at the body.

"It was... awful. I wanted to be sick. I asked him why he'd done it and what we were supposed to do now, but Vinnie just kept looking at the body and saying what needed to be done was done, and he'd done it in a way that would distract the cops and put them onto Dale."

Holmes nodded, voicing the very same thought that was now at the forefront of Watson's mind.

"By killing Gregory Smythe with a fountain pen, he thought he was framing Vanderpool."

Sophie just shook her head. "I guess. I don't know. I keep telling you, *I don't know*."

"Where did Vinnie get the pen from?" asked Gregson.

Sophie shook her head again. "I don't *know*. All I knew is that the guy was dead and we were in trouble. I didn't know what Vinnie was talking about, I just said we had to get rid of the body. I kept asking what Dale had to do with any of it, why he wanted to blame him for what Vinnie had done, but Vinnie just kept saying it was under control, it was under control.

"But I convinced him. I told him we had to move the body, get it out of the hotel, somehow. And then we'd run. Whatever the plan was, whatever operation Vinnie had been running, it was over. We were through."

"And he just agreed to that?" asked Watson, frowning. "Months of planning, an operation of this scale, and he was going to let you out of it?"

Sophie twisted her cuffed hands around. "I don't know. I was in shock, I guess. But he said yes, and he said we'd rent a car, use that to move the body. It was... I don't know, early morning by then. We took a series of buses out to New Jersey—he knew a place, he said, it was out somewhere I hadn't heard of, just outside of Jersey City. We got there when it was opening, and Vinnie used the same IDs we'd used at the hotel. I think that was part of his plan, keep the two linked together. Then we could go back, get the body and move it, then dump it and the car. It would be found eventually, but we'd be far away by then and the cops would still link it all back to Dale."

"Only that didn't happen," said Gregson. "Someone else found the body first."

"The security team from Mantis," said Holmes, "looking for their AWOL CFO."

"Right, right," said Sophie, nodding. "We got back to the hotel, the place was crawling with guys in black suits. They looked like Feds—I've seen a few in my time, trust me. They were all over the place. There was no way in. Then the police turned up and they started arguing with these guys.

"That was when Vinnie snapped—he was so calm, so controlled, and he sat there in the car and we watched the hotel and I asked what we were going to do and he didn't answer, and I asked him again and then he just yelled at me to shut up. It was the only time I'd ever seen him lose his temper.

But it was over in a second, like it had never happened. He calmed down and said he would drop me back at my hotel, and then he took off in the rental. He said we had to keep on with the tour. He told me to clean up, have a rest, get some food, and everything would be fine."

Holmes pursed his lips. "A little naive of you, wasn't it? You were a liability to him. You didn't think he would kill you the moment you'd helped him clean up the first mess?"

Sophie's jaw clenched. "I… I don't know. After we spoke he drove off in the rental. And that was the last time I saw him."

Sophie's water was replenished. She muttered a thanks, took a long gulp, then set the plastic cup back down on the table.

"It was later," she continued. "That same night. I tried to hold it together, but Trent knew something was up. So I told him. I had to. We made it through the talk but as soon as we were done Trent called Vinnie. He asked what the hell was going on, and they had an argument over the phone. I guess Vinnie had been right on the edge, and that call was the last straw. The plan was coming apart, and so was Vinnie."

Watson glanced at the others. "That's when Bell and I were taken backstage by Vanderpool, to the green room. We walked in on that phone call."

Holmes nodded, then looked at Sophie. "Can you tell us what your partners in crime argued about?"

Sophie frowned and shook her head. "Trent told me later. He was furious. He'd told Vinnie he was going to go to the police unless Vinnie explained everything—not just what happened at the Athena, but what the whole operation was, what we'd been doing for nine months. He also asked for something for our trouble, something to keep us quiet." Sophie shrugged. "It seemed like a risk, but Vinnie said yes, apparently. He said he'd work something out and be in touch.

"I didn't like it. I mean, I'd told Trent what Vinnie had done but, y'know, Trent hadn't *seen* it. Seen it with his own eyes. So I told Trent to be careful, that Vinnie wasn't who we thought he was. That made Trent angry too—he said he knew what he was doing, that he could handle it. We were in a mess and we had to get out—whatever Vinnie was going to give us, we'd take it and run. That would be easy—we'd done it enough times. Trent went on and on, saying we'd been suckered into a long con and the only people being conned were us."

Sophie chuckled quietly. "Perhaps he was right. But we went back to our hotel. Vanderpool wanted to have the usual after-show drinks but we fobbed him off. I tried to sleep, but I couldn't. I tried to talk to Trent but he just ignored me. He just kept pacing, staring at his phone. Every time I tried to talk to him he just snapped at me.

"Then he got a text, and he said that was it. And he went."

Sophie exhaled a long breath. "And that was the last I saw of him. I waited in the hotel, not knowing what to do. But of course I had to get out—the second lecture was that night but I just couldn't do it. Dale, he knocked on the door a few times, and then he called my cell, but I never picked up. So I got out of the hotel, waited around in a coffee shop just down the street. The next day I got the email from Vinnie, telling me to meet at the warehouse. It was from an old email address— maybe that should have warned me. I tried calling Trent, but it was no good. I thought maybe he was with Vinnie and they were going to finalize the deal, y'know, we'd get our payout and then we'd be out of it.

"But… I mean, I wasn't sure. It was crazy to go, a part of me knew it, but… I guess I was in shock, not thinking straight. I didn't know what was going on, but another part of me wanted to find out. So I decided to go meet him. But I was going to be careful—or, that's what I told myself anyway.

"Trent had a gun in his room. I don't like them, have

never used them, but I'm also not stupid and I know that sometimes, a life like ours, you need a little muscle on your side. I snuck back to the hotel, took it, then headed up to the Bronx and waited."

Sophie reached for her water cup again and then, as though remembering it was empty, withdrew her hand quickly.

She looked up at the captain. "So do I get protection now or what?"

Gregson brushed his chin with a finger, like he was thinking it over. "I can't make any promises right now, but if you can testify in court against Vinnie, then the DA might be in the mood to be lenient," he said. "Assuming, of course, that you're being honest with us."

Watson turned back to Sophie. Gregson had a point. She'd told them a story—a big one, at that—and she was displaying every indication that she found the details uncomfortable, upsetting. But Sophie was a career criminal, she freely admitted that. She and Trent—Carl—had made a living ripping people off, pulling scams. Grifting. According to her, the death of Gregory Smythe had shocked her, and its retelling had seemed to distress her.

But there was something in what Captain Gregson had just said that struck a chord with Watson. Sophie was a confidence trickster, one skilled in the art of deception and misdirection.

Perhaps it was all an act. Perhaps the story was just that—a story.

Perhaps she was as guilty of murder as the mysterious Vinnie Talben.

Holmes paced around the interview room a couple of times, then he stopped. He tapped his bottom lip, then pointed a finger at Sophie.

"Give me a name," he said.

Sophie blinked. She looked at the captain, perhaps

looking for support from the person who was supposed to be in charge. For his part, Gregson at least had the courtesy to ask Holmes for clarification.

Holmes waggled his finger.

"If we accept that Vinnie Talben is the killer, and for the moment take it on face value that you had no direct connection to the death of Gregory Smythe," said Holmes, "that still doesn't tell us what Vinnie was really up to, or who he works for."

Sophie sighed. "I told you, I don't *know* who Vinnie works for."

Holmes nodded, his finger back to tapping his lip. "No, no, I understand that. What I want to know is who your last target was. At the lectures, you targeted attendees from a list prepared by Vinnie. You got close, turned on the charm, perhaps wore a skirt a little shorter than the average. You, in point of fact, *stole* from these companies. Only you can't tell us what it was you took."

Sophie's jaw worked as she struggled for an answer.

"So," said Holmes, with a smile and a wave of the hand, "just tell us who your last target was. Just a name, or a company. Surely you can remember."

"I... ah..." Sophie rubbed her forehead again. "Ah... Allpress. Charles Allpress." She looked at Holmes. "He's a human resources manager at a place called Chemical Elements—it's a mid-sized chemical company in New Jersey. He was at the meeting in Newark, before we came to New York—his was the last company I visited."

Gregson took his glasses from inside his jacket and began jotting the details in his notebook. "Can you give us a full list of targets?"

"I can remember some, but not all." She glanced around the table. "We made sure not to keep a record."

"Okay, I think we're done here for now," said Gregson, standing. "Detective Bell can help you get started on a list."

Watson stood and followed the captain out, Holmes behind her.

The trio headed back to Gregson's office.

"As soon as we get a list of companies they targeted," said the captain, "we can get officers to contact each, see if they've reported any irregularities or other problems."

"It must be financial," said Watson, shaking her head as she tried to figure it out. "Vinnie promised them a big pay day at the end of the operation. They'd been working on the tour for months."

"Stands to reason," said Holmes. "Sophie—AKA Nancy Brennan—is a confidence trickster and a thief. Her partner, Trent—AKA Carl Warren—is, or rather *was*, convicted for insider trading. And Vinnie Talben—if that is indeed *his* real name—is a master identity thief and hacker. The object of his grand plan must be financial reward. And what better way than to simply ride the coattails of the great Dale Vanderpool speaking tour. It gave them every access."

They came to Gregson's office. The captain tossed his notebook to the desk as Holmes took a seat, Watson closing the door behind them.

"Which means," said Gregson, "that any irregularities should show up right away when we start taking a closer look at their targets."

"They will have covered their tracks well," said Watson.

"Their *actions*, Watson, yes," said Holmes, "but not their *tracks*. By the very nature of their business, they should by rights have left a veritable trail of destruction across the country."

"Okay," said Gregson. He reached for the phone with one hand and pointed over his shoulder with the thumb on the other, in the general direction of the interview room. "If what we were told in there is true, then this little crew has been active across multiple states. It's a federal matter, and I'm obliged to call in the FBI on this one."

At this, Holmes leapt out of his chair. He held both hands up to stop Gregson as the captain lifted the receiver. To his credit, Gregson put it down straight away.

"Okay," said Gregson, sitting in his chair with a sigh. "How long do you need?"

"Twenty-four hours. Possibly forty-eight, but I will appraise you of progress in due course and we can reassess."

"Twenty-four hours for what?" asked Watson.

Holmes turned on his heel to face her. "*Charles Allpress*," he said. "Their last target. While Sophie and the NYPD cooperate to prepare a longer list, I want to visit Mr. Allpress and the offices of Chemical Elements in person."

Watson nodded. "So we can find out what Vinnie's crew were doing, I get it," she said, "but shouldn't we be working on Vinnie Talben? He's still out there somewhere and so far he's killed two people."

"I am aware, Watson," said Holmes. He turned to Gregson. "But if you call in the FBI this will turn into a federal manhunt. Vinnie will already be lying low. He'll be wondering where Sophie went. Any suggestion he is being actively sought, he will disappear altogether. And while Vinnie Talben is undoubtedly a murderer, we also need to identify his boss. It's possible he was acting on orders as well, at least with regard to Gregory Smythe. We don't want whoever it is higher up the chain to vanish as well."

"If they haven't already," said Watson.

"That is a possibility," said Holmes.

Gregson nodded. "Okay. I can give you twenty-four, but that's gotta be it. Then I call the FBI. I'm sorry, but I have to."

"I am confident we can bring this case to a conclusion without them, and without any more needless deaths," said Holmes.

The captain frowned at him.

"I'm trusting you on this one. Don't let me down."

Holmes gave Gregson a tight-lipped smile, and he and Watson headed out of the office.

33

THE RISE AND RISE OF CHEMICAL ELEMENTS

Watson and Holmes left the Brooklyn brownstone early the next morning, heading off in her car for New Jersey and the offices of one Charles Allpress, human resource manager at Chemical Elements. By the time they reached the address in question, the sun was high and Watson was very grateful she'd insisted on a snack stop en route.

She wasn't entirely sure quite what she had expected the offices of Chemical Elements to be like, but, standing in a large parking lot in the warming morning, she knew it wasn't anything like *this*.

The office in question was located on the third floor of a slightly odd, mid-eighties building which looked like a series of blocky cubes of bronze-tinted glass balancing on top of each other like a giant, discarded corporate desk toy. It wasn't unpleasant to look at, and the developers of the business park, an hour west of Newark near the Pennsylvania border, had clearly been pleased with their architectural choice—the building was just one of six identical constructions, each separated from the others by acres of blacktop slowly filling with cars as the working day started. Watson estimated there were enough spaces for a couple of hundred vehicles in front of the building housing Chemical Elements alone, servicing not just that office but the others that shared the building. Each of the buildings in the park had its own dedicated lot, and some were more occupied than others.

That wasn't to say the parking lot outside the Chemical Elements building was empty—it was far from it. But Watson immediately noticed a conspicuous row of empty spaces, and as she drove closer she bypassed the spots reserved for visitors, instead heading for the empty row. She pulled in, the front fender almost touching the sign that was planted at the head of each of the empty spaces.

RESERVED
CHEMICAL ELEMENTS PLC

Now the pair stood by her car, taking in the scene around them. The bronze glass office block was directly in front, and as they stood there, a couple of people dressed in smart but not flashy office attire entered the building.

"Interesting, isn't it?" Holmes asked.

Watson looked around the lot. Every other company's allocated spaces were filled. The only free parking spots were a dozen marked for visitors, and the row reserved for Chemical Elements.

"So, what? Vinnie's crew pulled their scam on this company and forced them out of business?"

Holmes pursed his lips. "It would fit the picture we have thus far constructed. They go in, they extract valuable and highly confidential business information, and use that to cause maximum financial damage." He glanced at Watson across the roof of her car. "And make a profit for themselves in the process."

Watson sighed. "So we came all the way out here for

nothing? You did call first, didn't you?"

Holmes didn't answer, but he did point. There, at the very end of the Chemical Elements parking row was a silver station wagon. It had one space clear on either side—at first, Watson had thought it was parked up in the neighboring spaces reserved for another company, only she could see now that it was, in fact, parked in one of the Chemical Elements spots.

Watson wasn't so sure of the connection. "That car could belong to anyone. There are plenty of spaces free now. It doesn't mean that there is anyone in at the office."

"Perhaps, or perhaps not."

Holmes opened the rear door of Watson's car and, reaching in, pulled his tablet out of his bag. He unfolded the device's kickstand and balanced it on the roof of the car. Then, unlocking the device, he brought up a website and twisted the screen around for Watson to take a look.

The website on display was the one for Chemical Elements. The browser was pointed at the staff page, which showed a gathering of office workers standing outside their bronzed glass office block.

Holmes pointed to the tablet. "The reflection in the windows. Look."

Watson peered closer, then she turned to look over her shoulder, confirming the angle. The office block was directly behind where they had parked, in the row reserved for the company. Reflected in the photograph on the website was the row of cars—mostly obscured by the assembled staff members, but at the end, beyond the last person, were two cars—one of which was a silver station wagon. The same one that was parked in the spot it was in right now.

"Okay, so someone *is* here," said Watson, touching the back button to return the browser to the company's front page. "Does that mean that Chemical Elements are in business or not?"

Holmes reached over and tapped at the screen. The front page was replaced by a blog.

"Chemical Elements is a small firm," he said, "specializing in the manufacture and supply of just a small handful of individual components used in the mass production of various other chemical entities. Thanks to the practical business advice of one *Dale Vanderpool*, they shifted from in-house production to outsourced manufacture, reducing costs and allowing their executive staff to work *here*, rather than in some toxin-spewing factory in the middle of nowhere."

"Wait, it says 'toxin-spewing'?"

"I'm paraphrasing."

Watson shrugged. "Okay, and when Vanderpool himself was in town, they took the opportunity and sent a rep over to his lecture."

"Indeed," said Holmes. "That rep being Charles Allpress, head of HR."

Watson peered back at the tablet screen. "So what am I looking at here?"

"Being a small company, Chemical Elements are remarkably quick at adaptation and innovation—more of Vanderpool's teachings, no doubt. One staff member maintained a frequently updated, if exceptionally tedious, news blog on their site, a veritable cavalcade of the monotonous and unimportant happenings among the staff, including bake sales, school music recitals, and charity skydiving events."

Watson skimmed down the page. Holmes was right—the blog was nice, a quaint, homespun look at the lives of the company staff. Scrolling back to the top, she saw immediately what Holmes was getting to.

"The entries were made nearly daily, but the last one is more than a week old."

"Precisely."

"So they *are* out of business?"

Holmes folded the tablet shut and shoved it under his armpit.

"I suggest we go and find out."

Chemical Elements was still listed on the board at the building's main reception, and the woman behind the desk gave them directions to take the elevator to the third floor. It was worlds away from the rarified, paranoid atmosphere of Mantis Capital. The receptionist hadn't even asked who they were, or who they were here to see.

The company only occupied half of the third floor, as they soon discovered. Holmes led the way, following directional placards from the elevators until they came to a plain wooden door with the company logo Watson recognized from the website.

The door was framed on two sides by frosted glass windows, and there was an intercom buzzer set in the wall. While Holmes pressed the buzzer, Watson peered through the windows. She couldn't make anything out, except that the lights inside were on. There was no movement, and no answer on the intercom.

The two consultants looked at each other, then Holmes tried the door. It opened, and, after a moment's pause, he entered. Watson followed.

They found themselves in another reception area, separated from the main, open-plan office by just a low wall, beyond which was a sea of cubicles, each separated from the next by a low, gray, fabric-covered partition.

There was nobody there. More to the point, there was *nothing* there. The reception desk was devoid of anything, with a metal articulated arm stretched out at one side where a computer monitor had once been mounted.

Watson stepped around the reception desk and into the office proper. All the desks were the same—all empty, their surfaces devoid of anything save the metal arms, and in several cubicles the under-desk drawers were pulled out, showing that they were quite, quite empty. Watson tallied the detritus left behind, but counted only four computer cables of various types, a used notepad with the top half missing, and a pristine, unopened cube of sticky notes, still wrapped in their cellophane.

"You know," said Watson, "that *was* a long way to come to look at an empty office. *Please* tell me you called first?"

Holmes was looking around, standing on tiptoe as he scanned the office. "I did, in fact, call several times, but all I got was an out of office voicemail. And before you ask, yes I did check on the staff—as many social media accounts as I could find. Nothing to indicate anyone had changed jobs recently, and Charles Allpress himself still lists HR manager at Chemical Elements as his current position on one of his accounts."

"So now what? Get another name and company from Sophie and try them?"

"Perhaps," said Holmes, turning back to his companion. "Don't forget the car outside." Then he turned back around.

"Hello?" he yelled at full volume, loud enough to make Watson jump. His voice echoed dully in the empty office, but there was no reply.

Holmes turned with a sigh, and then Watson pointed. He spun back around on his heel.

A man approached from the other end of the office. He was middle-aged, his hair brown but not naturally so, his stomach stretching out a lime-green polo shirt. His bottom half was covered by cream chinos and he wore boat shoes.

"Sorry, I was just, y'know," said the man as he reached them, chuckling. "You can't hear the buzzer back there. So, did you talk to Cindy?"

Holmes and Watson looked at each other.

The man frowned. "From the realtor? She said someone was coming today to take a look at the office space—nothing to do with me of course, but I told her I'd be in this morning and was happy to show folks around." He checked his watch. "Wow, you're early! You must be pretty interested."

Holmes smiled politely, blinking at the man like he was speaking an alien language. "In?"

"Ah, the office?" the man waved his hand around. "Twelve hundred square feet. Done us well the last couple of years. Great facilities—you'll love the building."

"Oh," said Watson, "sorry, we're not here to look at the office."

"Oh?"

Holmes stuck out his chest, his hands clasped behind his back. "My name is Sherlock Holmes, my colleague here is Joan Watson. We're consultants to the New York City Police Department."

"Oh, wow, New York? You've come a fair way." The man stuck out his hand. "I'm Charles Allpress. How can I help you?"

Allpress took them to one of the meeting rooms at the back of the empty office. The room was smallish, with an oval table and six chairs, and the window-wall showed nearly a one-eighty view of the parking lots. In the middle distance, two of the other bronze cube office buildings were visible.

"Sorry I can't offer you much," said Allpress, as he pulled up a chair and sat at the head of the table. "The kitchen has been cleared out. I'm just here to collect the last couple of things—those rubber plants are actually mine."

He pointed out of the open door of the meeting room. Watson and Holmes leaned around to see, and indeed, there were two rubber plants, each at least six feet tall, against the wall on the other side of the office.

"I'm sorry about Chemical Elements," said Watson, taking a seat.

Allpress looked confused. He looked at the pair of consulting detectives, and then the pair of consulting detectives looked at each other.

Holmes lifted his clasped hands from his lap, gesturing to the former HR executive. "I'm sorry, we understood that Chemical Elements had ceased trading, given that your section of the parking lot is currently empty, as is the office itself." He closed his eyes and nodded. "Save, of course, for the rubber plants."

Allpress gave a small chuckle and waggled a finger at Holmes. He turned to Watson. "I like this guy! You're right on all counts there, Mr. Holmes, but there's nothing to be sorry about. Chemical Elements was bought, just two weeks ago in fact. Merged with one of our rivals, actually. True enough, nobody saw it coming, but hey, can't complain, can I?"

He spread his arms and he laughed again—laughter that died in the empty meeting room when he saw the looks on the faces of Watson and Holmes.

"Oh, um, I'm sorry," he said, "but what's this about? You said you were consultants or something…?"

"Do you know a woman called Sophie Absolom?" asked Holmes.

Allpress's face lit up again. "Oh yes! We had her in here as a consultant of our own, in fact. I tell you, she was *great*." The man shifted on his chair, sliding right to the edge as he bubbled over with apparent excitement at the memory of his time with the con artist. "She ran four sessions over two days, and then we had three days of one-on-ones with key staff. She was here for a whole week. I tell you, that was just *great*. Signing up to the Vanderpool lecture was the best thing we ever did. We were… oh, how can I describe it?" He stared off into the middle distance, then he snapped his fingers. "Energized! It was like day and night. Everyone felt it. It was like we were a whole new company. You know, we redefined our purpose. She helped us come up with new mission statements, key performance indicators, even a new way of handling performance reviews and business plans. The lecture itself was just the icing on the cake really—that was just me and Lucian, the managing director, who went along to that. That's actually where we met Sophie—she was working front of house, she came and spoke to me during the intermission, offering her services."

"For free, I take it?" asked Holmes.

"Yes! I mean, I wasn't sure, there's usually a catch—in fact, there was a little, we had to buy a pack of DVDs and books, enough for everyone at the company. But that seemed like a small outlay in exchange for personal workshopping."

Watson frowned. "But what happened to Chemical Elements? You just said you'd been bought out?"

"Oh, yes. We were. But that was two weeks ago—ah, that's not in the public domain yet. All our staff are under an NDA for another month."

Holmes crossed his legs and hooked his hands over his knee. "So Sophie Absolom comes into your business, revitalizes the staff and operations, the company is practically *reinvented*, and then it is sold out to a competitor. And, if you don't mind me observing, you seem quite pleased as punch about it."

Allpress shrugged. "Don't get me wrong, what Sophie did was nothing short of a miracle. But that has nothing to do with our acquisition. Like I said, that was a sudden move, out of the blue. But it worked out for the best—we get to take everything we learned from the Vanderpool program into the new company, so as an investment that still stands." He chuckled again. "Chemical Elements was a small company.

Every employee had shares in the company as part of their contract, so when we were bought out we all got quite a good little payout. And our new offices are much nicer than these. So yeah, all in all, I couldn't be happier. It was a great outcome, for everyone."

Holmes and Watson exchanged a look.

"I tell you," said Allpress, "attending that lecture was the best thing I've ever done for this company." He frowned and leaned forward. "Say, is the NYPD thinking of getting Sophie in? She'll change your life, I guarantee it."

Holmes inclined his head. "She is assisting the department, yes."

Allpress clapped his hands. "Oh, hey, great, that's just great. Say, you couldn't help me with the rubber plants, could you?"

"Well, that was *not* what I expected," said Watson, brushing the dirt from the rubber-plant pot from her hands.

They stood in the morning sunshine outside the former offices of Chemical Elements. Watson looked out across the parking lot toward the other blocks. After such an early start, and a long drive—and then helping to cart two giant rubber plants that weighed at least an imperial ton each into the main office reception—she was in need of refreshment.

Next to her, Holmes bristled, a grimace on his face as he squinted into the sun, arms held rigidly by his sides, bouncing a little on his heels. Watson could tell he was thinking the same thing, that this was not what he had expected either.

Watson cast one last look up at the bronze glass edifice of the office block, then led the way back to the car.

"Why was a company like Chemical Elements even targeted?" she asked, thinking aloud more to herself than trying to talk to Holmes, whose mood was continuing its rapid descent. "I mean, Vinnie's crew are talented—in their own way. But working the tour for months on end doesn't seem like a particularly quick or easy way to make a buck. Sophie and Trent would have been better off as grifters on their own."

"There you are correct, Watson," said Holmes, "but it does depend somewhat on the reward that Vinnie offered them. He was promising a big pay-off, so perhaps it was worth the investment of time for them—one last job that would send them all into an early and preferably obscure retirement."

Watson unlocked the car and opened the driver's door, but before she got in she paused and leaned across the warm roof of the car.

"There's not even any evidence of theft!" She waved her car keys at Holmes, who stood with his hands in his pockets on the opposite side. "You heard what Charles Allpress said— going to that lecture and getting the one-on-one treatment was the best thing that ever happened to the company. Sophie helped turn the company around, pushing it up to where it became an attractive takeover target."

Even as she said it, she realized what that meant. Holmes looked at her and nodded.

"Remember what I said about coincidences." He opened his car door. "It is also important to remember that it is not always *successful* companies that make for attractive buy-outs. Those whose share price is *falling* are equally enticing, if not more so, if they have other assets that are of interest to competitors."

Watson sighed. "So there *was* some kind of corporate sabotage?"

Holmes shrugged. "Vinnie Talben was extracting something from each of his targets, thanks to the way Sophie Absolom so elegantly ingratiated herself into each company. We just need to know what it was he was taking."

He got into the car. Watson joined him and found him composing a text on his phone. "I'm informing the captain of our progress," he said. "We only have twenty-four hours before the federal authorities step in to make a pig's ear of the situation and send Vinnie Talben underground."

"Ask Gregson to look into the financials of Chemical Elements," said Watson. "If Vinnie's activity had any impact on the company, we should see it. Their buyer would have filed official documentation with the SEC as well."

"An excellent suggestion," said Holmes, completing the text message, then pocketing the phone. "Hopefully by the time we get back to New York we shall have further information."

Watson nodded, started the car, and the pair headed back toward the state line.

34

WORD GAMES

It was early afternoon by the time Watson and Holmes got back to the brownstone, their journey from the wilds of New Jersey interrupted only briefly by Watson's insistence on stopping for this strange thing normal people call "lunch" at a highway service center.

While they had been away, the NYPD had indeed made progress. Watson and Holmes sat at the red table in the big downstairs room, on which was Holmes's phone, the pair listening as Detective Bell gave them an update on speaker.

So far, the news wasn't what Watson wanted to hear.

"You're sure?" asked Holmes, staring at the phone, leaning forward on his chair with his hands gripping his knees. Watson recognized the body language. More of the uncertainty and doubt, annoyance at his own lack of insight and the apparent failure of his deductive reasoning to draw an accurate picture of their combatant's plans.

Which, Watson knew, was precisely what Vinnie Talben now was to Holmes. The case was at a crucial stage: enough data and evidence had been gathered to form a picture of events, but it was a long-distance view, like looking down the wrong end of a telescope. Holmes could see what was happening, but they were lacking the final thread that would draw it all together.

"Yeah," said Bell. "We've been through almost all of the names that Sophie gave us. Nearly two dozen of them so far—we've got feed traders in the *Mid*west, plastic molding factories in the *south*west, a couple of shoe manufacturers near the Great Lakes, a paper supply company in Georgia. None of them have reported any financial irregularities. In fact, several said that business was booming. Of course we're only just hitting the West Coast companies now, with the time difference. But so far, no dice."

Watson leaned back, stretching her arms, and interlocked her fingers behind her head as she looked up at the brownstone's high ceiling.

"What's going on here? Whatever Vinnie was getting from his hacks, it wasn't money."

"We'll keep on it," said Bell. "And we're digging into the Chemical Elements takeover deal. Although we've got forensic accounting a little tied up with all this, so it might be a while before we learn anything."

"If there's anything to learn," said Watson, with a sigh, bringing her hands down to her legs with a heavy slap. "And we still don't even know how Vinnie knew to target the Vanderpool speaking tour as a vehicle for whatever scam he's trying to pull. The fact that he knows Vanderpool's history suggests it was more than just a long con."

"This Vinnie Talben character is a hacker, according to Sophie," said Bell. "Perhaps he just stumbled across Vanderpool's true identity accidentally, and thought he would be a good little piece of insurance if any of the companies he was targeting became suspicious."

Holmes pursed his lips and looked down at the phone. "That, my dear detective, is leaving the realms of ordinary coincidence and is heading very rapidly toward the quackery of synchronicity."

Watson heard Bell sigh over the phone. "Synchro-what now?" he asked, with a weary tone in his voice.

"*Synchronicity*," said Holmes, "is the theory that some coincidences are too powerful and deliberate to be mere chance, but that the universe is somehow conspiring to make events happen—"

Holmes stopped, and looked at Watson, his lips parted, his eyes wide.

Watson knew that look. She leaned forward.

"What?"

Without a word, Holmes leapt from the table, turned three-sixty, then picked up the phone and held it horizontally between himself and Watson.

"Contact the Federal Bureau of Prisons," he said. "We need his prison jacket sent over *immediately*."

"What prison jacket?" asked Bell. "San Quentin already sent it."

Holmes closed his eyes, his free hand curling into a fist by his side.

"Not *Hauer's* jacket! The file on that of his last cellmate."

"Who was?" asked Watson.

"One *Calvin Bennett*," said Holmes, "imprisoned for forgery and online fraud. There was a scant report in Hauer's file, which I managed to absorb when I sped-read *that* jacket."

From the cellphone in Holmes's hand came the sound of papers shuffling, then Bell came back on the line.

"Okay, Calvin Bennett, on it. You wanna explain why you need that one now?"

Without answering, Holmes passed the phone to Watson, and then marched into the front room and stood in front of the fireplace, his eyes darting around the photographs pinned above it.

Watson followed, carrying the phone. As she watched, Holmes tore off some of the pinned documentation, revealing a bare patch of wall.

There was a fat marker pen on the mantel. Holmes took it, removed the cap, and then wrote directly onto the bare section of wall in large, block capital letters.

CALVIN BENNETT

Once done, he continued to stare at the name while calling out over his shoulder, ensuring that Bell could hear what he was saying.

"While Calvin Bennett only shared David Hauer's cell at San Quentin for a short period, it seems that the latter made a rather distinctive impression on the former."

Holmes lifted the marker pen, and directly under the C of CALVIN BENNETT, wrote a capital V. Then, crossing out the V in the name above, he continued, adding letters in the row underneath the first, removing each from the name as he went. After a few seconds, there was a second name on the wall. Holmes stepped back and gestured to his work with an open palm.

Now Watson understood. Underneath the crossed out letters of CALVIN BENNETT was the name of the man they'd been chasing.

VINCENT TALBEN

Holmes gave a derisory snort. "And hackers think they are so very clever," he said.

Watson shook her head, then lifted the phone.

"Marcus, Vinnie Talben *is* Calvin Bennett. His current identity is just an anagram of his real name."

Holmes stepped over to Watson, and took the phone

rather roughly from her hand. Holding it to his lips, he turned to look at his handiwork.

"It is imperative you get his prison jacket as soon as possible," he said. He ended the call.

Watson joined him at his side.

"So that explains how Vinnie knew who Vanderpool was. But we still don't know who Vinnie is working for."

Holmes nodded.

"That, Watson, is precisely the problem."

35

THE SCHEME REVEALED

The precinct house was a hive of activity when Watson and Holmes arrived. They were met by Detective Bell, who took them straight into a meeting room, laptop under his arm.

"We've got all the financials on Chemical Elements and their recent deal," he said, setting the computer up in front of Holmes. "They were bought out by a company called Elements Materials and a new entity was formed, going by the catchy new name of Chemical Elements Materials. Staff are all under an NDA, but like Joan said, everything had to be filed with the SEC as a matter of course."

Bell let Holmes drive the computer, plowing through pages and pages of legal documents and forms. After a while, Holmes nodded.

"Looks like an entirely legitimate business transaction," he said. "No doubt anything out of the ordinary would have been flagged by the SEC as a matter of due diligence."

"Right," said Bell, as Holmes kept cycling through documents. "Forensic accounting is still looking through it all, but there's nothing here to suggest any laws were broken."

Holmes flew through the documents too fast for Watson

to keep up. Surely he wasn't taking it all in, was he? But then, as Bell had said, if there was anything unusual in the transaction, it would have been flagged already.

A spreadsheet flickered past. A moment later, Holmes stopped scrolling and went back to it. He studied it for a moment, then nodded.

"As I suspected," he said, pointing to the graph on display. "Chemical Elements' share price. They were a modestly successful if completely nondescript company highly unlikely to make any lasting impact on the world. Their share price reflected that fact."

He was right. The chart, which plotted share price over time, was more or less flat for the last several quarters.

Until…

Watson pointed at the screen.

"The share price shoots up… what, two months ago?"

Holmes nodded, tapping his chin with his index finger. "And then just a few weeks later it crashes completely, and it never recovers."

"So, things were going pretty well," said Bell, "until something happened that nearly wiped them out."

Watson nodded. "Making them an ideal target for a cheap takeover by their rival."

"But, vitally, at a share price still higher than their initial valuation," said Holmes, scrolling the spreadsheet sideways to show the very beginning of the company. "As Mr. Allpress told us, all of the company's employees were issued shares as part of their contracts, so each will still have received a nice enough payout, despite the tumbling fortunes of the company."

Bell gestured at the screen. "The price crash I can understand. Vinnie took some information, maybe did some insider trading, something that affected the value of the company. But the spike before, that I don't get."

"Look at the dates," said Watson. "The share spike is in

the period just after Sophie went in and gave the company their week of free workshops. Charles Allpress was telling the truth—she did wonders for the company."

"Until Vinnie Talben brought it all crashing down," said Holmes.

"Wait a minute," said Bell. "This kind of legal paperwork is hardly my department, but there's a pattern here, reminds me of something…"

He pulled the laptop toward him, and, closing down the files on Chemical Elements, went into the precinct network to his personal drive, and brought up what looked, at first glance, to be the same kind of documentation. Then he angled the laptop back so the others could see, and began flicking through pages of data.

"These are the financials of Mantis Capital," he said. "We're still going through them—there's a hell of a lot here—but check this out."

He stopped at a spreadsheet. Only this one wasn't share prices, it was financial holdings.

Watson frowned. It was hard to follow the detail, but something was very clear.

The spreadsheet had a lot of columns—dozens of them—and a *lot* of them were red.

Very, *very* red. Negative numbers in the hundreds of thousands, all of which added up, at least to Watson's untrained eye, to financial ruin.

"Mantis Capital has had a run of bad luck," said Bell. "*Very* bad luck. One thing's for sure, you wouldn't want to have your money tied up with their funds and investments. Clients and customers would have stayed well away."

"Like rats fleeing the proverbial sinking ship," said Holmes as he studied the data. "At least until things picked up."

"Right," said Bell. He scrolled down. The red columns all turned black. Watson blinked at the sums of money listed.

"That's quite the comeback," she said.

"More than that," said Holmes, with a frown. "Nothing short of a financial miracle. Mantis was very much on the way out."

"Until it was blessed by the investment gods," said Bell.

The three of them sat at the table for a while, Holmes idly flicking through more of the documentation. It all told the same story. Mantis just about went bust, then it somehow came back from the brink.

Watson rubbed her forehead. "So Mantis stages an amazing reversal of fortune," she said, "while across the country, small firms coached by Sophie experience their own transformations." She sighed. "So the mystery man Vinnie Talben was working for *must* have been Gregory Smythe. He was the CFO of Mantis." She gestured at the laptop. "Maybe he was hiding the state of the company from *his* boss, at least until he found a way of refilling the accounts."

Bell nodded. "Right, so he recruited Vinnie and they ran some kind of stock market scam, using confidential information stolen from the target companies to manipulate share prices and make a nice profit? And they spread the targets across the country, so none of the NYSE watchdogs would get suspicious."

"Then the profits were syphoned back into Mantis," said Watson, "while Vinnie and his crew skimmed their own share from the top."

Holmes said nothing. He merely pulled at his bottom lip as he sat back from the table, staring at the laptop.

Watson turned to him. "Sherlock?"

He dropped his hand. "It's time to get Vinnie Talben into custody," he said.

"And how do we do that?" asked Bell.

"The answer is simplicity itself."

"Oh?"

"We just use Sophie—Nancy—as bait. And I have a feeling he will be very eager to find out where she has been."

36

TO CATCH A THIEF

The diner was called The Skyscraper, but as Watson cast her eye over the exterior through a set of small binoculars, she thought the name was a little... well, ostentatious, for a single-story grimy establishment wrapped in peeling, painted panels like an old streetcar. Maybe the place had been something once, but its peak had most definitely passed, unless you had a hipster's penchant for faded glamor.

The diner had two long, continuous windows radiating out from either side of the main double doors. The windows offered an excellent view of the unremarkable downtown street for the diner's patrons enjoying their short stacks and coffee. Those windows also made it rather easy for someone on the outside to look *in*.

That was why it had been chosen as the meeting place.

Watson sat in an unmarked police car on the other side of the street, diagonally opposite the diner. It had rained and the sun was beginning to disappear behind the Manhattan skyline, casting an orange glow over the street and diner alike. Watson didn't need the binoculars to count the bodies inside the restaurant, but she wanted to make sure she kept a close eye on Sophie and, she hoped, their target, who was due to arrive in just a few minutes. A couple of hours ago, Holmes had set their meeting up via text from a burner phone.

Sophie sat in the corner of the diner, as instructed, her profile to Watson. As she sipped on another bottomless mug of coffee, Watson panned the binoculars toward the main doors. There, on the other side, seated at the diner's main counter with their backs to Watson, were Gregson and Bell, the former still in the suit he had been wearing at the precinct—he looked enough like a jaded office worker to not require a change, Holmes had said, much to Gregson's annoyance—while Bell was now in jeans, sneakers, and a green New York Jets hoodie.

Watson swung back to Sophie, then sighed and dropped the binoculars. Sophie was a pro, a career criminal with a string of confidence tricks and cons to her name. But here, now, she was nervous. Obviously so.

Watson didn't blame her. This was a different kind of con. In her chosen career, there was always the risk of discovery, of capture. She'd even done a little time. But there was not much in the way of real physical danger.

Here, she was afraid for her life. Her boss, Vinnie Talben, had killed twice, and perhaps had killed others—the original tour manager and publicist for the Vanderpool roadshow sprung to Watson's mind, making her shudder—and even if she wasn't shaking like a leaf, he would be immediately suspicious of her demeanor, and Sophie would know that. While it was unlikely that Vinnie was going to do anything out in the open, in the diner, Watson could easily place herself in Sophie's shoes, imagining the emotions as she sat there, fueled by fear and caffeine, ready to face a man she knew was a cold-blooded killer.

The police radio sitting on the passenger seat of Watson's

car squawked as, from another unmarked vehicle parked nearby, another police officer reported with just two short, simple words.

"He's here."

Watson ducked down in the driver's seat, perhaps instinctively, but she knew that unless he came right over to the car, Vinnie would never spot her. She and Holmes had been on dozens of stakeouts, more than she could really remember. She knew what she was doing as she watched the target arrive at the scene.

Vinnie Talben emerged from a shapeless blue Chrysler, Voyager car rental sticker on proud display in the windshield, which he'd parked at a free spot—covertly arranged by the NYPD—just down the street. He came walking toward the diner from Watson's left, his muscular physique wrapped in a tight black denim jacket over a white t-shirt, his blonde hair hidden by a baseball cap—the same cap that had featured in the security-camera footage from both the Athena Hotel and the Voyager office.

But if Vinnie was trying to keep a low profile, he wasn't making much of an effort—even from across the street, Watson could see his blonde goatee clearly. It was as distinctive as his huge footballer's frame.

Vinnie walked quickly, not looking at anything in particular, and certainly not looking around. He passed by the window at which Sophie was sitting, and Watson saw her stiffen as she recognized the figure heading for the main doors.

Vinnie went inside, and walked straight to her table, sitting with his back to the majority of the diner—Gregson and Bell included—but with a good view of the outside through the long curved window. Watson saw him glance around. He was keeping a lookout, but if he suspected that Sophie was cooperating with the authorities, then he clearly didn't think that the diner might already have police in it.

At the bar, Gregson and Bell glanced surreptitiously over in his direction.

Sophie wasn't bugged—Holmes, back at the precinct, going over the financial records with a fine-toothed comb, insisted that speed was of the essence, and the meeting had been set up hastily. Also, hidden microphones and other surveillance might make for great crime drama on television, Holmes explained, but in the real world, it often posed too much of a risk. While the meeting between Sophie and Vinnie was in a public place, they wanted to do nothing that might heighten the target's suspicions.

Besides which, this wasn't a trap that required taped audio surveillance. It didn't matter what the conversation was. All they had to do was get Vinnie Talben out into the open, and, once the police determined an arrest could be made without endangering Sophie or a member of the public, they could move in and apprehend the target.

But Watson was still curious about the conversation. She lifted the binoculars and watched the pair talk—Holmes, of course, would have been able to lip read most, if not all of the conversation. Sadly, Watson didn't have that skill, and whatever the topic being discussed was, Vinnie was putting on a good act. He was smiling while Sophie shivered, and at one point he even reached forward and moved her bangs off of her face, like they were just two lovers out for an early dinner.

Watson felt her skin crawl.

That was when Watson saw Vinnie's other hand. It had been impossible to see when he initially sat down, but now as he shifted, reaching across the table toward Sophie, Watson could see that he was holding his other hand inside his jacket, like he was reaching for an inside pocket. To anyone in the diner, it would have been impossible to see, and nobody walking past would have taken much notice either, had they cared to look in.

But with the binoculars, Watson had a clear view at what Vinnie was holding with his hidden hand.

He had a gun.

A gun, *dammit*.

Watson lowered the binoculars, then raised them again, as though she expected to see something different the second time.

Nope. Vinnie Talben was armed. No wonder he was looking so relaxed. But... surely he wouldn't pull it in the diner? Of course, Watson knew he didn't have to. All he'd have to do is tell Sophie he had it and that she had better listen to him and listen carefully.

Watson lowered the binoculars again, and then her heartbeat kicked into high gear as she saw Gregson and Bell shifting at the counter, the captain preparing to stand while Bell, now fully turned around on the stool, watched the apparent lovebirds in the corner.

No, no, no, no, no, *no*.

Watson scrambled for the radio on the passenger seat.

"Do not engage, do not engage!" she said. "Tell the captain. The target is *armed*. Do *not* engage!"

The radio squawked and somebody said something she hoped was an acknowledgement—she couldn't speak directly to Gregson or Bell; she had to rely on her message being relayed via the other officers listening.

Seconds ticked by.

Gregson took a step forward and Bell stood up from his stool.

Gregson reached into his jacket, no doubt ready to bring out his NYPD badge when he made the arrest.

Watson squeezed the call button on the radio again, opened her mouth to speak—

Inside the diner, Gregson appeared to cough into his fist, then he turned and sat back down. Beside him, Bell turned around on his stool and went back to leaning on the counter.

Watson breathed a sigh of relief. She quickly trained the binoculars on Sophie and Vinnie.

Sophie was alone.

Watson swore and dropped the binoculars again.

There. Vinnie was at the counter, grabbing a... coffee to go? He was standing right next to Gregson, who turned and looked Vinnie up and down, a common enough piece of body language at any run-down diner in town. At the table in the corner, Sophie sat still, her back ramrod straight, as she watched her former associate.

The meet had *not* gone as planned. There was no way to tackle Vinnie cleanly—it was just too dangerous now they knew he was packing. And once he was out the door, he was as good as gone—it was rush hour, the sidewalks and streets getting progressively busier and busier. They had no choice but to let him walk back to his car and leave. With the suspect armed and dangerous, a pursuit by car was also too much of a risk. Maybe they could grab him somewhere else, but it would take time, and there would be no guarantees.

And then Watson had an idea.

He walked back toward the car, one arm swinging and in his other hand a tall cup of hot, fresh coffee to go.

He checked the street as he left the diner. Looked right. Looked left. People and cars and busses passed. He turned to his right, and walked off, and he sipped his coffee.

The car was where he left it. He put the coffee on the roof as he squeezed a hand into the front pocket of his jeans. He removed the car's key fob from his pocket, took his coffee off the roof, opened the door and got inside.

Then he inserted the fob into the slot next to the steering column, pressed the panel down under the radio to make the cup holder pop out and he put his cup of coffee in it.

And then he froze and didn't move a muscle as someone in the back of the car sprang up from the footwell and shoved something very hard into the back of his seat.

Then he glanced in the rearview mirror and saw an Asian woman with long black hair and a mean expression looking back at him. She shoved the back of his seat again and he winced as the hard object dug into his back.

"Don't try anything," said the woman, and the man didn't try a single thing.

Watson leaned back against the police car, hands in her pockets, as she watched three officers in NYPD windcheaters go over the Voyager rental car. All four doors were open and the trunk was popped as the interior of the vehicle was pulled apart.

There was another marked police unit parked just across from the first car. The rear passenger door was open and an officer in uniform and Detective Bell in his civilian clothes spoke briefly to each other while, seated in the car, Vinnie Talben scowled up at them. His hands were cuffed behind him. He didn't look at all comfortable.

Bell nodded at the other officer, who swung the passenger door closed, and then the detective headed over to Watson.

"That was some quick thinking," he said, with a smile. He pointed at Watson's hand with his pen.

Watson grinned and lifted the silver preserve spoon. "It was a souvenir from the last case Sherlock and I worked on. And the first thing I grabbed out of my bag."

"That was also exactly the kind of risk I don't like anybody taking. You least of all."

Gregson came around the front of the car, hands deep in the pockets of his jacket, his chin pressed into his chest in what Watson instantly recognized as the captain's patented look of disapproval.

She slipped the spoon back into her bag.

"You're right," she said, "but after all this, we couldn't let him just drive away."

"We would have got him," said Gregson.

Watson waved at the Voyager car. "Well, *now* you have."

Gregson frowned, but if he was going to argue any further the conversation was interrupted by one of the officers looking over the rental car. At his call, Gregson, Bell and Watson peeled off from the cop car and walked over.

The officer was by the front passenger door of the rental. In one gloved hand he dangled the floor mat, but in the other he held something far more interesting.

"Found this," said the officer, somewhat unnecessarily. "Doesn't look like it was hidden, just discarded."

It was a ballpoint pen, an ordinary disposable one with a shaft of stiff yellow plastic that was, in this case, split down the middle. The writing end of the instrument was coated in something dark and thick, almost like the pen had sprung a leak and the ink had dried into a sticky mess.

Except Watson knew it wasn't ink.

It was blood.

"Bingo," said Bell, and at this the captain nodded.

"Bag it and bring it in," he said. "I think we just found the second murder weapon."

37

VINNIE TALBEN TALKS

Vinnie had been here before. Watson could tell. She'd seen it in many, many suspects they'd brought back to the precinct to be interviewed. It was the way they sat, the way they looked, the way they drank coffee, even the way they *breathed*.

And she was right, of course. Vinnie had been in situations like this many, many times before. As she sat next to Gregson at the table in the interview room, she glanced down at the folder in front of the captain. There it was, all laid out. A life's history of misdemeanors and felonies. Police records, mug shots, the works.

Next to that open manila folder lay another one. This one was a mottled red-brown, and it was closed. The prison jacket, sent over from the Federal Bureau of Prisons. The complete incarceration history and report for one Calvin Bennett, AKA Vincent Talben.

As had been the case with Sophie Absolom after they'd brought her in, Vinnie hadn't yet spoken. But unlike Sophie, Vinnie wasn't scared. He wasn't even a little bit nervous. He sat and smiled and sniffed, and sometimes he scratched an itch with his cuffed hands. He was still wearing the black denim jacket that seemed a little too small to contain his impressive frame, but the baseball hat was gone. His hair, like his goatee, was pale blonde, and with sparkling blue eyes he almost looked Scandinavian. And perhaps, Watson thought, some of his false identities used this to their advantage.

Watson blinked and drove the thoughts away. She was drifting, the rush of adrenaline from the events outside the diner fading, only to be replaced by fatigue, which was in turn now being fueled by the interview. She'd spent so long in this room over the last day or so, and now they had been sitting in the room for yet another hour and Vinnie Talben looked like he was prepared to sit there without saying a single word all *night*. Watson wondered where Holmes had got to, and thought that *he* really should be here, not her.

Captain Gregson seemed to be faring a little better than Watson. A veteran of long hours squeezing information out of uncooperative suspects, he sat back in his chair, tapping the prison jacket with his pen, looking at Vinnie. Watson knew full well that the captain could go on for as long as it took, and that it would be Vinnie who broke first.

"You do realize that the game is up, right?" Gregson asked. It was the first time anyone had spoken for a full minute or so. "You're going down for two murders, maybe another two. We know about the other tour manager and publicist, the ones you had bumped to make room for your two little pets."

Watson folded her arms. This wasn't true, of course— likely, perhaps, or to be truly objective, *possible*. But otherwise pure supposition.

At the moment, anyway.

Gregson cocked his head. "Who else was there, Vinnie? Two in New York City—now, they were necessary. I get it. You had no choice there. The other two as well—they were in the way. You needed to move the pieces around the board, get it all lined up. But maybe there were more? I mean, let's forget about whatever con you're working on at the moment. I'm talking about in the last year. The last *two* years. What are we going to find when we start digging up your past? Easy enough to get rid of people when they're in the way. We've seen that. So I'd say you've done it before."

Vinnie sniffed again and scratched his cheek.

"Listen," said Gregson, "you're going to go away for a long, long time. I don't really see what you have to lose if you cooperate."

Vinnie looked blankly at the captain. Watson took the moment to jump in.

"You're smart," she said. "We know that. You're a hacker, a master forger. Two skills that makes identity theft just a game to you. You're good. We know that too. And planning a con this complex is impressive. The jury is going to have a hard time getting their heads around it, but believe me, we'll make sure they understand every last detail."

Gregson looked down at the folder in front of him and made a show of leafing through some papers.

"So we've got life, life again, add a couple more, then there's identify theft and forgery, industrial espionage—"

At this, Vinnie's carefully managed, placid expression flickered. Gregson must have seen it, because he stopped and he looked up at the suspect over the top of his glasses. Vinnie's gaze shifted between the captain and Watson.

"Industrial… *espionage*?" Vinnie asked.

"And more," said Watson.

Gregson slipped his glasses off. "It might even go beyond life, once the Feds start digging into all this. This is bigger than just the NYPD, you know."

"Wait," said Vinnie, "you didn't say anything about this being *federal*."

"What did you think was going to happen, Vinnie?" asked Gregson. "You and your crew have blazed a trail across a dozen states. The FBI will be here to take over, oh—" Gregson checked his watch, flourishing it theatrically as he pulled the sleeve of his jacket back to get a better look "—anytime now."

"Hold on now, hold on now," said Vinnie, then he paused and he scratched his cheek again, harder this time, hard enough to leave a red mark. "Look, the reason I'm not saying anything is because I know I'm going down, and like you said there isn't much I can do about that now. But listen, I was just doing my job, okay? I was just doing what I was asked to do."

"Funny," said Watson, "that's what Sophie Absolom said too. She said you were the brains behind the whole operation."

Another white lie, thought Watson, but in the heat of the interrogation room, it was fair game.

Vinnie shook his head and rattled his handcuffs on the table as he held his hands out, like he was grasping for an apple. "No, she wouldn't have said that, I know she wouldn't. I mean, yes, I did the work, but look now, I was just following the word from above. I ran Nancy and Carl—I mean, *Sophie* and *Trent*. But look now, I wasn't in charge. There was someone else. I just got the calls, passed it on, y'know."

"No, we don't know," said Gregson, "but I'm just dying for you to tell me."

Vinnie sat straighter in his chair, and his hands disappeared under the desk. He looked at his two interrogators and sniffed. "I need some kind of deal, y'know. I lay it out, I get something back."

But Gregson just shrugged. "You've been in this game long enough," he said. "You should know how this goes. I can't put anything on the table until I see what you got."

Vinnie shook his head. "Look, man, I ran the op. Sophie and Trent. Trent steered the tour, Sophie did the glad-handing, got on the *inside*. I wrote some software, the stuff that Sophie would use to crack company servers, secure file vaults, that kind of thing."

"We know all this," said Watson. "What we don't know is who you claim you were doing it for, and why."

"Hey, look now, I'm getting there, I'm getting there." *The thought of the FBI getting involved really seems to have rattled him*, thought Watson. Gregson's estimation of the maximum penalty might have been a little much, but Watson wasn't sure Vinnie knew that.

Now—*now*—he was running scared.

"What did you pull out of the companies you targeted?" asked Gregson.

"Ah, lots of things. The boss wanted it all. Full financial and purchasing reports, internal memos—anything that wasn't publicly available information. Sensitive commercial data, y'know. Like, say, how much grain a farming conglomerate was forecasting to warehouse the next season, that kind of thing. Anything that might affect share price, y'know. I mean, I don't know how the boss cut it all together. I kept working on the data mine algorithm, but the program kinda pulled anything and everything."

"Information that could be used to manipulate company stocks, generating a profit, whether the target company survived or not," said Watson.

Vinnie nodded.

Gregson pursed his lips and glanced at Watson, then he turned back to the suspect.

"And don't tell me, you and your boss had a little disagreement. Maybe you asked for a bigger cut. Maybe things were getting too hot and too heavy."

"I… what? No, we never argued. I did what I was told."

Gregson ignored him. "You disagreed, you fought, and you killed him. It was easier that way, right? You knew what to do now. You could do it yourself."

Vinnie looked at Watson. "What the hell is he talking about? I didn't kill the boss."

Watson frowned. "You're saying you didn't kill Gregory Smythe?"

Vinnie's jaw dropped. "Smythe? He wasn't the boss."

Watson and Gregson looked at each other. Vinnie noticed, because then he sat back and his expression changed.

"Look, I'll give you the name. I'll tell you the works. But only if you can put a word in with the DA. The federal prosecutor too. I mean, look, yes, I killed Gregory Smythe and I killed Trent... I mean, Carl. But I was only doing what I was told. The boss gave me the job, I did it. That was the deal."

Gregson pulled on his bottom lip. "And now you want another kind of deal, that it?"

"Sure. There's gotta be something in it for me. I mean I did the wet work, but someone else ordered the hits. That's gotta mean something, right?"

Gregson and Watson shared another look.

"*Right*?" asked Vinnie again, his voice rising.

That was when there was a thumping from the two-way mirror on the wall to Watson's left. She jumped at the interruption and saw the glass wobble in its frame, and then she heard a voice shouting something, something she couldn't make out.

"Sherlock?"

Footsteps, a slammed door, and then a moment later the interview room door flew open. Holmes marched up to the table. He leaned over it toward Vinnie.

"No deal!"

Gregson sighed. "Holmes, what's going on now? You can't just burst in and—"

"I said no deal." Holmes turned to the captain.

Watson stood. "Why not?"

"Because," said Holmes, with a smile. "There is simply no need. I know exactly who the boss is."

38

THE BOSS

The lights of Manhattan glittered like a universe of stars as Watson looked out through the vast floor-to-ceiling plate-glass windows that formed just about every outer wall of the offices of Mantis Capital Investment. Just a few blocks away, the Empire State Building was lit up in a slowly changing mix of red, and green, and yellow, the light show most likely commemorating an anniversary or special event that Watson couldn't quite bring to mind. It was getting late, and the office was down to just a few last stragglers as they finished up for the evening.

The view was beautiful, spectacular. People paid an awful lot of money for a view like that. For a company like Mantis Capital, it was a triviality. They could afford the best offices in the city. And for the company CEO, Darcy Kellogg, well... she got the best office of them all.

Except she wasn't here.

Watson turned around to see Detective Bell loitering nearby, lifting the visitor's badge with the large red block V on it to get a better look, then checking his watch, not paying much attention to the opulent surroundings. Captain Gregson stood over by Kellogg's huge slab of a desk, while

Holmes himself sat in one of the chairs in front of it, hands clasped, apparently studying the piece of modern art hanging on the wall behind the desk. Watson glanced at it—she didn't recognize it, nor could she place the artist, but she could probably take a guess at its value.

"I'm sorry to have kept you waiting, gentlemen."

Kellogg breezed in, computer tablet swinging in one hand as she headed for her desk. She nodded at her guests, then saw Watson and gave her a smile. "And *ladies*," she said, correcting herself. Seating herself at the desk, she motioned for the others to sit. Gregson and Watson obliged but Bell stayed on his feet, offering a polite wave and a small nod to indicate that he was fine just where he was.

Kellogg glanced around her desk—whether to check what was next on her agenda, or to check whether anything had been moved out of place by her visitors, Watson wasn't entirely sure—then looked up.

"I'm sorry this is a little rushed. I always find myself run off my feet at the close of play, and those last meetings always seem to overrun."

Holmes gave the CEO a radiant smile. "That's quite all right, Ms. Kellogg. I think we all fully understand how the wheels of business turn."

Kellogg seemed to relax, sinking back into her chair. "I'm very glad I can help with your investigation," she said. "I understand there are a few things you'd like to go over with the case?"

"Thank you, ma'am," said Gregson. "My colleagues have—"

"Remarkable man," said Holmes, interrupting the captain. All eyes were on him.

Kellogg cocked her head. "Ah... I'm sorry?"

"Gregory Smythe," said Holmes, lifting his hands from his knee but keeping them clasped as he emphasized his words. "I have to congratulate you on his appointment as Chief Financial Officer." Holmes turned to the others. "It is a rare thing for someone to become an expert in one field, only to change careers so late in life and become an expert in another. Smythe's work as a security analyst was formidable, but his success in steering a hedge fund like Mantis Capital perhaps even more so."

He turned back to Kellogg, and he gave her a slight bow with his eyes closed. "As I say, congratulations on finding such a hire. You must have been very pleased with his work."

Kellogg frowned and glanced at the others in the room for support while Holmes continued to beam at her. Then the CEO sat more upright and reached forward to adjust the position of the tablet on the desk in front of her.

"Gregory Smythe was an excellent officer of this company, yes," she said. "And thank you. He was not only a good hire, but a very good fit for our culture."

Holmes laughed. "And so modest." He turned back to Gregson and Watson sitting next to him. "Gregory Smythe was more than just another CFO. He was a business *genius*, virtually unparalleled in corporate history."

There was a glint in his eye, a look Holmes passed to Watson, one perhaps only she would understand.

And oh, yes, she understood where this was going. Watson lifted an eyebrow very slightly, and Holmes did the same. If Kellogg noticed, it didn't matter.

It was time for the endgame.

Kellogg laughed, perhaps nervously. "I'm sorry, I'm not sure where this is going...?"

Holmes pursed his lips and glanced at Watson. Taking her cue, she followed through on the trap he had set.

"Gregory Smythe was somehow able to predict movements in the stock market with uncanny accuracy," she said. She reached down and opened her bag, and took out a slim manila folder. She passed it across the desk to Kellogg. The CEO looked at the folder for a second or two, then took it and flipped it open. Watson leaned forward to point out what the data showed.

"After the portfolios of Mantis Capital were nearly wiped out, Smythe managed to refund nearly all of them."

"And," said Gregson, "all before any investor had the slightest clue what was going on."

"I…" was all Kellogg could manage. Watson could see it in her face, her body language, as she cast an eye over the numbers. Because that's all she was doing, casting an eye. She was familiar with the numbers. Very familiar. She'd seen them, studied them in great detail.

"It is true that we had some… issues," she said, then she looked up, a large but rather cold smile on her face. "But let me reassure you, Mantis Capital is in a strong position. We realigned our investment strategy, took on new traders, and with the markets improving globally we were able to turn our fund portfolios around."

Holmes nodded, his lips pursed as if he considered Kellogg's words to be particularly insightful.

"If you will forgive me, Ms. Kellogg," he said, "but a bigger load of dingo's kidneys I have hardly heard."

Kellogg stared at Holmes. The consultant was looking at the CEO with narrow eyes, the smile, the pleasant demeanor, suddenly gone.

"Excuse me?"

Holmes bristled in his chair. "Hogwash. Pure and simple, unadulterated hogwash. Such a turnaround is impossible, and in any event, Gregory Smythe had nothing to do with it, did he?"

Kellogg squared her shoulders and turned to Gregson.

"I'm sorry, Captain Gregson, I'm going to have to ask you and your… *colleagues*… to leave. If you need to communicate with me or my company in future I am happy to supply you with the details of our legal representation—"

"Oh, thanks," said Gregson, sitting back in his chair in a comfortable slouch. "And you're right, I think you'll be wanting to get your lawyers involved pretty soon."

Kellogg's face drained of color. She stammered, and then turned to Holmes as he spoke.

"Tell me," he said, "did you enjoy high school?"

"High school?" Kellogg laughed and shook her head. "Okay, we really are done here." She made a move to stand from her chair, but as she did so, Bell took a step forward from his position farther back in the office.

"Ma'am," he said, "if you could answer the question."

Kellogg laughed again, but she lowered herself back into her seat anyway. She squared her shoulders again and looked down at the desk.

Watson could sense what the CEO was doing. She was running through her options, trying to figure out how much they knew, what they had on her, if there was anything she'd overlooked, any mistakes she'd made.

But they knew a lot. Holmes had been locked away in the brownstone for hours while the others had grabbed Vinnie Talben and questioned him back at the precinct. After interrupting that interview, the information Holmes had laid out was nothing short of a unique piece of detective work.

Watson wondered if he'd had help from Everyone. If you had a tool, it was stupid not to use it.

But she suspected he hadn't. It was the gleam in his eye as he had explained it, the heat, the passion she could see rising in him like a furnace.

Kellogg recomposed herself, and then looked at Holmes again, like she was chairing any other business meeting with a client she didn't much like.

"High school?"

"Yes," said Holmes. "You went to Green Oaks High School in Sacramento, California."

Right on cue, Watson pulled another piece of evidence from her bag. Another printout, showing a grid of passport-sized photos. She handed it to Kellogg, who took it and looked at it, her brow creased in confusion.

"Yes," she said, after a beat, "I went to Green Oaks. But you seem to have found that out already. You really are a *great* detective."

She held up the paper, printed side toward Holmes, one eyebrow raised in disdain. Watson glanced over it, scanning the photographs for the *n*th time since Holmes had produced it back at the precinct.

It was a page from the Green Oaks yearbook, senior class of 1983. In the middle of the fourth row of pictures, a teenage Darcy Kellogg smiled back out at them across the decades.

When Holmes didn't take the paper, Kellogg tossed the printout onto her desk and leaned back in her chair. "What exactly does this have to do with the death of my CFO?"

"The difficulty we had," said Watson, "was establishing the nature of the connection between Gregory Smythe and the Vanderpool speaking tour. We knew there *was* one, we just didn't know what it was."

"And to answer your question," said Holmes, "Green Oaks senior class of 1983 has *everything* to do with the murder of Gregory Smythe."

"The murder," said Gregson, punctuating his words with a stab of his pen, "that you ordered."

"This is *beyond* ridiculous!"

"And the answer to *our* question, Ms. Kellogg," said Holmes, "is that, actually, yes, you did enjoy high school. Very much so, in fact. You particularly enjoyed the time spent as organizer of the Green Oaks Gaming Club, and the countless teenage years whiling away the hours playing Dungeons and

Dragons with your club mates. *Advanced* D and D, of course. In particular, you enjoyed the company of another classmate who soon became the club's regular Dungeon Master."

Watson reached forward and grabbed the yearbook printout from the desk. She quickly found who she was looking for, and, marking the place with a finger, she turned the sheet back around to Kellogg.

"Calvin Bennett," she said. "Currently using the alias *Vinnie Talben*."

Kellogg stood up and pressed her hands into the top of her desk. "This is nonsense. How and why you dug up my high school records, I don't know. But it doesn't show a damned thing. If you don't leave now, I will be forced to call security."

"The connection was actually rather easy to discover," said Holmes. "Green Oaks very recently instituted a new digital information policy, and is in the process of scanning their entire archive of school publications into one giant, publicly accessible repository. All that was required was a simple Internet search, correlating the names of everyone at Mantis Capital with the names of our other persons of interest. In fact, you and Calvin Bennett's connection popped up as the second result."

Kellogg rose and leaned forward over her desk.

"What was it you said before? Hogwash, was that it?" The color had returned to Kellogg's face. In fact, she looked positively furious, the pulse pounding in her neck. "Well, that's what this is." She turned to the captain. "I'll be registering a formal complaint with the department. I don't know if you normally carry out homicide investigations in this manner, just letting your, your... *associate* here, run amok over everything."

Gregson waved at Kellogg, motioning her to sit down.

"Take a seat, please. I can assure you you'll have full opportunity to register any complaint you like, Ms. Kellogg.

But we're going to have a lot more to talk about first."

"See," said Bell, with a smile, moving closer to the group, "while we've been here, your apartment has been searched by the police. Apparently it's a big place with lots of hidey holes, but they found your collection."

Kellogg stared at the detective, and then she finally complied with Gregson's instruction and sat down, slowly, almost gingerly.

"Stuffed into a tote bag, hidden in an air vent," said Gregson. "That doesn't seem a very nice way to treat a collection of very, very expensive vintage fountain pens." Gregson looked over his shoulder at Bell. "How many was it?"

"Thirty-three," he said, "including five LeFevres." Bell grinned. "Good vintage too, all pre-1986."

Kellogg lifted an eyebrow. "A good vintage?"

"LeFevre didn't introduce serial numbers to their pens until after that year," Holmes said, "makes it rather hard to trace their owners." Then he reached into his pocket to pull out his phone. "*But*, interesting thing about fountain pens, particularly vintage ones, is the *nibs*. They are extremely durable, usually composed of an alloy that uses metals from the platinum group. A quality nib can last years—*decades*, even—and still perform perfectly."

Holmes brought up an image on his phone, which he leaned forward to show Kellogg. It was a strange, angular shape, showing an object that looked sharp, a little gritty, that was silvery-gold in color. An extreme enlargement of a fountain pen nib, shown in microscopic detail.

"What makes fountain pen nibs interesting," Holmes continued, "is the way they wear in, at an angle unique to the handwriting style of the person who uses the pen. That's why it is often advised that you do not lend your fountain pen to anyone else, as not only will it not write very well for them, but it will create a secondary wear surface, spoiling your own writing. Of course, with more modern nibs and newer alloys, this is no longer a real issue. But as I said, on vintage pens…"

Holmes trailed off and sat back in his chair, slipping his phone back in his pocket. His eyes never once left Kellogg's.

"In 1995," said Watson, "in Chula Vista, California, a man named David Hauer killed someone with a fountain pen. He stabbed him through the *eye*. The wear on the nib of that pen was a match for another in Hauer's possession."

"The pen used to kill Gregory Smythe, on the other hand," said Holmes, "has wear that matches yet *another* pen. Several, in fact, including the five LeFevre writing instruments we found hidden in your air duct."

Kellogg said nothing.

"Gregory Smythe was murdered by Vinnie Talben," said Holmes, "or as you know him, Calvin Bennett. Vinnie has already confessed to that killing, and to the subsequent murder of Carl Warren, who was at the time using the stolen identity Trent Absolom. But Smythe's death was ordered by you, Ms. Kellogg. Not only did you 'outsource' the task to Mr. Talben, but you provided him with the murder weapon. The LeFevre pen, one from your personal collection."

Holmes stopped there, and smiled at Kellogg.

"It was the turnaround of Mantis Capital that gave us the final clue," said Watson. "There is no way a company like this could have been saved from disaster without some shady dealing. Only your CFO wasn't behind it, was he?"

"On the contrary," said Holmes, picking up the narrative, "it was he who found the irregularities in the first place. The failure of the investment portfolios had been *hidden* from your clients. Mr. Smythe discovered the strange activity, and the way that the portfolios were miraculously being regenerated, and had no doubt brought it to your attention, as any conscientious financial officer would."

Gregson shifted in his seat. "So whatever it was you were

doing with Vinnie Talben, Smythe had found out, and he now became a liability. He was going to blow the whole thing wide open." He then turned in his seat and lifted a finger, indicating to Bell. Bell nodded and walked over to the glass walls of Kellogg's office, lifting his phone to his ear. He murmured something, and moments later, the group turned to watch through the glass walls of the CEO's office as Mantis was filled with police in full uniform, and others in blue jackets with FBI written in bold yellow letters on the back.

Bell turned around. "The FBI are taking every scrap of paper and every digital file you have. Whatever you were up to, however you did it, it's over."

Kellogg looked out at the office, at the men and women who were now sitting at computers, who were carrying stacks of collapsed cardboard boxes, ready to seize everything in the office. Those few Mantis staff who were left were standing around, looking confused and concerned. Almost as one, they all turned to look at their boss.

Inside the office, Darcy Kellogg stared at Sherlock Holmes. She licked her lips, and then she said:

"Fine."

39

THE FALL OF GREGORY SMYTHE

Darcy Kellogg took a deep breath and turned her chair to watch the police and federal agents at work. She smiled, faintly, to herself.

"Calvin and I had a thing in high school," she said. "We were both geeks. We met at the games club. It didn't last long—nothing does, not at that age—but we were friends. We lost touch a little after we graduated, but we were both in the same town, we ran into each other now and again. We both went to college in the state. He did computers and economics—a prestigious course, I think. Later I found out he'd been arrested for hacking and financial fraud."

At that she barked out a laugh, which died quickly in the silence of her office.

"I felt bad, I think," she continued. "Like it was my fault, somehow. Like I should have done something, back in school. I don't know. So I got in touch, we rekindled that old friendship. When he got out of prison I tried to help him, gave him money, but he was drifting a little, I think. He seemed to be doing okay. But he and I… well, it was a relic, an echo of the past. He faded away. I think I did too, to be honest. It was easier to just get on with life. To move on."

She straightened herself in her chair and turned her eyes back to the others.

"I founded this company six years ago," she said. "We were successful—*I* was successful—until we weren't. A series of bad investments, some internal sabotage from some bad hires, sent us into a spin. I was able to hide it in the short term, but I needed guaranteed results sooner or later or the whole hedge fund would collapse."

Holmes pursed his lips as he listened. "So you called him. Calvin Bennett, the old flame."

Kellogg nodded. "I was desperate. I was going to lose everything I'd worked for. All of it. So I called him and we met and we talked it over. I laid it out, told him what I needed, and he came up with a plan. It sounded crazy, but he knew what he was doing. Or I believed he did."

"And the fact that your old friend had done time inside for financial fraud didn't ring any alarm bells, Ms. Kellogg?" asked Gregson.

She shrugged. "I helped him when he was in trouble. Now he said it was his turn to repay the favor."

"And get a cut for himself in the process," said Watson.

Kellogg shrugged again. "I had nowhere else to go. We worked out a plan to target companies that were potential investment targets, to get the inside scoop on their businesses so we could buy or sell shares based on data the market didn't know. Of course it wasn't legal, but Calvin said he had it all worked out. He had what he called the 'perfect vehicle', one that provided an exit —'insurance', he called it. An escape route, one that wouldn't lead back to us if we had to take it."

Holmes nodded. "David Hauer, Calvin's former cellmate. AKA Dale Vanderpool, now a successful business speaker."

"I don't know anything about David Hauer," said Kellogg, "but Calvin talked a lot about Dale Vanderpool. He'd been to several lectures, trying to get his life back together after

ELEMENTARY

prison. It's not easy for convicted felons, you know. The rest of the world doesn't want anything to do with them."

"So you had your plan," said Watson, "and Calvin—now using the alias of Vinnie—assembled his crew. Sophie and Trent, two 'freelancers'."

"I didn't know who they were," said Kellogg, "but Calvin said he knew the right people. I guess it's a small world."

"You don't seem to know a lot of things. Ignorance is the best defense, right?" asked Bell, his voice dripping with sarcasm.

Kellogg just looked at him.

"The fountain pen was perhaps Vinnie Talben's most canny ploy," said Holmes. He smiled at Kellogg. "It was *payment*, wasn't it? Vinnie was smart there, at least, asking for a tangible asset, a vintage fountain pen. The most secure form of payment, in fact. Wire transfers can be anonymized, but even when routed through shell companies and offshore accounts, they leave a trail of some sort. Cash can be marked, serial numbers can be logged. But a *physical* object, something small and valuable, easily transportable, easily hidden. Something like a vintage LeFevre fountain pen."

Kellogg nodded. "I was surprised when he asked for it, but I guess he saw me using it. He wanted it as a down payment. I just assumed he knew what it was worth. I said I would arrange for him to receive it once the job was done."

"Except Vinnie had another use in mind for it," said Watson, "and he asked for it early, didn't he?"

"Yes," said Kellogg. "I… Really, I had no idea at all what he was going to do. He said he needed a down payment, on top of the expenses I was funneling to him."

"Gregory Smythe had to be eliminated," said Holmes. "As did Trent Absolom, when he discovered what Vinnie had done and threatened to expose the entire project. Vinnie's so-called insurance policy was Dale Vanderpool, his former cellmate. He was to be the scapegoat for several murders."

288

Holmes paused and cocked his head. "Including your *own*, Ms. Kellogg."

The CEO's eyes widened, then narrowed just as quickly.

"Me? What makes you say that?"

Holmes crinkled his nose as he considered, then he continued. "Vinnie was running a long operation, *months* in the planning and execution. But when it was all over, why on earth would he simply hand the profits over to Mantis Capital? On the contrary, he could have it all. First he simply had to eliminate his two employees—Trent and Sophie—and then his own boss. Knowing Vanderpool's past, and learning that his new employer had a collection of vintage fountain pens, Vinnie had the perfect framing device. All he had to do was get the pen, which was to be handed over in exchange for the next batch of company data."

"Which was what the exchange here at the office was about," said Watson. "Sophie dropped off a package of the USB sticks from the last batch of jobs, which contained stolen company data, while the package she picked up contained the pen." Watson smiled coldly. "It was just a shame that your CFO got involved. Vinnie had to change his plan."

Kellogg leaned forward over her desk. "Listen to me. I had no idea what Vinnie was planning to do with the pen. All I knew was that he wanted it as partial payment, and that made sense to me."

"But Smythe had to be eliminated, didn't he?" asked Holmes.

Kellogg said nothing. She just stared at the detective.

Holmes continued. "He was suspicious. Perhaps he reviewed Mantis trade activities regularly. Perhaps he merely decided to take a look one day. But he found out what you were doing."

"Which is understandable," said Gregson. "He was a security analyst before moving into the financial world. That was one of the reasons you hired him in the first place."

The Mantis CEO sighed and steepled her fingers under her chin. She averted her gaze to her desk, like she was reading from a script.

"He was a suspicious bastard," she muttered. Watson wondered if the hint of regret in her tone was natural or an affectation. Kellogg knew she was going down. Perhaps she was trying to mitigate the damage now.

"It was Philadelphia," said Kellogg, suddenly looking up at Gregson. "I went to the Vanderpool lecture there, to meet Vinnie. But I didn't tell anyone where I was going—I entered it into my company calendar as a visit to Toronto, but Greg— well, he was watching me. Once I was gone, he accessed my cellphone tracking, which showed me in Philly."

"More precisely," said Holmes, "it showed you at the Vanderpool lecture. He was curious, wondering what his CEO was doing at such an event, wondering what was happening to the company. He knew something was going on, but he was unable to work out precisely what. Indeed, Mantis was doing well. *Too* well. And, foremost in his mind, was the fact that his CEO was lying to him. So he decided to see for himself. He found the next lecture was going to be in Newark."

"And," said Watson, "that's where he saw Sophie. He'd seen her before, of course—making the delivery to the Mantis office. That was the final link he needed—a direct connection between the speaking tour and your company."

Kellogg's gaze was now unfocused, lying somewhere in the middle distance beyond where the guests in her office were seated. When she spoke her voice was equally distant.

"Vinnie called me. He said that Smythe had confronted Sophie. I didn't know what to do, but Vinnie said that he would take care of it. I didn't know what that meant."

"What that meant," said Gregson, "was *murder*."

The captain stood and motioned over his shoulder at

Detective Bell. Bell walked around the side of the desk, handcuffs at the ready. Kellogg remained where she was, but as Bell waved at her to stand up, she didn't protest. She just stood and turned, holding her hands out behind her.

Bell slipped the cuffs on.

Then Kellogg looked at Holmes.

"Why did he have to interfere? Why wasn't he happy that I was turning the company around? I was *saving* Mantis Capital! Why couldn't he see that?"

Holmes remained tight-lipped.

"Why couldn't he see that?" the CEO repeated. "We weren't hurting anyone."

"On the contrary," said Holmes. "Two men died in this city because of your actions, and two more were also killed by your *associate* in order for your plan to be enacted."

"But I didn't *know* that!"

Bell tugged at the CEO's arm and led her away. Gregson followed.

When they were gone, Holmes remained seated where he was for a long, long time, and Watson sat and watched him. Holmes didn't speak, he merely tapped his chin.

And then he stood and left.

Watson followed.

40

AN INTERRUPTED PERFORMANCE RESUMED

Watson taped the last of the document boxes closed, then heaved it up and dumped it onto the shortest of the several stacks that sat in the front room of the brownstone. The FBI would be collecting the boxes in the morning as part of their investigation into Mantis Capital. Watson was pleased the complex case was now out of their hands; she was looking forward to taking a break.

As she walked to the kitchen to make some tea, she found herself running over the events in her mind yet again. While it was satisfying to bring their investigation to a conclusion, she felt affected by the case in an unusual way. The case *itself* had been unusual—certainly one of the more complex criminal enterprises they had uncovered—but the motivation was the saddest part.

Money.

It all came down to money. A failing hedge fund, a CEO desperate for results at all—at *any*—cost.

Including people's lives. True enough, Darcy Kellogg had denied all knowledge of Vinnie's activities, and Watson thought that might be at least partially true.

But it didn't mitigate the crimes, or Kellogg's actions. She was as much responsible as Vinnie Talben.

Actually, it was Dale Vanderpool she felt the most sorry for. He'd done more than just turn his life around after his imprisonment—he'd created an entirely *new* one, and had found his true calling, only for his past to come back to haunt him in a way he couldn't possibly have imagined. While Watson thought there was a good chance a sympathetic DA would keep his name out of it, she doubted he would want to continue with his current business after all this.

Well, at least until he got an idea for his next book.

In the kitchen, Watson filled the tea kettle and put it on the stove. While she waited for it to heat up, she went over to the big table. Clyde's terrarium was on it, the little tortoise happily basking under the heat lamp. Next to the terrarium was a fresh bag of lettuce. Watson tore a leaf off, tore the leaf into small pieces, and offered them to the tortoise. Clyde lazily drifted over to the offering and began taking tiny, tortoise-sized mouthfuls.

The sound of bare feet padding across the floorboards alerted Watson to the presence of her housemate.

"Ah, there you are," said the great detective. "Excellent, excellent."

Watson glanced over her shoulder to see Sherlock Holmes, wearing a Japanese kimono tied only loosely at the waist, walk to the fridge, from the bottom of which he extracted a polystyrene container about the size of a shoebox. Giving Watson a courteous nod, he placed the box next to Clyde's terrarium.

He stood and stared at the container. Watson raised an eyebrow, then went back to the stove where the kettle was beginning to boil.

"Aren't you going to ask me what's in the box?" asked Holmes. He sounded ever so slightly disappointed.

"No," said Watson. Instead, she opened the cupboard

above the kitchen counter to look for a mug.

"Well," said Holmes, turning around. "I'm afraid that since my little dramatic performance for Everyone was unfortunately curtailed before reaching the grand climax, they have requested a couple of additional numbers as recompense."

Holmes lifted the lid of the polystyrene box with both hands and placed it carefully on the table. Reaching in, he lifted out a whole fish. He held it carefully by the tail as it glistened under the kitchen lights.

Watson froze, watching Holmes, one hand on the door of the cupboard.

"What are you planning on doing with that?"

Holmes smiled. "Actually," he said, sticking his chin out a little. "I was hoping to obtain your assistance."

He reached his free hand into the box, and extracted another, identical fish. "The next part of my performance really works better if there are two participants."

Watson sighed, then closed the cupboard, turned off the stove, and took the tea kettle off the heat.

"You know what, I think you'll do just fine by yourself. I'm going out for dinner."

She headed for the door. Behind her, she could hear Holmes replacing the lid on the polystyrene box with a squeak.

"Your loss," he called out, "but I will be sure to record the next act for you to enjoy later."

Wow, won't that be great, thought Watson as she closed the front door, leaving Holmes and the damp smell of fresh fish behind her.

ACKNOWLEDGEMENTS

My thanks as always to my editor, Miranda Jewess, whose boundless enthusiasm for, and bottomless knowledge of, Sherlock Holmes continues to make these modern-day New York adventures a joy to write. And to my agent, Stacia J. N. Decker of Dunlow, Carlson & Lerner, for her expert eye and guiding hand.

Part of this book was written over a few cool spring mornings in Christchurch, New Zealand, when I should have been doing other things. My thanks to Bruce and Carol for their indulgence as I locked myself in their caravan and drank all of their tea as I vanished into a Manhattan mystery. And my thanks to their daughter, and my wife, Sandra, who puts up with a very great deal more than that.

ABOUT THE AUTHOR

Adam Christopher is a novelist, comic writer, and award-winning editor. His debut novel, *Empire State*, was *SciFiNow*'s Book of the Year and a *Financial Times* Book of the Year for 2012. Recent books include *The Burning Dark* and *The Machine Awakes* in the *Spider Wars* series, *Made to Kill*, the first novel of the *LA Trilogy*, and *Elementary: The Ghost Line*. Born in New Zealand, he has lived in Great Britain since 2006.

For news and information about books and events, sign up to his author newsletter at www. adamchristopher.ac and follow him on Twitter @ghostfinder.

ELEMENTARY

THE GHOST LINE

A summons to a body found riddled with bullets in a Hell's Kitchen apartment is the start of a new case for Sherlock Holmes and Joan Watson. The victim is a subway train driver with a strange Colombian connection and a mysterious pile of money, but who would want to kill him? The search for the truth will lead the detectives into the hidden underground tunnels of New York City, where more bodies may well await them.

"Like all the best tie-in fiction it's like we're watching an episode of the TV show"

Starburst

"A fun, fast-paced detective yarn... It will satisfy fans of the series, intrigue fans of the original Sherlock Holmes stories, and appeal to those who love a good murder mystery"

Nudge Book

"It felt like Adam Christopher had put the hours in and come up with something that would have made a budget-breaking episode."

SF Crowsnest

For more fantastic fiction, author events, exclusive excerpts,
competitions, limited editions and more

VISIT OUR WEBSITE
titanbooks.com

LIKE US ON FACEBOOK
facebook.com/titanbooks

FOLLOW US ON TWITTER
@TitanBooks

EMAIL US
readerfeedback@titanemail.com